Lake Wobegon Summer 1956

Garrison Keillor is the best selling author of *Lake Wobegon Days, Happy to Be Here, Leaving Home, We are still Married, Radio Romance, The Book of Guys* and *Wobegon Boy*. He is the host of *A Prairie Home Companion* on American public radio and a contributor to *Time* magazine. He lives in Wisconsin and New York City.

AUTHOR OF

Happy to Be Here
Lake Wobegon Days
Leaving Home
We Are Still Married
Radio Romance
The Book of Guys
Wobegon Boy
Me

FOR CHILDREN
Cat, You Better Come Home
The Old Man Who Loved Cheese
The Sandy Bottom Orchestra
(Co-written with Jenny Lind Nilsson)

GARRISON KEILLOR

Lake Wobegon

Summer

1956

faber and faber

First published in the USA in 2001
by Viking Penguin Inc. New York
First published in Great Britain in 2001
by Faber and Faber Limited
3 Queen Square London WC1N 3AU
This open market edition first published in 2002

Printed in England by Bookmarque Ltd, Croydon

A CIP record for this book
is available from the British Library

ISBN 0-571-21029-5

2 4 6 8 10 9 7 5 3 1

To my darlings—winter was so long
And soon will come again, meanwhile
This story from when I was young
I hope will elicit a summer smile.

O my Lord God almighty and everlasting, grant me a prayerful heart. Even in the tumult of prosperity and all ordinary distress, give me words to address to Thee, O great Attender to misfortune, and when my spirit is defeated and my faith is an ash pit, yet grant me a silent prayer, O Merciful, O Giver of Life and Creator of this day, this piece of wood.

—ST. JOSEPH THE WOODCARVER

Lake Wobegon

Summer

1956

1

A Summer Night

Saturday night, June 1956, now the sun going down at 7:50 P.M. and the sprinkler swishing in the front yard of our big green house on Green Street, big drops whapping the begonias and lilacs in front of the screened porch where Daddy and I lie reading. A beautiful lawn, new-mown, extends to our borders with the Stenstroms and Andersons. The dog under the porch scootches down, pressing his groin into the cool dirt. A ball of orange behind the Stenstroms' house, flaming orange shining in the windows, as if the Mr. and Mrs. had spontaneously combusted because of a faulty fuse, a frayed electrical cord, or a box of oily rags in the basement. The shadow of their elm reaches to our porch, a wavery branch flickers across my right arm in gray shade. I wish my cousin Kate would come by. She said she would but it doesn't look like she will. I wrote her a poem:

Kate, Kate,
She's so great
I would wait eight hours straight
To attend a fete
For Kate.

Daddy lies on the white wicker daybed in his blue suit pants and sleeveless undershirt and black-stockinged feet, exhausted from a long week at the bank. He is the head cashier. Daddy doesn't like dealing with people. They wear him out. Their ridiculous demands. Their utter ignorance of sound fiscal practices. He pretends to be reading C. H. McIntosh's *Commentary on the Ephesians*, but really he's listening to the Minneapolis Millers on the radio. Mother is upstairs lying down with a headache, and the big sister is on the telephone complaining about boys and how dumb they are, and the big brother is at the University, studying math, the big brain of the family. I am taking it easy. Reclining on the porch swing, nestled in four pillows, a bottle of Nesbitt orange pop within easy reach. I am fourteen. In 1958 I will obtain my driver's license and in 1960 graduate from Lake Wobegon High School. In 1963 I can vote. In 1982 I'll be forty. In 1992, fifty. One day, a date that only God knows, I will perish from the earth and no longer be present for roll call, my mail will be returned, my library card canceled, and some other family will occupy this house, this very porch, and not be aware that I ever existed, and if you told them, they wouldn't particularly care. Oh well. What can you do? I hope they appreciate the work I did on the lawn. Here's a little-known fact: *Saturday* contains the world *turd*. How many of you knew that? *Librarian* has a *bra* in it. Words are so interesting. *Breastworks*, for example. *Peccary. Pistachio. Cockatoo. Titular. Interred. Poop deck.*

* * *

I lie on the white wicker swing, *Foxx's Book of Martyrs* before me, reading about the pesky papists piling huge jagged rocks on the faithful French Huguenots and crushing them, while listening to the Minneapolis Millers on the radio lose to Toledo thanks to atrocious umpiring that killed a rally in the third inning. Eruptions of laughter from the *Jackie Gleason Show* at the Andersons' to the east of us, the Great One glaring at Audrey Meadows. *One of these days, Alice—pow! Right in the kisser!* At the Stenstroms', Perry Como sings about the tables down at Morey's, at the place where Louie dwells. We are Sanctified Brethren and do not own a television, because it does not glorify Christ. I know about these shows only from timely visits to the home of my so-called best friend, Leonard Larsen. Tucked inside my *Martyrs* book is a magazine called *High School Orgies*, lent to me by Leonard, opened to an ad for a cologne made from "love chemicals" that will turn any girl to putty in your hands. You dab some behind your ears and hold her in your arms and suddenly all resistance in gone, she is whispering for you to thrill her, fulfill her, do what you like. Plus a book of surefire pickup lines with a bonus chapter, "Techniques of Effective Kissing." Daddy is also worn out from killing chickens today at Grandma's farm. He and Aunt Eva dispatched forty of them, forty swift downstrokes of the bloody hatchet, forty astonished heads flopping into the dirt, the scalding, the ripping of feathers. The evisceration, the cleaning and wrapping. Usually, my job is to chase the birds and grab them by the ankles with a long wire hook and carry them to the killing block, but I didn't go today, because I wanted to mow the lawn and besides Eva is mad at me. Daddy grew up on that farm. He doesn't like to visit, because Aunt Eva has weepy spells and Daddy can't bear to be around anyone crying, but he has to kill chickens for Grandma, because the ones sold in stores carry deadly bacteria. The bacteria doesn't seem to bother us, but it would kill her.

Ten eye-popping mouth-watering stories in every issue of *High School Orgies*, and the first is the story of Jack and Laura, tenth-grade teachers at Central City High who have the hots for each other. She is blonde, him too, and common sense is no match for spring fever, no match at all. *She felt his eyes devour her resplendent globes as she bent to squirt mustard on her ham sandwich in the faculty lunchroom—why had she worn this blouse with the plunging neckline??? What was she thinking of???* Whatever it was, he was thinking of the same exact thing, and in no time flat they find themselves in an empty classroom tearing the clothes off each other with trembling fingers.

"There is a hole in a screen somewhere," Daddy says. "Mosquitoes are coming in all over the place." I listen and hear no mosquitoes. "You run around with bare legs and arms and you never use bug repellent, for crying out loud. I keep telling you and it's in one ear and out the other." He lies looking up at the ceiling, talking to himself as the announcer Bob Motley says, "We'll be right back after this important message," and a male quartet sings, "From the land of sky-blue waters, Hamm's, the beer refreshing." Daddy: "You ever hear of encephalitis? Know what that is? It's an inflammation of the brain. They have to drill a hole in the top of your skull and stick a tube in and drain it. And if you get an infection—*pfffffffffffffft.* You're a goner. You'd be a vegetable. You couldn't use a knife and fork. I saw this over and over in the Army. But

4

don't listen to me. What do I know? If you want to be a cripple for the rest of your life, go right ahead."

This is pure Daddy. He is a woofer. He's only happy when he can get upset over something. If a toilet is running, if he walks into a room and finds a light on and nobody there, he barks from one end of the house to the other. What are you people thinking? *Do you think I am made of money?* After Elvis sang on the Tommy Dorsey show—even though we have no television—Daddy woofed about that for weeks, the corrupting effect of it on the youth of our nation.

From one mail-order house, you can purchase nifty magic tricks, a correspondence course in ju-jitsu, novelty underwear, and powerful binoculars that can see through clothing. A cartoon man aimed his binocs at a high-stepping mama and his eyes bugged out and his jaw dropped and drops of sweat flew off his brow.

The cologne makes girls "eager to respond to your every wish, as if in a hypnotic trance," which sounds like a good deal, but what if someone like Miss Lewis came under your spell? You'd have a scrawny horse-faced old-lady English teacher in your arms. Maybe a guy should settle for the binoculars. And learn ju-jitsu in case somebody tries to steal them.

"Where does the word *Saturday* come from?"

Daddy grunts. He thinks it comes from the Roman god Saturn.

"But it's not Saturnay. It's SaTURDay."

"It got changed, I guess."

"Why would they change Saturnay to *SaTURDay*?"

"Got me."

This is not an important matter to Daddy.

5

I spring the next question. "Do you think it's right for Christians to use the names of pagan gods for the days of the week?"

He grunts. I have caught him in a small inconsistency of faith. But in matters of faith, could any inconsistency be said to be "small"?

We are Sanctified Brethren, the Chosen Remnant of Saints Gathered to the Lord's Name and Faithful to the Literal Meaning of His Word, the True Church in Apostate Times, the Faithful Bride Awaiting the Lord's Imminent Return In Triumph in the Skies, whom God has chosen to place in Lake Wobegon, Minnesota, a town of about twelve hundred in the center of the state, populated by German Catholics and Norwegian Lutherans, whom Scripture tells us to keep clear of, holding fast to the Principle of Separation from the Things of the World, Avoiding the Unclean, Standing Apart from Error, which is not such a big problem for my people, because we are standoffish by nature and not given to hobnobbing with strangers. Separation is the exact right Principle for us.

The Brethren are opposed to having a TV because it doesn't honor the Lord, but does it honor Him to refer to Saturn or Thor or Wotan when you plan a family picnic? Should we not testify to our faith by changing Saturday to Saintsday? How about Spiritday?

Daddy ignores this suggestion. He is good at shutting out matters he prefers not to address. Daddy is large and slow-moving, balding, with soft pink hands, smelling of Lifebuoy soap. He and the big brother (the genius) got in some bitter arguments before the genius went away to the U—Daddy yelling, "If you knew the actual number of communists in the federal government today, it would make your skin crawl!" and the genius simply ignoring him, employing his own separation principle—because what is the point of arguing with an old woofer like Daddy? You only make him woof harder. Above his head hangs a glass-bead contraption that dingle-dangles in the breeze. It glitters like a kaleidoscope. The dingling drives him nuts, like a phone that nobody answers, but it can't be thrown out, because it belonged to Grandpa, Mother's dad, and Grandpa is dead. This wicker porch furniture was his before he went to heaven to be with the Lord. He sat in this swing in his house on Taft Street and read from Deuteronomy and Leviticus and all about sacrificing calves and what was an abomination unto the Lord and how many cubits long the Temple should be, which made more sense to Grandpa, a practical man, than the Beatitudes ("Blessed are the meek"—what is *that* supposed to mean?). He was reading from God's Word and got up to go take a leak and he slipped on a loose rug and fell and broke a hip. What got into the hired girl's head that she had to go and wax that hall floor? The fool had too much time on her hands, evidently, so she had to go torture an old man, as surely as if she had set out a leg trap for him. Better she should have put cyanide in his prune juice or blown his brains out with a rifle. Poor Grandpa was hauled to the Good Shepherd Home, where he lay weeping and gnashing his teeth for two years, refusing TV, refusing crafts, until God finally called him home; meanwhile, we had been enjoying his furniture, knowing he'd never need it again.

Her hand brushed against the bulge of his maleness and suddenly his body seemed to rise as if on an ocean wave. His passion was too powerful to resist. "Oh, Jack," she moaned. He leaned forward so she could better sniff his secret cologne and she began to tear at his shirt buttons. He had viewed her often through his binoculars and well knew the delights that would soon be his.

And suddenly, on the radio, Bob Motley is in a white froth, yelling, "Goodbye, Mama, that train is leaving the station!

Whoooooooooooooo-eeee!"—his trademark home-run cry—and Daddy perks up his ears, but it isn't a homer, it's a long fly out for Miller slugger Clint Hardin. ("That ball was on its way out of here, folks! And the wind got hold of it and it's a heartbreaking out to right field for a great ballplayer and just a wonderful guy! What a shame! And now Wayne Terwilliger comes to the plate.") The crowd goes back to sleep.

The noble Huguenots, our Protestant ancestors, are perishing under the rock piles dumped on them by papists, and with their dying breaths the Huguenots pray for God to forgive their tormentors, a truly wonderful touch. A papist sneers at a lovely Huguenot girl as she raises her hands to heaven, as a load of rocks is piled on her. *Expertly, Jack's tongue probed her hot mouth as his lovestick hardened. Laura moaned audibly—she loved it, the little vixen!* And now out comes the older sister from the kitchen, all hot and bothered, and cries out, "Why does he get to lie around and read books while everybody else has to do the work around here? I even had to do his laundry today—boy, talk about disgusting!" She makes a face, at the thought of unspeakable things. "And he's supposed to dry the dishes and he just waltzes away and the pots and pans are sitting there in the dish rack!"

I close the *Book of Martyrs* carefully to conceal Jack with his lovestick. But the book is too small! The magazine pokes out!

Quickly I shift *High School Orgies* from *Foxx's* to my *Collier's Encyclopedia* (Volume XI, Passover–Printing), but the sister got a glimpse of the lovestick man. I'm pretty sure she did. She doesn't miss a trick. The sister smelled the wine on my breath that Sunday morning weeks ago. Walked in and sniffed it and knew instantly where it came from. It was the Blood of the Lord. People go to hell for things of that sort, as she was quick to point out.

She stands over Daddy, hands on hips, her broad butt in the yellow Bermudas, her pale pimply piano legs. "It takes two minutes to dry a few pots and pans, and he can't even be bothered to do that much!"

I explain to her the principle of evaporation, whereby the air absorbs moisture, and objects such as pots and pans become dry in a short period of time with no need for human hands.

"Why do you have to be so stupid?"

I am only being reasonable, I explain.

She leans over Daddy and touches his shoulder, to bring him back to the point. "Why do I have to do my chores and his too? It isn't fair!" You'd think she had spent ten years on a chain gang.

I open my encyclopedia, which conceals Jack and his lovestick. A handsome book from Grandpa's sixteen-volume set, of which each grandchild received a volume. My volume includes Pax Romana, peacocks, the peanut, *The Pearl Fishers* by Bizet, explorer Robert Peary, the Peloponnesian Wars, the Pend d'Oreille Indians, penicillin—I wish that Penis were here, illustrated, so I could check my own for normality (why does it hang slightly to the left?)—Pennsylvania, the pentatonic scale, the periodic table, the perpetual calendar, perspective, photography (illustrated), the Pimpernel (Scarlet)—Wayne fouls off a Toledo fastball—a full page of Scottish plaids by clan, the planets, the various genuses of plants, the Poets Laureate of Britain, poisons and their antidotes, poker hands, polo, Catholic popes, Presidents of the United States from Washington to F.D.R., the prevention of forest fires, a history of printing—

how could a person not love such a book? And right in the middle, surrounded by Scottish plaids, Jack is doing a push-up over Laura with her luscious orbs and his lovestick is between her legs, vanished into a thicket of hair. *"Please, Jack, don't stop!" she murmured, as a wave of pulsating pleasure hit her like an express train and the life-giving sperm suddenly shot over her proud globes of flesh.* They were teachers at the high school and suddenly it was spring, they opened the windows, and now look at them. Wayne Terwilliger fouls off another pitch. "It's a waiting game," says Bob Motley. "Wayne's looking for the inside fastball."

Daddy says he wishes I would be kinder to my sister and do my share of the chores.

"I do the lawn." And this is surely true. When the genius went away to the University I took over the lawn, which he, being a genius, had allowed to go to rack and ruin, and now take a look for yourself. Thick, green turf. Dandelions: vanquished. Massed on the Anderson border, they launched a seed barrage that fell to certain doom, thanks to vigilance. Crabgrass: ditto. "It would mean so much to Daddy if you'd take over the lawn," Mother said to me in early April, and that very same day I became the Lord of the Yard, Genghis Khan of the Lawn, the Conqueror of the Crabgrass Race (but to impress Mother, not Daddy)—I fertilized and raked and watered and poked it with steel rods to aerate the soil and fought off two moles by whacking their tunnels flat and flooding them and inserting poisoned Twinkies. I spent several Saturdays prying out dandelions with a two-prong fork, stemming the yellow tide from the Andersons' jungle, I patted chunks of sod into bare spots caused by winter blight or dog pee. And I was surprised myself at how verdant and thick and green it got by the end of May. I cut it close and soak it regularly and the result is a lawn worthy of millionaires and Hollywood stars—if Clark Gable had our lawn, he'd sit on it every day and grin for the photographers. Every day Daddy looks at this perfection, and once, prompted by Mother, he said, "It's looking pretty good," but mostly he searches for flaws, a ragged edge, a few brown blades, a lone clump of skunk cabbage, and he delights in pointing these out. But still—you don't hear me whining about my sad lot in life. Everybody knows Daddy's not the backslapping type. But the sister has him wrapped around her little finger. She works him like a marionette. She stands behind him, touching his shoulder, and he tells me to go dry the pots and pans. Even though I have today mowed the entire lawn. "I will," I say. "In a minute."

"Why can't you do what you're told to do?" she hisses at me.

"Don't make a federal case out of everything." Wayne fouls off another pitch. Still looking for the inside fastball.

She looks daggers at me, poor ugly thing. A big shovel-faced girl with Christmas cookies for titties and Percheron legs and chubby thighs and cheesy hair and a very very bad personality. And that is the problem here, ladies and gentlemen. This is not about pots and pans. This is about a personality problem.

I tell her that a person can't poke along washing the dishes and complaining about everything under the sun and expect me to stand and twiddle my thumbs and wait for her to finish in a week or two, can she. And steady Wayne Terwilliger takes a called third strike ("Un-believable! Un-believable, folks! That pitch to Twig was *in the dirt*, ladies and gentlemen! How can a man be expected to hit a pitch like that? In the dirt! And the fans here are letting home-plate umpire Larry Cahoon know they're upset about that call!") and the Millers are set down, scoreless, and there's a commercial for Rainbow motor oil and then the Burma-Shave Boys

("You can put on suntan lotion, where the ocean meets the sand. / Find he-man perfection and a complexion well tanned. / You can dream of sweet *amore* on your surfboard on the wave, / But listen, pal, you'll get your gal if you use Burma-Shave.").

She says, "I just finished washing your underwear, and if that isn't a disgusting job. Did nobody ever show you how to use toilet paper?"

A low blow. I ignore it.

Daddy says, "I come home from butchering forty chickens and I'm on the verge of a nervous breakdown and you kids can't give me one minute of peace."

I have given him plenty of peace. It's a peaceful night, the sprinkler swishing, school is out, and the humiliations of phys ed are over, I am quite content here with my reading material, but this porky little whiner, Miss Misery, comes and ruins a perfectly lovely summer night, simply because someone knows enough about the scientific process of evaporation to let the pots and pans sit and DRY BY THEMSELVES instead of running in to dry them at her beck and call. This is the issue here.

"Go dry the pots and pans," says Daddy. "How many times do I have to tell you?"

"As soon as I move the sprinkler, I will go and put away the pots and pans, which are undoubtedly dry already."

"So move it, then," he says.

"I'll go check and see if it's ready to be moved." I set the encyclopedia down on the porch swing, with the lovestick inside, and set a pillow over it.

The sprinkler is placed at the exact point where it douses a quadrant of front yard from the birch tree to the sidewalk, allowing a slight overlap. I check the grassroots. Wet but not soaked.

"Not ready to be moved yet," I say.

Daddy says, "Make sure you move it before it floods, for heaven's sake. Or we'll have to resod the whole thing. And sod doesn't grow on trees, either. It grows on the ground." He chuckles at his little joke. I chuckle too. There is much to be gained by laughing at Daddy's little jokes.

The sister is not amused. She shakes her head and stomps into the house, her big yellow butt like two pigs fighting in a laundry bag. And then she comes charging right back.

"The pots and pans have big water spots on them!"

I point out that pots and pans will still conduct heat and cook food even with a few water spots.

I step to the door and stand, one ear cocked to the game, the sprinkler whirring, the circle of drops flung glittering out into the gathering night. Faint in the distance the chugging of a tractor. *They lay side by side on the classroom floor, their love juices spent, breathing softly, and then he felt her hand on his thigh, reaching for him, leaning against him, her resplendent breasts, and he thought he'd like to get a hand on those puppies.*

"Boy, you never know how kids are going to turn out, do you," says Grandpa, looking out the window of heaven, wearing his best wool suit and starched white shirt with the armbands, his hair perfectly combed. "I used to think that kid might become a preacher. Now I don't see how he's going to stay out of prison. Nobody in this family ever went to prison for sex crimes. He'd be the first."

"Yes," says Jesus, "you never know about these things."

He and Grandpa are drinking cups of coffee and eating ginger snaps. Grandpa says, "When are you planning to return to earth?"

"Soon as I finish this coffee," says Jesus. "Pretty good, isn't it."

"Never tasted better in my life," says Grandpa.

Back when he was on earth, Grandpa used to drop in on Saturday and cry out, "Who wants to go for a ride?" And for years I said "Me!" and went with him, and then one year I said, "I can't. I have homework. I'm sorry." Three lies in five seconds. I hated riding around and listening to Grandpa reminisce about who used to live in that house and everybody they were related to. Once I liked it okay and then I didn't anymore. I wonder if Grandpa remembers how I treated him, inventing excuses to get away from his perorations against Hollywood, drink, Democrats, Catholics. He was even hard on the Lutherans. Flatheads, to him.

"Why don't you just go and dry those pots and pans?" says Daddy. "It'll take you five minutes."

"The pots and pans are probably dry by now," I inform the sister. "All that needs to be done is to put them away in the cupboard, and I'll come in and do that in a moment. Soon as I'm done reading about the Huguenots."

"It's not pronounced *hug-you-nots*," she says. "For your information, it's *hue-ge-nots. Hue-ge-nots.*" I thank her for elucidating this. Her eyes narrow to chinaman's slits and she leans down and quick as a snake she snatches the naked couple out of the encyclopedia.

"*Give it back. Please.*" She grins at me all bony and wolfish, and her muzzle twitches at the smell of blood. She backs away, clutching *High School Orgies.*

"Please give me back that magazine," I say firmly.

She gazes at it. "What is this?" Her eyes widen in mock horror as she flips through a few pages. "Oh my goodness." She looks to Daddy, but he has spotted a pair of houseflies and is stalking them into the corner, a swatter in hand. Daddy is a sworn enemy of flies. Flies walk around in fecal matter, and if you don't kill them you may as well be eating your dinner off the barn floor with the hogs.

"You really need to go see a psychiatrist," she says.

"I don't know what you're talking about."

"Talking about this." She waves the magazine at me, wrinkling the cover. "*Touch not the unclean thing,*" says the sister, who is getting a bad Scripture-quoting habit. "*Whatsoever things are pure, whatsoever things are holy, let your mind be fixed on these things.*" I could club her.

"I have no idea what you're talking about." She wants me to beg for mercy, but remorse is an endless highway where she's concerned, I know her, so I must take the 100-percent denial route. I never saw those pictures of that naked couple and their hot love juices. I know nothing about this magazine. I have no idea where the sister found it. I had no idea she was interested in such things. Frankly, I'm shocked.

"You know this would break Mother's heart. She would cry her eyes out if she knew," she says.

"If she knew what?"

"You know what," says the sister. "You know." She tosses her head and reminds me that the dishes are waiting to be dried and wheels toward the kitchen, *High School Orgies* in hand.

I will swear up and down I never laid eyes on it, I will lie my face off, tell fibs until I am tied in knots—deny everything. Mother looks at me, hurt, tearful, holding the filth in her hands. *How could you, my son?—I never saw that magazine in my life, Mother. I demand a polygraph test! Call in the FBI, Boston*

Blackie, Sam Spade. Get me City Desk! We'll get to the bottom of this! Find out who is defiling our household with this despicable literature! But Mother will know. Mother knows all. She will know.

The tears run down her cheeks, her voice trembles. "I never thought a child of mine would sink to such depths of degradation. What pleasure could you possibly get from this—this *trash?*"

And now my eyes are full of tears and one tear rolls down the side of my nose and into my mouth, bitter salt, and, not wanting anyone to see me cry, I slip into the dark living room and up the stairs and into my bedroom and lock the door and in safety now release a gush of tears and a wrenching sob.

I sit on the bed. What a wretch I am. What a gink. A hayseed Herkimer Jerkimer from the sticks and also a freak and a sicko. A despicable sinner, as Grandpa can see from up in heaven, and soon this will become general knowledge, and Mother and Daddy and even Aunt Eva will turn away from me in shame.

I will be sent to a hospital with rolls of barbed wire around it, and men in white uniforms will place copper electrodes on my temples and throw a switch and scorch my brains so I never have another dirty thought in my life, and I will return home a placid moon-faced boy with an IQ of 45 who sits on the porch steps all day with his dog Scooter and eats big bags of potato chips and waves bye-bye to passing cars.

The village idiot.

Which is exactly what I looked like in the movie Daddy made on New Year's Eve, 1955.

Everyone has seen this movie twice and the memory of it burns like acid.

O friends, Romans, countrymen.

2

Mr. Tree Toad

We Sanctified Brethren are people of the Word and the great cadences of the King James Version of 1611. We don't hold with Literature and its godless drunks and wastrels, but we hold fast to God's Literal Truth in Scripture. Yea, surely. But Daddy is a man of the picture and he loves his Kodak box camera. At family picnics he loves to arrange family portraits in the backyard and place Al next to LeRoy and Uncle Sugar and Aunt Ruth and Mother in her new green dress and Aunt Flo, all in a row beside the hydrangeas, and cry "Cheese!" and dash into the gap between Ruth and Mother and grin as the shutter goes *click!* Then get one of LeRoy mugging and get the earnest Al to hold out his hand for a trick picture in which he seems to be holding Flo's head in his palm. We have pictures of various dogs wearing hats and neckties. An old snapshot of Sugar (with hair) holding a chamber pot. Aunt Bertha from behind, bending over her petunias. The older brother, tall, stone-faced, on roller skates, arms at his side, concentrating on remaining upright. The big sister in Camp Fire Girl neckerchief, trying to look normal and friendly. And me.

I look like a tree toad who was changed into a boy but not completely. There is still plenty of toadness there. The dark amphibian eyes blinking, the pipestem arms and wrists, the high-water pants, the flappy clown-shoes, the Herkimer hair, the steel-rim glasses. There I am at the end of the row of family, hunkering, as if waiting for a tasty dragonfly.

Daddy gave himself a Revere movie camera for a Christmas present, and on New Year's Eve, as Mother and I sat playing Monopoly and listening to Ben Grauer live from Times Square, with Guy Lombardo and his Royal Canadians standing by at the Waldorf-Astoria, and Mother having just traded me Boardwalk for two railroads and Baltic Avenue, the camera started whirring and a floodlight blazed and I turned and Daddy said to smile and I leered at him (and at posterity) and these eleven seconds, my fellow countrymen, will forever live in the annals of shame.

0–3 sec. Side view of pencil-necked geek, his glasses, his hopeless hair shaved high on side of head, visible shaver-marks, unmistakable signs of home haircutting kit. His big Adam's apple bobs as he swallows a bite of oatmeal cookie.

4–6 sec. His head jerks in reaction to off-camera command and he turns head, still chewing, and smiles his hideous toad grin, the little yellow toad teeth showing between the slimy lips.

6–11 sec. More of the leer, his trademark Norman Ninny

glasses riding low on the oily nose, and then he attempts to boost them by screwing up his face—it looks like a spastic in mid-seizure! The feeb's entire face scrunches up, and then he boosts the glasses with his little toad finger.

Here in this facial convulsion you can see why girls do not chase after this boy. Here is the reason he has never kissed a girl. (Okay, *one girl*, but a cousin. More on this later.)

No sensible woman would marry a guy this creepy. Take a look and you see: this person will never be a normal American. He will live alone and suffer from psoriasis and hemorrhoids and halitosis and earn $$$$ at home through taxidermy and selling salve and he will never have true friends, only other geeks, who remind him too painfully of himself, but what choice does he have? So he meets them at the Spastic Center to compare stamp collections, play chess, solve algebra problems, do geek-type things. He may never obtain a driver's license. He'll ride his Schwinn bike to and from Ralph's Pretty Good Grocery and his old classmates will zoom past in their late-model cars and think, "Whatever happened to old Gary? The creep-o. The spaz. Haven't seen hide nor hair of him for years." *ZOOM!* And there I am, the old guy on a bike, the old galoot who totes his necessaries around in a plastic bag, a rubber band around his pants leg, reflective tape plastered on the sleeves and back of his plaid jacket, and a reflector pinned to the back of his hunting cap, eating a Little Debbie Snack Cake. *"You thrill me so," she whispered as she kissed him, her back arched, her luscious orbs gleaming in the moonlight*—this type of thing will not happen for that guy, any more than he will sing and dance in a Broadway musical. That guy's lovestick will never be a lovestick that any babe thinks of with anything but mute disgust.

The *High School Orgies* story about the boy in home-ec class.
This will not happen for me. The girls are sewing dresses and the
boy sews a tiny leopardskin bathing suit and models it for them.
The girls inspect it closely, admiring the handiwork, and suddenly
he bursts a seam and soon they're all naked, their love juices flow-
ing. I find this tremendously exciting, those girlish fingers poking
at his pouch. I am going to hell. This is becoming increasingly
clear. As Aunt Flo says, you don't get to be a Christian by sitting
in church any more than sleeping in a garage makes you a car.
What sort of Christian can open up *High School Orgies* to the picture of the home-ec girls' breasts with pointy nipples and feel that
happy twitching in his shorts?

I am going to spend eternity in hellfire for what is twitching in
my mind right now.

Here I am in my room, weeping for my carnal sins, on a warm
summer night, and what if the Second Coming is scheduled for
nine-fifteen P.M. Central Time and in exactly five minutes the
saved of earth will rise into the stratosphere and I will find myself
left behind with the heathen?

This could be the case. What if I tiptoe downstairs *right now*
and Daddy isn't lying there on the daybed listening to the Millers
on the radio—what if all of the Sanctified Brethren have whooshed
up to the sky, Sugar and Ruth and Al and Flo and LeRoy and Lois,
and I am left behind with the Catholics and the atheists and the
drunks at the Sidetrack Tap? And Bob Motley says, "Folks, it's the
damnedest thing but all of a sudden—I'd say about a thousand
fans—they were here in the stands enjoying the ballgame and
suddenly they weren't here, folks! I can see their half-eaten hot
dogs, their scorecards, their shoes and clothes and, yes, even their

doggone underwear! But they're gone! I don't know what the hell is going on!"

And then I stand in front of God's Throne squinting up at His blazing glory and He says, "You had your opportunities, boy. But did you listen? No. You went on heedlessly reading that garbagey magazine with pictures of naked girls in it. How juvenile! I gave geese more sense than that."

Please, God. I'm only fourteen years old. A teenager. Have mercy. Be loving.

"I was," says God. "For eons. And look at what it got me. You."

God turns in disgust, just the way Daddy does. "Sorry, but I'm the Creator. I take it personally. There are slugs and bugs and night-crawlers I feel better about having created—I mean, there are *sparrows*—I've got my eye on one right now. Is that sparrow consumed with lust? No. He mates in the spring and that's the end of it. Consider the lilies. Do they think about lily tits all the time? No. They look not and they lust not, and yet I say unto you that you will never be half as attractive as they. Therefore, I say unto you, think not about peckers and boobs and all that nonsense, and your Heavenly Father will see that you meet a good woman and marry her, just as I do for the sparrow and walleye— yea verily, even the night-crawler and eelpout. But I've told you this over and over for nineteen centuries. And now, verily, it's too late. Time's up, buster. Lights out! Game's over!"

I close my eyes and squeeze tight until bright sparks appear. In this way, I manage to hold off the Second Coming for a moment. I say a quick preventative prayer *(Lord, I'm a sinner, come into my heart and save me and let me go to heaven)*, but I've said this prayer hundreds of times before and doubt its efficacy. It's only words. God looks on the heart and in my heart is a whole bevy of naked women beckoning to me.

I return to the porch. Toledo is at bat in the bottom of the seventh, their shortstop Denny Davies, who poked the triple in the second, now knocks out a single—he is three for three—and the sister is there, having stashed the magazine for blackmail, sitting beside Daddy, her hand on his hand. "I think Gary has something to tell you," she announces.

Daddy looks at me. "Go dry the dishes."

"I will in a minute."

I will not surrender. I never saw *High School Orgies* in my life and have no idea where she found it. I will go to the kitchen *when I choose* and dry the pots and pans *when I choose and not a moment before.* You let the sister start calling the shots and you will become her indentured servant, and there will be no end to it.

She leans down and whispers, "I'd be very careful if I were you, because you're not going to get away with this. You are going to be in very very big trouble. You smile like you think I don't mean it. I do mean it. I could have that filthy magazine in Mother's hands in two minutes!"

And just then, out comes Mother, my old ally and defender, iced tea in hand, in her green linen pants and white sailor blouse, barefoot, her bushy blond hair tied back, and settles down in the white wicker chair with the *Minneapolis Star.* "What a lovely evening," she says.

"He won't dry the pots and pans," says Miss Misery. "And there's one more thing—"

Mother looks up. "They're dry. I put them away in the cupboard."

The sister seethes. She steams, she fumes, she foams at the mouth. Oh, great is her rage thereof! Verily she is pissed. She glares at me, her pupils like shards of glass, and she heaves a sigh as big as North Dakota and stomps out. She stops in the living room to grind her teeth and then stomps upstairs in a white froth. Poor thing. This is what comes from anger, boys and girls. It chews up your brain and poisons your heart. Anger eats up your innards and is vile and displeasing to God and it availeth naught. It gets you nowhere. And now she stomps back down. And is standing in the doorway. She informs Daddy that the pots and pans had to be rewashed because flies had walked all over them for the past half-hour due to my disobedience. They are in the dish rack now and await my dish towel.

He looks over at me on the porch swing, a pillow behind my head, glancing through the *Collier's*, reading about peanuts, a leguminous plant *(Arachis hypogaea)*, bearing underground nut-like pods.

—Go do what you said you were going to do before I completely lose patience.

—I have to move the sprinkler again. I don't want to overwater the grass. I've worked hard to get the lawn looking good and I don't want to ruin it just because somebody is too weak to put away a few pots and pans herself.

—Then go move the sprinkler now.

—It isn't watered yet.

—Move it anyway.

—I will, as soon as the mosquitoes are gone.

Daddy peers into the dark.

—There are clouds of mosquitoes swarming there. They'll go away in a little while, and then I'll move the sprinkler.

The sister addresses Mother in a small cold voice: "Everything he wants, he gets. He's treated like royalty around here. He's spoiled rotten and everybody says so. I don't think you realize all the things he's up to. Maybe someday you'll find out and then you'll wish you had exercised a little more discipline." Her day has been ruined, poor thing. She stands, silent, defeated, proud, a moral bastion and bulwark who will be proven right in the fullness of time. She is a prize-winning born-again Christian who agrees 100 percent with Daddy that Elvis is evil and can't sing one bit, the rock-and-roll craze is ridiculous, it's those pelvic gyrations that are driving the youth of our nation crazy and inspiring paroxysms of lust and causing so many teens to go wrong.

I walk down the front steps. Frames of porch light stretch over the beautiful grass, and drops of water fly into the light. Thousands of drops enjoying a split-second life as individuals before mingling in the ooze. The grass is drenched, the ground soused. I pick up the green hose and crimp it to shut off the spray and drag the hose around to the side of the house, and in the shadows the Stenstroms' cat, who knows my accuracy with water, slinks for cover in the lilacs.

I set the sprinkler so it waters a sphere of backyard from the cellar steps to the tomato plants to the clotheslines, and I come in the back door into the kitchen, where the sister sits smirking at the table. "Life is no bowl of cherries for anybody," I tell her. "People around here are tired of hearing your complaints. We have enough troubles of our own." I tell her she really ought to do something about her personality. And also her appearance. And she hisses at me, "Fornicator!" and stomps upstairs, and I dry the three pans and one pot she has rewashed, the ones that flies purportedly trod on, and as I put them into the cupboard I sneeze and a string of snot lands in the pot and I open the cupboard under the sink to get the detergent and there is *High School Orgies* hidden in a dish basin. *Yes! Thank you, Lord! I appreciate this favor!* I slip it under my shirt, and return to the porch and plop back into my nest on the swing and sit, pretending to read about peanuts, the evidence hidden safely under my shirt.

3

Ricky

Mother sits in the white wicker chair by the driftwood lamp, her legs crossed ladylike at the ankles, sipping her Salada iced tea, reading the *Minneapolis Star*, which she enjoys for its extensive coverage of heinous crime. Politics doesn't interest her one whit, sports makes no sense whatsoever, she isn't interested in the love lives of Marilyn Monroe and Elizabeth Taylor; but a good murder brightens Mother's day considerably, she gets all giddy and chilly reading about it and mulling it over in her mind. The Lutheran minister who was telling his wife of thirty-one years that he couldn't understand why people want to go to Europe when there are so many wonderful things to see right here in Minnesota and she blew off the back of his head with a Colt revolver. *Blammo.* Never shot a gun before in her life. Bull's-eye. The St. Paul milkman who poisoned three old ladies on his route. They poured cream on their cornflakes and opened up the newspaper and ate their breakfast and fell face-first into the comics. He told the cops that he knew them well, they were lonely old ladies, and their great pleasure was reading *Winnie Winkle* and *Bringing Up Father* and *L'il Iodine* and *Gasoline Alley*. They looked forward to their cup of coffee and the funny pages every morning, and how fitting for a lonely old lady to fade away in a moment of pleasure. The Richfield man who wanted to move with his wife to Florida and decided to rob a liquor store, having read about attempted robberies and feeling that he could do it better, so he picked a big liquor store miles away and donned an eyemask and robbed the store at gunpoint at closing time, when the till was chock-full of cash, but the clerk happened to be an old high-school classmate and recognized him despite the mask, and the police pounded on his door as he was telling his wife the good news about Florida and called on him to surrender, and he emerged, holding a gun to the back of his wife's head, demanding a ride to the Northwest Orient terminal at Wold-Chamberlain Field or he'd kill her, sure as shooting, and she turned and said, "You've done dumb things before, but this is the dumbest thing you did in your life, Joe," and she dashed for cover, and the cops gunned him down in a fusillade of hot lead in his own front yard, the poor dope. He collapsed on the grass he had mowed all those years and his life ebbed away, he died looking at a birch sapling he had planted that spring which had died and he'd meant to dig it up and now he never would.

Tonight Mother is in a lighthearted mood because Aunt Doe is sick and can't come up from Minneapolis to decorate Grandpa's grave on his birthday.

"She called and said she has a bad case of the trots," says Mother. "Poor thing." Daddy breathes a long sigh of relief. Doe is a weeper, a sob sister of the first water, and Daddy cannot tolerate crying, he has to evacuate the room whenever it rears its head, one sniffle and he is up and out of his chair.

Doe is a skinny minnie with mouse-colored hair who tries so hard to be no trouble to anybody and stay out of everyone's way and make no demands whatsoever on anyone, and if you ask her what she'd like to eat for lunch, or what she wants to do after lunch, she only whispers, "Whatever you have left over. Don't fix anything special for me. A piece of bread is more than good enough. Whatever you have extra of. Water is fine. If you want to go someplace after lunch, I can just sit here and look out the window. I'm happy. It's fine with me. Make it easy on yourself. I'm quite content to look at an old magazine and listen to the radio. I don't need anybody to entertain me. You go do whatever you like and just pretend I'm not here." Her visits place a huge weight on our household. The weight of meekness. Aunt Doe is sort of the Billy the Kid of meekness, a professional meeker, she has out-meeked the best of them, she can meek you to death.

Mother is the only cheery one in that family, come to think of it—the others are a bunch of damp rags. Brother Ed works for the railroad in Chicago, a mournful little man indeed, and brother Jim is a lost cause in Duluth, a collector of defeat, and then there's Mother. "Why carry rocks in your pocket?" she says cheerfully. "What's past is gone." Emphasize the positive. Why dwell on the past? Smile and you get a smile back. Look for the silver lining. Tomorrow is a brand-new day. What's done is done and you can't look back, you have to look to tomorrow.

If she knew what I have under my shirt, she would tell me to throw it away, and then tomorrow she'd be her usual self, bygones forgotten, water under the bridge.

If Daddy knew what's under my shirt, he'd tell Mother and have her deal with it.

If the big sister had her way, I'd be sent to an institution for the sex-crazed. A dark stone building surrounded by a ten-foot fence, with steel mesh over the windows, and the hallways smell of piss and boys lie strapped to bunkbeds with thick leather straps—a place like the place Grandpa died in, except for sex lunatics, and the cure is to dunk them in ice water and zap them with electricity and give them anti-sex drugs and if necessary slice off their wieners so for the rest of their lives they have to pee sitting down, like girls.

Tonight Mother is engrossed in the story of Ricky Guppy, 17, of Millet, eight miles away, who got in a loud argument with his mother yesterday, around 4:37 P.M., after she refused to give him ten dollars on the grounds he'd only fritter it away on pinball and cigarettes, as he had done in the past. Ricky had arrived home from Lake Wobegon High School, where he is enrolled in summer school to make up for two classes he flunked in the spring, and he yelled at her so loud that neighbors two doors away heard it. She was cooking him a hamburger for his supper, thinking he had to be to work at the HiDeHo Club in St. Cloud at seven-thirty. Actually, Ricky had been fired by the HiDeHo for tardiness and was intending to take his girlfriend Dede to see James Powers in *Give It the Gun.* The boy was enraged by her refusal to give him ten dollars and threw several china plates at the kitchen wall, busting them to smithereens, and cursed her and tried to kick her, causing the cast-iron skillet to slip from her hand and spatter her with hot grease and causing serious burns to her arms and legs. He then seized the skillet and flung it through a window, and swiped fifty-eight dollars from her purse and also her car keys and sped away in a two-tone green-and-brown 1955 Ford station wagon and picked up Dede who was awaiting him at her house in St. Rosa. Instead of tooling in to the Starlite Drive-In for the twin feature, the two of them headed west at a high rate of speed. An all-points bulletin has been issued. Ricky's parents have urged him to turn himself in. Authorities in North and South Dakota are on the alert. The Civil Air Patrol sent out several flights in search of them. The FBI has been brought into the case. Kidnapping is a federal offense and so is transporting a minor across state lines for immoral purposes. The FBI searched Ricky's room and found records by Elvis, Little Richard, and the Sh'Bops and also some pictures of rock-and-roll singers and a scrapbook with lyrics apparently written by young Guppy himself, which FBI agents characterized as "amateurish." Mother can't get over the fact that this took place eight miles away from our home and she is reading about it a day later in the Minneapolis paper.

"What is this country coming to when a boy kicks his mother because she won't pay for his cigarettes?" wonders Mother.

"Wake up and smell the coffee," says Daddy. "That's where this country has been headed for a good long time now. Look around you. The disrespect for parents and authority. You see it everywhere. Lookit who this kid's brother is. Go ahead. It's right there in the paper."

Ricky is the youngest brother of James Guppy, 22, better known as Jim Dandy, a singer in a local pop group called the Doo Dads. Another brother, Ray, 21, is an inmate at St. Cloud Reformatory, serving a sentence for robbing a gas station, and a third brother, Roger Guppy, 19, is a rookie pitcher with the Lake Wobegon Whippets.

"Quite a family," says Daddy. "In no time, our town will be famous as the gangland capital of the North. A hotbed of robbery, rock and roll, and matricide."

"Do you know these young men?" asks Mother, looking at me.

"Sort of."

"Everybody knows them. I know them," says Daddy. "James is the guy with the long hair and mustache who lounges around town in his white Chevy convertible and talks about how he's going to hit it rich someday. A two-bit piker, if you ask me. I repossessed that car for nonpayment. Twice. Fancy new car and the guy doesn't even have a regular job. Ding Schoenecker lets him do PA for the Whippets, and last year he was peddling Christmas wreaths and gewgaws and giving dance lessons, and whatnot. Lives in the basement of his uncle's house. A place over near Bowlus, the backyard is full of junk cars. But the whole family is like that."

I could say a word in the Doo Dads' defense, but why ask for trouble? They are all from around our area and very popular not only here but in the Twin Cities. They are an excellent singing group. They appear every Friday night at the HiDeHo Club in St. Cloud. If I could, I'd go see them perform. I've heard their music over WDGY (Wonderful Weegee) played by a late-night DJ named Big

Daddy Fats. I have a tabletop radio I take to bed under the covers to listen to his show. He is "four hundred pounds of rambling boy, built for comfort, not for speed," who eats *ten giant one-pound cheeseburgers* during his "Midnight Jukebox Jamboree" (which actually starts at 10 P.M.) and he does a Cheeseburger Countdown and hollers, "Okay, all you duck butts and skinny minnies, time for Big Daddy to TIE ON THE OLD BURGER BAG! HOO-YA!" and a lion roars and bells ring and there is a mammoth munching sound and an elephantine belch and then Big Daddy announces the next tune with his mouth full. Somebody said they'd seen him riding on a flatbed truck in the Aquatennial Parade, stretched out on a rhinestone-encrusted divan like King Farouk, wearing shades, rings on his fingers, a gold jacket, pink shoes, and that he really was about four hundred pounds. Other kids said it was all a big hoax.

Toledo has now pounded the Miller hurlers for six runs in the eighth inning and Bob Motley is moaning and Daddy turns down the radio. He wouldn't be surprised if Ricky is a raging psychopath and Dede winds up in a ditch with a bullet in her brain. Some men are like that, and if a girl won't listen to her parents, what can anybody do? But that's the trend of things nowadays. Kids listen to this music and, believe me, the lyrics are NOT about saving your money and planning your future, no, it's all about grabbing what you want and to heck with everybody else. Go off and do whatever you please and never mind the consequences, and if somebody gets in your way, kick them and spatter hot grease on them.

Mother doesn't see it that way. She thinks they're two kids in love. It's all a big misunderstanding, and if somebody could just sit Ricky down and talk some sense into him, the whole thing could be worked out. There's no need for the FBI. Ricky only needs some good advice. Somebody like Art Linkletter or Arthur Godfrey. She's worried that the two kids might be cut down in a fusillade of police bullets like that nice man in Richfield.

"Nice men don't rob liquor stores," says Daddy.

"He only wanted to give his wife a vacation."

According to the *Star*, the Guppys' neighbors described Ricky as "quiet and well behaved and always polite to grown-ups."

"The neighbors obviously don't know that kid from a bale of hay," says Daddy.

I think Ricky and Dede should go to Canada and change their names and get married and forget about ever coming home.

Then Daddy looks at me, as if he heard that thought, and says, "You don't hang around with kids like that, I hope."

Of course I do. Quiet and well-behaved kids are who live in this town.

"Did you know him?" asks Mother.

"Not really. I saw him around. Some. He was in my gym class, I think." *He and I tried to sneak out of doing the rope climb because we were so bad at it. We kept going to the back of the line, pretending to tie our shoelaces, dawdling at the water fountain, killing time, but Mr. Foster was on to our tricks and made us climb.*

"Did you notice anything odd about him?"

"He hated gym class."

"Why?"

"He didn't do very well on chin-ups." *Neither did I. Two chin-*

ups was all I could do. Ricky and I were peas in a pod. Both of us with skinny arms and legs, glasses. His were half-rim, mine steel-rim, but the same thing. He wrote poems too. Leonard saw some of his poems. Mr. Foster grabbed Ricky and me by the arms and said, "Come, girls," and made us do the rope climb. The phys-ed class laughed their butts off. Two long ropes hung from the rafters, with knots for handholds. Mr. Foster showed us how as if we were morons—"You grab hold of the rope, pull yourself up, get a foothold. Pull up, foothold, pull up. It's simple." Ricky grabbed his rope and I grabbed mine. I remember seeing the goosebumps on his legs and the glitter of sweat on his brow. The class tittered when I hauled myself up, then Ricky went up, then we went up another knot and hung. Then Ricky dropped off, his shoes squeaked on the floor, and I clung to the rope for another few seconds, trying to muster the strength to go farther, but my feet lost their hold and swung free and I dangled there, turning slowly—the Great Tree Toad—See Him Cling to the Rope, Gentlemen! See Him Dangle & Spin! See His Toad Legs Flail & His Eyes Bulge! See the Sweat Pop from His Slimy Forehead—See His Lips Glisten with Spit! Hear Him Wheeze & Groan! And I dropped. "Thank you, gentlemen," said Mr. Foster. Ricky and I resumed our place in the back of the class as Mr. Foster hauled out the wrestling mats for the next event, tumbling. The back of the class was where Ricky and I felt safe. We didn't talk. We knew what we needed to know about each other.

"It's the direction this country is going in nowadays." Daddy again. "You've got fornicating music on *The Ed Sullivan Show* on the CBS Television Network, for crying out loud. You've got singers shaking their pelvic areas, lighting pianos on fire, jumping around like monkeys—it's no wonder a kid attacks his own mother. This group, the Doo Dads—didn't they get in hot water for some obscene song of theirs?"

He is referring to "Hot Rod Alley," which Big Daddy Fats played on Wonderful Weegee—*If you got a Ford, you're on board; a Chevrolet, you're okay; an Oldsmobile, you're the deal; a Mercury, you're in for free; a Pontiac, she's on her back.* With Jim Dandy the bass guy making sounds of rumbling mufflers and Earl the Girl doing the screeching tires. Some Baptist preacher got his picture in the newspaper by kneeling in prayer at the gate of the Weegee radio tower, holding a big sign: *Father, forgive them for they know not what they do.* The preacher had hair as long as Jim Dandy's and held a big white Bible up in the air and his eyes were squeezed shut and the agony on his face was like someone tied a knot in his lovestick. It was no skin off Big Daddy Fats's nose, he played the Doo Dads every chance he got. His theme song was their song.

> *My baby took one look and she just*—ran away!
> *Haven't seen my buddies for a*—year and a day!
> *I went to church and they*—locked the door!
> *Even my mama doesn't*—love me no more! (Oww!)
> *I went to the doctor and he scratched his beard.*
> *He gave me a test.*
> *He said*—"Man, you're weird!"
> *Even my buddies, they all*—disappeared.
> HEE HEE HEE HEE HEE HEE
> I'M WEEEEEEEEEEEEEEEIRRRRD!

And then Daddy says, "I don't understand how people can sit back and let these things happen. Well, I guess I better hit the sack," and he's gone. Poor Daddy. It's a relief to see him go through the door. He has so little to say, really—how most people pay too much for stuff they could get cheaper, and the immorality of the Democratic Party and its communist wing in particular, and the decline of standards and the sheer waste and people expecting something for nothing in America nowadays, and the ridiculous things people do for status and prestige such as gad about Europe or go to museums full of modern art that chimpanzees could do better than or buy expensive stuff that isn't nearly as good as what you'd pay half that for, and the dangers of infection, and the evil of rock-and-roll music. That is pretty much Daddy's entire repertoire.

I loved it when he toddled up to bed and Mother and I stayed up late. For Daddy, ten-thirty was a moral boundary, the time when decent people put on their jammies and brush their teeth and gargle and crawl into bed, and the only reason for staying up later is to do things you wouldn't do if decent people were awake to see you do them. But all Mother and I wanted to do was listen to the Trojan Troubadour and drink ginger ale and carry on civilized conversation.

"How about a game of Rook?" she said.

"How about Monopoly?"

The Troubadour came on at ten-fifteen right after Cedric Adams and the news—you heard a rippling melody on a piano and a soft, familiar voice say, "Top of the evening, everybody, it's just your old Trojan Seed Corn Troubadour Tommy Thompson coming by for a neighborly visit—to sing some old favorites and also tell you about the amazing production records set by Trojan's new Golden Victor, the talk of the seed-corn world for months now. But before we do—" and then he launches into a song.

> Moonlight on the plains of Minnesota,
> I sit here on the front porch feeling blue.
> Tomorrow it's a year since we parted, dear,
> Still my mind keeps going back to you.
> I rue the day when I walked away,
> Playing the fool as cool as could be.
> Moonlight on the plains of Minnesota.
> How I wish that you were here with me.

I always beat Mother at Monopoly, because she prefers Baltic and Mediterranean (she likes the names) and the railroads and utilities and she passes up the red or yellow or green ones or Park Place and Boardwalk because they are too expensive. I scoop up everything I land on and if necessary I borrow from the bank, which she allowed in a game a few years ago when I had the mumps.

—Is that in the rules? she says.

—We've always played that way.

Mother does not borrow, it is not in her make-up to borrow. She sits tight and gets creamed. I race around the board, acquiring property, building hotels, winning, winning—it's easy to see the importance of unlimited credit. I am very contented late at night when it's just Mother and me. I pretend my ginger ale is gin and I tell her jokes out of *Reader's Digest* and she says, "I don't know how you do it, I can't remember a joke for two minutes," and she's right, she can't. You can tell her a joke twice in one night and she enjoys it as much the second time as the first.

* * *

—Did this Ricky Guppy have many friends at school?
   —A few.
   —What was he like?
   —Quiet.

All is peaceful on Green Street. The televisions are quiet. The sprinkler whispers *shh-shh-shh-shh* in the backyard. A train whistle blows, faraway.

This may be the last summer for Monopoly. Next year I'll be 15 and I'll have a job, I'll be going to parties.

On the other hand, who would invite me? Name one person. I can't. The cool kids in my class—the Guntzel girls, the Jacobsons, the Petersons, the Bunsens, the Nilssons—do they want a tree toad lurking in the corner at their parties, licking his lips, blinking his eyes? No, surely not. I may be playing Monopoly with Mother for years to come.

—Tell me about when I was born, I say.
   —I've told you all about that before. More than once.
   —Tell me again.
   And she does.
   First, there is a certain settling of herself, and rustling, and tinkling of ice in the glass, and then she starts the story as she has always started it.
   —It was February and they were forecasting a blizzard.

4

Paradise

I was born in the great blizzard of 1942. February. It struck at noon, obliterating the roads, and the streetlights were turned on to assist the schoolchildren of Lake Wobegon in finding their way home. The country kids went to their assigned Storm Homes. Daddy was all set to drive Mother to the hospital in Willmar as soon as the pains got bad. The St. Cloud hospital was closer, but it was Catholic, and the nuns were known to put rosaries in the cribs of newborns and smear oil on their foreheads, and why go through all that nonsense? The radio bulletins said to stay home, and that only stiffened Daddy's resolve to get to Willmar. Luckily, his old Packard wouldn't start. Engine failure may have saved my life. There were ten-foot drifts of snow across the state highway and we could have run into a ditch and all three of us frozen to death. Or—I might have survived in Mother's belly and been surgically extracted and put up for adoption. The Blizzard Baby—Tiny Survivor of Nature's Frigid Onslaught—Adopted by

41

America's First Couple of Stage and Screen, Alfred L'Etoile and Jean du Nord, who read of infant's plight in the papers—"Our hearts were touched. We had to help," she sobbed—Private Plane Dispatched, Piloted by the Lone Eagle Himself, Colonel Lindbergh— Child United with New Mom and Dad in swank suite at Hollywood Roosevelt Hotel, where the celebrated pair go before RKO cameras Monday to shoot *And Away We Go!* directed by Raoul Oahu. But the engine wouldn't turn over, so Mother walked three blocks through the blizzard to Dr. Bjork's house and had me there. Mrs. Bjork was a nurse, she did the delivery, and Dr. Bjork sat in the kitchen and finished his supper. According to Mother, it was liver and onions, and she was nauseated by the smell of frying liver forever afterward.

A child born in February / Is often stubborn and contrary / And if he's born in heavy snow / Will follow his own way to go.

On Mother's side, I am descended from pale bookkeepers with thick glasses and soft hands and pink-cheeked Methodists who lived with utmost caution, gingerly, regretfully, in little stucco bungalows in south Minneapolis around 38th Street and 42nd Avenue and rode the old yellow streetcar to work and once a year packed a trunk and rode the Great Northern *Lakeshore Limited* to their summer cabin on Lake Wobegon and waded into the water up to their waists and paddled around in the shallows and fretted about wasps and the dangers of botulism and black-widow spiders and bull snakes and lightning and escaped lunatics and were grateful to return to the city and their daily routine.

On Daddy's side, I am descended from country people who woke before sunrise and clambered out of bed and dressed in coveralls or print dresses that smelled of lye soap and took their porcelain chamber pot to the outhouse and emptied it and washed their faces in cold water from a steel basin and made porridge and corn-bread for breakfast and after breakfast read a chapter of Scripture and said a prayer for their loved ones and the President of the United States and then went to their work outdoors, sun or snow, raising cows, pigs, and chickens, and corn and hay.

The farm was small, about 160 acres, in rolling sandy hills a few miles north of Lake Wobegon. Daddy grew up on the farm with his five brothers and sisters, and by the time I was old enough to figure out who was who, all of them had moved to town except Aunt Eva, who never married and stayed on the home place with Grandma. The land was rented to a neighboring farmer, Mr. Wal-berg, a man with immense black eyebrows. Grandma and Eva bus-ied themselves cleaning and cooking and washing and tending the garden and raising chickens, as they had always done. Nothing had changed there in a hundred years except Grandma owned an old Studebaker, and they had a telephone and electric lights, though Grandma liked to keep kerosene lamps around, the sour smell reminding her of her girlhood.

When I was 3 years old, Daddy went away to Fort Lee, New Jersey, to serve in the United States Army as a paymaster's clerk and Mother and I and the older brother and sister went to live on the farm, and thus began the paradise part of my life, my earliest memories. Mother and the Olders shared a bedroom, and Eva and I shared a bedroom. It was small, under the eaves, with a sloping ceiling, and I imagined we lived on a ship. The wallpaper pattern was little bouquets of blue flowers tied with pale-pink ribbons. The bed had a valley running down the middle, and we slept under a quilt and flannel sheets in winter, a blue chenille spread and percale sheets in summer, and Eva told me stories in her soft twang and sang me to sleep with sweet sad songs about the days of yore, "The Old Oaken Bucket," and "Mother's Not Dead, She's Only Sleeping in the Baggage Car Ahead," and the babes in the woods who lay down and died and the robins spread strawberry leaves over them, and the death of Old Rex, who found Little Jimmy in the storm and lay beside the sleeping form and thereby kept the child warm. When rescue came at break of day to the hollow where they lay the faithful dog had passed away. Somewhere around that time, I began to think of Eva as a mother. She wasn't Mother, but she was the warm body who lay next to me and whose smell I loved. I took an old dress of hers and curled up with it for my afternoon nap. She was my Eva. My Queen of Heaven.

She was a fireplug of a woman, with thick legs and small hands and a flat face, who all her days went around in one of two or three identical cotton print dresses, or the ancient navy-blue thing she wore to town for the Breaking of Bread on Sunday morning. She had no children and so she belonged to me and was available for my adoration. She was perfectly nice to the Olders but she preferred me. She didn't have to say so; it was quite clear.

She liked the same exact things I liked. Meat loaf. Fried-egg sandwiches. Devil's-food cake. Fresh tomatoes from the garden eaten warm right off the vine. Sneaking up on people and listening to them. Farts. Talking late at night. We loved the same radio shows. *Burns & Allen* and *Fibber McGee & Mollie* and *Lum & Abner* and *Footlight Favorites* with the Radio Toe-Tappers and *The Post Toasties Cavalcade* with Spike Hopper and His Jazz Equestrians originating from the famous Tom-Tom Room at the Hotel Oglallah on New York's fashionable West 49th Street. The

Jiggs Wahpeton Show starring "the gal in the know," gossip columnist Jiggs Wahpeton, sponsored by Hercules Cleaning Crystals. *Hold on to your hats, ladies, back in a moment with another juicy morsel after this word from Hercules!* Monday night, it was *Jack Cassidy and His Air Cadet Squadron,* sponsored by Happy Baked Beans. An evil gelatin came squooshing in the windows of the Johnson house and started eating their furniture and then it ate the dog, Rusty, while the family clung to a chandelier. The gelatin was climbing the walls toward them, gurgling and sucking, and they were about to lose their grip on the light fixture, and just then we heard the drone of airplane engines and knew that Jack and the boys were on their way, and the Air Cadet Chorus came back to sing:

> *Happy Baked Beans are nutritious,*
> *Help you live the natural way.*
> *They are nature's fruit, have a healthy toot*
> *With baked beans every day.*

Eva woke us up in the morning by calling out, "Daylight in the swamps." She just liked the sound of it. She had a whole raft of phrases. She said, "If wishes were horses, then beggars would ride." She said, "What we lack in our heads, we must make up for with our feet." If you couldn't find the pitcher of cream sitting right smack in front of you, she said, "If it were a snake, it woulda bit you." Or "None so blind as those that refuse to see." If you burped at the table, she said, "Bring it up again and we'll take a vote on it." She enjoyed jokes of all kinds, knock-knocks or Little Willie riddles, moron jokes. We tossed a softball back and forth and she complimented me on my arm. She also told me how well I read to her out loud from the Psalms and *McGuffey's Reader*, where we never wearied of Longfellow, the village smithy under the spreading chestnut tree, the smith a swarthy man was he, and listen my children and you shall hear of the midnight ride of Paul Revere, and the forests primeval of Evangeline, and the song of Hiawatha and the lovely Nokomis and the waters of Gitche-Gumee.

"I love to hear you read out loud," she said. "You have the loveliest voice."

I basked in her praise, coveted her praise, set my hat by it. Mother was the one who checked my ears for earwax and cautioned me against nose-picking and reminded me to make the bed and do my chores and worried about spoiling me. Eva didn't worry about spoiling. She told me that I was the brightest little boy she knew and that I would grow up to be a great man like Franklin D. Roosevelt or Jack Benny.

It was a big day when Daddy finally came home from New York. Mother and the Olders and I drove to the Great Northern depot in Minneapolis and met his train as it came steaming in under the long shed, the dark-green cars, a trainman riding on the steps, and a car passed and through a window I glimpsed a couple smooching, and then Daddy hopped off, rumpled and tired and (I thought) not so happy to see us. He groused about us wasting all that gasoline to come meet him when he could just as easily have taken the bus.

Mother had warned us not to make too much noise, so we rode home in silence, listening to Daddy complain about the Army and its inefficient practices.

The farmyard was full of cars, all the relatives drove out to see him in his uniform and his campaign hat, ribbons on his chest. Grandma cried. We posed for pictures. There was fried chicken and corn on the cob at a long table on the lawn. We stood around the piano, Aunt Eva playing, and sang hymns. And not so long after that, Daddy went away again.

Mother says it was almost a year later. I remember it as three or four days. My earliest memory is of Daddy not being there, and then he was, and then he wasn't.

Mother explained to the three of us that Daddy could earn a great deal of money if he went to work for the Air Force in Greenland, in a place called Tooley, but spelled Thule. He would earn better money than he could ever hope to earn in Lake Wobegon, so—because he loved us all so much—he would go away for a while and then come home and we'd be able to buy a nice house in town.

I didn't care about a house in town, I was perfectly happy where I was.

We kept a map of Greenland in the living room, over the couch where we knelt and prayed every morning after breakfast, and a red pin marked where Daddy was, and while everyone else prayed to God for Daddy's safe return, I silently prayed that he would not come back and that I would live on the farm forever with Eva and Grandma and Mother.

He was gone for three years, coming home for a week in the summer and a week at Christmas, and those were good years for yours truly.

People said, "You must miss your daddy a lot," and I nodded

yes and made a brave face, but it was all a big lie, I loved things as they were.

Mother was a town girl, slender and pretty, she had worked as a secretary for Brown & Bigelow, taking shorthand and typing, and liked to dress well and do up her hair, and the farm was a long exile for her. She never ventured into the woods or the hayfield. She took a job at the bank and bought a Model A Ford and kissed me goodbye every morning and went off for the day. She boarded the Olders with Aunt Flo and Uncle Al in town, so they could attend school there and not the one-room country school. Several times Mother left me with my beloved Eva and took the train to New York and met Daddy there. I did not mind this at all.

"You're a brave boy not to cry when your mother goes away," said Grandma, but the truth was, I didn't mind.

I loved the little white house with the big kitchen and tiny parlor, the old black spinet, Grandma's bedroom downstairs, the creaky L-shaped wood stairs and the two bedrooms above, the woodstove and the red water-pump on the kitchen counter by the sink, the pantry with floor-to-ceiling shelves of jars of canned corn and beets and pickles. The paradise of red-oak woods and pasture where Mr. Walberg's mournful Holsteins lay in the shade and chewed and thought cow thoughts and ignored the corncobs I tossed to them. Empty sheds to play in, the machine shed smelling of motor oil and full of coffee cans of bolts and nuts and screws and a long-deceased Ford tractor that was my Spitfire, my B-27. The big spooky old barn where you could climb up the side of the mow and leap down onto the loose hay, or stand on the highest promontory of bales and orate into the sweet grassy air.

My cousins came around to visit and eat Grandma's gingerbread cake, and we'd all play Starlight, Moonlight, and Eva tore around and flushed us out of our hiding places in the shadows and galloped after us through the tall weeds toward the yard-light pole that was the goal. She and I were It together and put our foreheads against the pole, counting loudly to fifty, and then she trotted off into the dark to flush the others out and I stood waiting to catch them, and the last one caught was always my cousin Kate, who was fast as the wind and sneaky. She had short dark hair and a mischievous look about her. She knew songs like "The horses stood around with their feet upon the ground, / O who will wind my wristwatch when I'm gone? / We feed the baby garlic so we can find him in the dark, / and a boy's best friend is his mother." She knew "Two little children lying in bed, / one of them sick and the other near dead. / Send for the doctor, the doctor said, / 'Feed those children on shortnin' bread.' " She would pee outside in the bushes, without a blush. She climbed trees. She told secrets. When it got past bedtime and Uncle Sugar and Aunt Ruth stood in the light calling "Katie! Katie!" she took her sweet time coming in. She was my favorite cousin as long ago as I can remember.

Eva could hypnotize chickens by cradling them in her arm and stroking their foreheads, ten or twelve strokes between the little yellow eyes and down the beak, and the chicken, dazed, stood motionless for several minutes before awakening from the trance and falling over in a feathery heap. She never killed a chicken without first putting it into a hypnotic state. She took us swimming in the river and there performed her trick of standing on her head, her two big white legs sticking straight up out of the water. She was the only grown-up to behave this way; the others sat in the kitchen and drank coffee and spoke of serious matters, such as the soul. She could recite the 23rd Psalm at top speed backwards or rattle off the eighty-seven counties of Minnesota, "Aitkin, Anoka, Becker, Beltrami, Benton, Big Stone, Blue Earth, Brown, Carlton, Carver, Cass, Chippewa"—a blur of sound and I loved hearing it. She could play several pieces on the piano by heart, one was by Chopin and the others were not. The Chopin one was sweet and sad and made me think of a drawing of Confederate officers bidding farewell to their wives on a veranda before riding north to die in the swamps of northern Virginia.

At night she would hum me the Chopin tune as we lay in bed, or "When I Survey the Wondrous Cross" or "Abide With Me, Fast Falls the Eventide," and I snuggled up against her broad back and fell asleep in her auntly smell and then the room was bright with sunlight and I dressed and trotted out back to pee and washed my face and sat down to breakfast. And if it was summer, we would stroll out to the garden down a dirt lane beyond the machine shed and hoe corn and weed the onions and beets and tighten up the twine that the beans twined along, and then she said, "How about a nice ripe tomato?" And we each picked one, hot in the sun, and wiped off the sand, and ate it, the juice running down our chins.

5

Precious

Daddy came home from Greenland finally in the summer of 1950. He bought us a big green frame house on Green Street, under a canopy of elms, three blocks down the hill from the high school, two blocks up from Main Street. I stood at the end of our cement walk and a boy rode up on a new red bicycle. He was Leonard Larsen. He asked if I liked reading books. Yes, I said, I do. Mother and Aunt Flo scrubbed and painted and varnished the floors, and Daddy and Uncle LeRoy hauled the furniture in from LeRoy's garage, where Mother had stored it, piece by piece, and I stood with Leonard and watched it float in the front door. He asked, "Where are you from?" I said, Minneapolis, not wanting to be thought of as a farm person. Our new home was exactly what Mother wanted. The Olders each had a room; the brother filled his with books and model planes and science projects, the sister with fussy grandma furniture and her very own Bible plaques—*Jesus Christ, the Same Yesterday, Today and*

Forever and *Where Will You Spend Eternity?* and *Prayer Changes Things*—and I had my room with a bed, a maple desk, a bookshelf, a dresser, a print of the "First Minnesota Repelling Longstreet's Advance at Gettysburg." Downstairs was our dining room with walnut paneling and built-in buffet and an arch between it and the living room, which had a brick fireplace. A majestic thing, with brass andirons. Mother's fairy tale come true. Being Mother, she didn't gush or cry or make a big speech, but you knew she was supremely happy, directing where each chair and table should go, straightening the lace curtains, supervising the hanging of pictures—a wolf on a snowbank, an old man praying over a loaf of bread, *The Harvesters*, and a plaque, *Jesus Christ, the Silent Listener to Every Conversation, the Unseen Guest at Every Meal*, a spooky thought to me, God as Spy.

I didn't invite Leonard into the house, for fear of what he might think of us. Especially the Bible plaques.

Kate came over. She and Ruth and Sugar lived in a stucco house just around the corner, with no garden in back, one of the few homes in town that didn't care about fresh tomatoes. "Now you two will really be able to get to know each other," said Ruth. She had no idea how right she was. Kate walked into our kitchen and reached into the sugar bowl and got out two cubes and sucked on them. "You got any pop?" she said. We had a cola. Daddy considered it as good as Coke at half the price. I poured us two glasses and we sat on the back step that looked toward the birdbath, the clotheslines, the garden, the garage, the wires on the poles in the alley. She asked me if I knew what *parallel* means. I did and I even could spell it. She was impressed. "How about *shitty?*" she said. I laughed. I'd never heard anybody in our family say such a word aloud. *Shitty.* She spelled it. *S-h-i-t-t-y.* "Now use it in a sentence," she said. I said, "I feel particularly shitty today." Actually I felt excited and pleased at having said this word out loud. It certainly filled a blank in my vocabulary.

I was a very good boy right up until the age of 11. Everybody said so. I stayed out of people's way and didn't ask too many questions. I sat up straight at meals, and when visiting other people's homes, I said, Thank you for the lemonade, and Please may I use your bathroom? I never picked my nose except behind closed doors, and when grown-ups spoke I was attentive. I was often pointed out to other children as an example. "Why can't you behave like Gary? Look at him, he doesn't wriggle around like a trapped squirrel during Prayer Meeting, he sits up straight and listens and Gets Something Out of It."

And then, one day in 1953, I said out loud, "Oh, to hell with it," in connection with a sack of garbage Daddy told me to take to the garbage can. I was standing on one side of the screen door and he on the other. I was wearing khaki trousers and an old Boy Scout shirt of the older brother's. I was surprised to hear these words myself. They just sprang out, like a sneeze, "Oh, to hell with it." And a great darkness fell over the earth.

Daddy was on the verge of apoplexy. He thought I had said, "Go to hell," to him. He marched into the kitchen and thundered around for a while and then Mother came out to speak to me.

"You upset your father terribly when you act that way. Do you realize that? And do you know how sad it makes God to hear you say such a thing?"

The Creator, the Hanger of the Stars and Planets, the Unseen Listener, He Himself mourned for my saying the terrible word.

"Why did you say it?"

Good question. I had often heard men condemn things to hell at various times around town, and it seemed like a powerful thing to say. But Daddy was the wrong one to say it to.

I was sent out to sit in the car. It was a hot day, the sun beat down. I sat in the back seat, the window rolled down, pretending I was on a train to Chicago. Kate came by. I told her what I had said and she grinned. "You're up shit creek now," she said.

And then Daddy came out and drove me to the farm. He talked about how hard he worked as a boy and how Grandma brooked no backtalk and if you didn't toe the mark it was the leather strap for you, but of course Grandma never was like that to me at all. He said, "You go spend a few days on the farm and maybe it'll make you think twice about the language you use."

We were quite different, Daddy and I. What he conceived as punishment was often quite enjoyable. "Go to your room and stay there!" Thanks. I'd love to. Why not? My books were there, my tablets, pencils, I could write stories. "Go spend a few days on the farm." My pleasure. Please don't throw me into that briar patch, Brer Daddy!

Aunt Eva was tickled pink to take charge of me. Daddy told her I'd said a swear word, and after he left, she cut me a slice of chocolate cake three inches thick with a glop of whipped cream on top. She said that everybody thinks swear words sometimes and there isn't much difference between thinking them and saying them, according to the Gospel. When she was young, she said, she used to go to the barn and say every bad word she knew, and that way she got it out of her system.

I asked if I was going to hell and she said, "Don't be ridiculous." And then she did something that nobody in our family did, ever, she told me she loved me, and she threw her big arms around me, and I took a deep breath of her, and she squeezed and said, "I wish you still lived with me, precious."

I was so happy. It was a blazing-hot summer afternoon. Grandma was taking a nap. Eva said we'd go swimming later in the river. We sat in the shade on the back steps. I asked, "What would you do if you had a million dollars?" I would take a trip around the world, I said. This thought didn't seem to interest her. She picked up a bucket, and we headed out past the machine shed to the garden drenched in sunshine, picked a dozen ears of sweet corn, two cucumbers. Bees busied themselves among the vines, the pea vines and melons and pumpkins and squash, the whole jungly spread of vinous stuff, dipping under the broad fuzzy leaves. Eva picked a few crimson tomatoes. I picked one and wiped it off and bit into it and sucked up the warm juice. Eva didn't. She was listening. Then she hissed at me to get down.

We hid behind the tomatoes and I heard a tractor coming and soon Mr. Walberg appeared, sitting up tall on his Allis-Chalmers like a skinny scarecrow, wheeling along the road and raising a cloud of dust in his wake. He flew past us and up through the gate and into the back pasture.

"What would you do if he saw us and stopped?" I said.

She shuddered at the thought and we hustled back to the house.

"You understand, don't you, precious?" she said when we got to the house and went up the steps and into the coolness and safety of the kitchen. "I don't care to be stared at by strangers. People can say whatever they like, but I refuse to be gawked at."

"Nobody's gawking at you."

"They would if they could," she said.

I found this conversation troubling. Everybody knew that Eva hated to go to town and only went for the Breaking of Bread and wouldn't shop in the stores. She'd make a beeline for the house if the postman drove in. Grandma thought nothing of jumping in the Studebaker and gadding about and visiting with neighbors, but Eva never accompanied her. This was not commented on, any more than you'd comment on any other piece of common knowledge, but it struck me now as embarrassing. If Mr. Walberg had glanced over and seen us two hunkered down in the tomatoes, I'd have hopped up and waved to him. *It's my aunt who's crazy, I was only doing it for a joke.*

Daddy came and took me back to town.

—How's Eva and Grandma?

—Fine.

—Did you think about how you need to control what you say?

—Yes, I did.

—And what did you decide?

—I'm not going to swear.

—I hope you mean it.

—I do.

And in my head I thought, *I've got to get the hell out of here, damn it.*

6

What Foul Blast
Is This?

was not such a good boy ever again after that. On a field trip to
the Science Museum in St. Paul, I was the one who got the other
boys to crouch at the head of the glass case with the Egyptian
mummy inside and peek down into the mummy's shorts to see
his petrified pecker. On a trip to the Como Park Zoo, I pointed out
the monkeys eating their own poop, and the one with a blazing-
red butt playing with his pecker. Girls glared at me. How could I
have such a filthy mind? I don't know. The *Boy Scout Handbook*
recommends that you get plenty of exercise and avoid spending
time alone, but this doesn't work in all cases, apparently.

And then, last spring, I caused tapioca pudding to come squirting
out the nostrils of Leonard Larsen, a remarkable accomplishment
as he considers himself the class intellectual and everything. We
were sitting across from each other in the gloom of the high-

school cafeteria and Leonard was talking about how he wanted to write a term paper about James Dean and Miss Lewis wouldn't let him, though James Dean was truly a great man, and he was all worked up over James Dean, James Dean, and I said, "He made that movie *Booger Without a Cause*, didn't he?" And it just hit Leonard a certain way and his eyes got teary and his face rubbery and two thick strands of tapioca pudding came out his nose. Long ones. I said, "You have tapioca snot, Leonard." And he choked and yarked up some pudding. It was just one of those stupid jokes that happen to hit a person at the right time. He choked and gagged and turned dark red and put his head between his knees. I never had such a big effect on anyone before. Of course, Leonard always was wound pretty tight.

He gagged as if his whole macaroni lunch might blow out of him, and Miss Lewis, our eighth-grade teacher, came flapping over and pounded Leonard on the back, and when he settled down, she said to me, "It's not funny, so wipe that smirk off your face. A person could choke to death like that."

"I'm sorry."

"You ought to be. What did you say to him?"

I told her. "That's not funny," she said. "That's just stupid."

A few classmates gathered round, sensing an emergency, hoping for something gory, perhaps with major hemorrhaging, and then Mr. Halvorson, the school principal, appeared, a short, chinless man with a watery gaze and a permanent pained expression, and she reported on my homicidal behavior, and he looked down at me and shook his head. "It only takes one to ruin it for everybody," he said gravely. That afternoon, Mr. Halvorson dropped in on our class in the middle of Emily Dickinson and gave us a lecture about taking responsibility for our behavior—that small careless deeds, no matter how innocent they may seem, can have horrible consequences. "You could snap someone with a towel— for fun—and injure him so that he will never be able to have children," said Mr. Halvorson. "You didn't mean to, but you're still responsible." We pondered this, the sting of snapping cloth against our testicles. "Or you could make a thoughtless remark while someone is eating and he could choke on his food and die. It's happened. I don't want it to happen here." He stood next to me, his hairy fingers tapping on my desk—"Do you have any idea what it's like to choke to death?" The room was still. And then his body sort of tensed up and gave out a low ripping sound, and suddenly a terrible sour shitty smell was all over the place. It smelled like the outhouse burned down. And the smell didn't go away. This was no ordinary 59-cent fart but one of those quiet, deadly ones, a sizzler, mean and dark, a stink submarine.

Like anyone else, I maintained a healthy interest in farts, all ten varieties—the silent but deadly, the slow leaks, the hissers, fizzers, poppers, croakers, bangers, cheek-flappers, tail-gunners, and cargo farts, the ones that deliver a load—and this one was in a class all its own. A small dark cloud of a fart such as an alien from outer space might deliver to Earth, necessitating the evacuation of cities. But Mr. Halvorson kept right on yakking about personal responsibility while his handiwork hung in the air. No apology from him whatsoever, no "Gosh, boys and girls, that was a ripe one, wasn't it," no nothing. I stared at the poem in front of me—

> *The voluptuous Tapestry*
> *Of day is done*

Behold — the Majesty
Of Setting Sun.
The darkness — like Ocean Currents
Descends — and soon
The chaste Appearance
Of the Orphan Moon.

And what Foul Blast —
Is this — dark Breath —
That holds us fast —
Who else — but Death?

And I let out a sudden high-pitched whinny that could not be held in. And he turned and smiled his phony Educator of the Year smile and said, "Did you think of a joke, Gary?"

I shook my head. No, sir. Not me, sir.

"It must have been a good one to make you chortle like that."

No, sir. There is no joke, sir.

"I'm sure we'd all appreciate a really good, funny joke right now. Wouldn't we, class? Why not share it with everyone?"

I looked down at the Emily Dickinson poem. He said, "Go ahead. We'll just wait until you're ready to share it with everyone, whatever you were thinking." And so I told him. My face turned blazing red but I said, "That's the worst fart I've ever smelled. It smells like a badger fart."

His smile immediately faded. He turned to the class, who were all in a tizzy *(What did he say? A badger what?),* and thanked them for their attention and said what a fine bunch of individuals they were and what a privilege it was to be their principal and out the door he scooted. Miss Lewis gave me a dirty look. "I'll deal with you later," she said.

Two hours later, Mother is waiting for me in the kitchen, in her gardening outfit, blue jeans and an old white shirt. Miss Lewis has spoken to her and informed her that I spoke insolently to the principal and used a vulgar word, a word Miss Lewis could not bring herself to repeat over the telephone. When School calls, Mother listens. She is not a questioner of authority. What word was it? she asks. "Tell it to me."

So I do.

She shakes her head. "What sort of Christian witness will you have if you go around talking like that?"

"He asked me what I was thinking, and I told him. Should I have lied and said I didn't know what was on my own mind?"

"Scripture says we're to avoid giving offense. Promise me you won't use language like that."

"I only use the word *fart* when one occurs."

"I hate dirty talk. Men hanging around the tavern, talking about damn this and the hell with that. He's a bastard and she's a bitch. It's ugly. It's not pleasing to the Lord."

I point out that I didn't use any of those words. Just the word *fart*.

"Well, please don't," she says.

"What word should I use instead? *Poot?*"

She says she doesn't see why people are so fascinated by what goes on in toilets.

"But that's the point! He didn't do it in the toilet! He did it three feet away from my face! He cut this tremendous stinker. And then he pretended it wasn't his. It hung there in the air and he acted like it was a bouquet of daisies."

And she giggles against her will, and turns away. "Your father is very disappointed when you do things like that," she says, her back to me. But I can tell that it doesn't matter so much to her. And Daddy is *always* disappointed, regardless. So that's the end of the conversation. But not the end of my troubles.

Leonard Larsen was impressed by the joke about *Booger Without a Cause,* even though it caused him to exhale tapioca. He told me I had a quick mind. He even invited me over to his house.

The Larsens lived in a new rambler with yellow siding up the street from the Lutheran church. They were Methodists, a bunch the Brethren looked down on as a weak-tea religious outfit, once staunch and now fallen far down the slippery slope of moderation and modernism, their preachers preaching civics lessons from the pulpit, their idea of a hymn "Beautiful Isle of Somewhere." Leonard's dad was a big muckety-muck at St. Cloud Teachers' College and they had piles of books around the house. In Leonard's room was a bookshelf full of big picture books about the Vikings and World War II and Great Paintings of the Renaissance and railroad locomotives and the Wild West and other stuff that I coveted but was cool about. I glanced at the spines, and said something complimentary about the quality of the binding.

Whereupon he reached in between the Vikings and the Renaissance and pulled out a copy of *High School Orgies,* a magazine for the connoisseur of the female form. "Return it whenever you're done with it," he said. "I've got more."

I sat down on the bed and opened it to the first story, "Sex in the Library," which featured a photograph of a naked woman. Completely naked. I had never seen such a thing before. I looked closely to make sure. Not a stitch was she wearing. That was all her. She stood holding an armload of books in front of a bookshelf, and a young man was peeking at her interesting breasts through the shelves.

"What do you think?" said Leonard.

So as not to hurt his feelings, I read the story.

Pete needed a manual on automotive repair so he could fix his jalopy. He found Miss Perkins the librarian in the stacks, bending over to shelve an armload of books, and there inside her blouse were the two prettiest bazooms he'd ever seen. "Oh Pete," she said. "You surprised me." He looked left and right. Nobody else around. "I need a manual, Miss Perkins," he said. "Call me Lorelei," she replied. "I'll give you a manual and a lot more." Her hot mouth sought out his and she unbuttoned her blouse. She slipped to the floor and he knelt in front of her. She arched her back and unclasped her brassiere to afford him access to her luscious orbs. His fingers slipped into her jeans. She was hot as a furnace. Soon his manhood throbbed against her as she lay in the aisle between the shelves, squirming with pleasure, pulling him on top of her, the hungry little bitch. She began to thrust violently against him. She knocked down several stacks of dusty tomes in the process but she didn't care. They slammed together like steam pistons, her legs wrapped around his waist as waves of pleasure seized her willing body that had been deprived of sexual fulfillment for much too long now. "Oh God!" she screamed, and spasmed as the first of several orgasms struck her. They dressed quickly and he helped her pick up the books they had knocked over. "Oh Pete," she said, smiling. "I hope we can do this again soon."

"It's interesting," I said, not wanting to offend him by suggesting that it was written for morons, though this thought did occur to me.

"You can jerk off to this," he said. I had no idea what he meant. "Jerk off what?" I said.

"Beat the bishop," he said. "Pound the peenie. Choke the gopher. Give yourself a hand job."

"Oh," I said. "Sure." But I had no idea what a hand job was, except probably a job that you did by hand, but what exactly?

7

My Literary Career

Leonard and I go way back. We were boys who loved school. We were spelling champs and math champs and reading champs—we went through the shelves like a prairie fire, all the *Doctor Dolittle* books and his voyages to Africa and South America and the Moon with Polynesia the parrot and Jip the monkey and Dab Dab the duck, and Black Beauty abused by the vile Nicholas Skinner, the adventures of Joe and Frank Hardy racing their power skiff or roadster around Bayport helping their dad, detective Fenton Hardy, and Hans Brinker and his poor sick papa, and Heidi happy on her mountain with the Grandfather and Peter the goatherd and the Alm-Uncle, and Peter Pan with Captain Hook crying "Floreat Etona!" as he is swallowed by the crocodile, and Robinson Crusoe washed ashore after the shipwreck, and my favorite book, *Little Britches*, with the boy Ralph selling his mother's pies from door to door. During class discussions, our hands flew into the air before all others and we waved at Miss

Schauendienst and she smiled and looked past us and asked David Magendanz instead, Who is John Foster Dulles? And his piggy eyes narrowed and his tiny brain considered various possibilities— football player? movie actor? dull person?—while Leonard and I were screaming inwardly, *Secretary of State! Secretary of State! Foreign policy! Brinksmanship! Massive retaliation! NATO! SEATO!*—as Miss Schauendiesnst patiently dropped clues for David: the federal government . . . the State Department . . . State Department, David . . . State. . . . And finally she wrote it on the board, *Secretary of State,* and asked him to read it. He did. He didn't know what it was but he could pronounce it.

Leonard was my best friend, who sat next to me in the cafeteria, and also he was my deadly competitor, at my throat daily, questioning, poking, probing my store of knowledge, and when he found a weak spot, he couldn't contain his happiness. He shrieked, "You don't know what *indigenous* means? *Indigenous??*" He once said to me, "You have green teeth, you know," hardly a friendly remark, and though I detected no mossy tinge in the mirror, I was careful after that not to smile if I could help it. I wanted to ask Mother, "Are my teeth green?" but was afraid of the answer. *(Well—yes, sort of.)* Leonard was a pain. But he was my only friend so I had to grin and bear it.

I tried to lord it over him once on the subject of poets laureate of England, which I knew about from *Collier's,* and I was declaiming on Tennyson as the epitome of lyricism and Leonard caught my one tiny mistake and leaped on it. "Epi-tome!" he shrieked. "*EPI-TOME?* It's not pronounced *epi-tome,* it's *e-PIT-o-me! E-PIT-o-me!* Everybody knows that! *E-PIT-o-me!*" We were in the

lunchroom, standing in line with our trays to get a plate of hamburger hotdish, and he turned to share his incredulity with the
world at large. "He thinks *epitome* is pronounced *EPI-TOME*,"
yelled Leonard, and Cousin Kate, who was half a foot taller than
Leonard, stopped and gave him her patented withering look *(Oh
my, aren't WE something)* and said, "You're the epitome of dumb,
Leonard. You're the king of the idjits." And a boy behind me in
line let out a high cackle and you could see Leonard shrivel as if
someone dumped ice in his pants. He turned red and his eyes got
watery and he turned away in shame. The heat of his shame was
like a torch.

I loved being smart. I was smarter than Leonard in math, and
every day when we arrived at math I smiled up at Miss Schauendienst, a smile of triumph. King of the Hill. Mr. Math. I was
thrilled to go to the board and solve a problem. In math, you could
be exactly right and ring the bell, and when you absorbed one
idea, it opened the door to the next and the next and the next; you
tore straight through the house of math, from multiplying fractions to factoring (20 is 2×10 and it's also 4×5), and this leads
to algebra, where you factor for x $(x + 2 = 5)$, and what is $2/3$ of
$3/5$?—$2/5$, of course. It was thrilling to hold the chalk and do the
problem in a few quick strokes, whack, whack, whack, whack, even
if some classmates despised me for it and the Magendanz twins,
Daryl and David, glowered at me ("You think you're smart, we'll
show you how smart you are, dumbhead") and once Daryl chased
me home after school, four long blocks, and if Daddy hadn't been
walking along the street, I'd've been a goner.

"Don't run like that," Daddy said, "you could trip and fall and land on something sharp and tear your insides open. People have died from infections they got from puncturing an intestine with a tree root or something." I clung to his side and Daryl walked past, whistling.

Thanks to Miss Schauendienst's appreciation of my superior math skill, I was in danger of getting my head broken. The Magendanzes were rangy boys with big hands with red bruised knuckles. They liked to lay for a boy during recess and leap out at him and whale on him fast and hard. They did this to Donnie Krebsbach and depantsed him and painted his testicles with iodine. They beat up Richard Paulson because he spilled a few drops of milk on Daryl's shoes. They beat kids up out of sheer meanness. They were bad. They came from a bad home, where the parents sleep off their hangovers on Sunday morning and have beer for breakfast and the television is always on and there are no books. They were always being reported to Miss Lewis or Miss Schauendienst and made to sit in the cloakroom, which they didn't mind at all, they snuck down to the furnace room and smoked cigarettes there. They smoked from fourth grade on and they drank beer. They had a hangout in the woods where they and their cohorts did things. And every so often they gave me that look that meant they were thinking about beating me up, I was high on their beat-up list.

Leonard, who was supposed to be my friend, told the Magendanzes that I knew the secret of the deadly sleeper hold made famous on *Saturday Night Wrestling* by Vern Gagne, which involves getting a leg scissors around Mad Dog Vachon's neck and giving a couple tight squeezes and sending the heinous Mad Dog off to sleepyland.

Leonard told me he thought it would make them leave me alone, but in his devious way he was trying to get me slaughtered. I knew the mind of Leonard, and it was as cruel as theirs.

You would think the Magendanzes could see that I didn't know beans about the sleeper hold, but suddenly they got chummy with me and invited me to sit near them in the lunchroom, which I knew was a ruse to lull me into complacency. I knew they would be laying for me, crouching in the limb of a tree like cougars, waiting for me to come galumphing along, the expert on sleeper holds, and leap on me with furious force and pound the snot out of me.

And then, one day at lunch, I told Daryl a booger joke and a bright grin appeared on his ugly mug and he asked if I knew any more. Of course I did.

I wrote a whole list of Booger Books, and though he and David didn't read books, they got a big kick out of my list (*Little House in the Big Booger, Ten Thousand Boogers Under the Sea, How Green Was My Booger, Anne of Green Boogers*, and so forth), and for each title I wrote a little booger tale. Fifty words was all it took and to the Magendanzes you were a genius.

Up until then, my literary endeavors had been of an elevated nature. Poems for dear Miss Schauendienst, who got all dewy-eyed from reading and read them aloud to the class as an example of what wonderful things a young person could do in this world—*O maple tree with leaves so bright, / You whisper to us through the night. / How lightly do your golden boughs / Brush against our little house.* And then, thanks to Magendanzdom, I learned the benefits of taking the low road. *Charlotte's Booger. The Secret Booger. The Little Booger That Could.*

I could go high or go low, either way: *O garden set in perfect rows, / Clean of bug and weed. / Thy sweet corn and thy tomatoes / Are good reward indeed.* Or, *Mr. Halvorson bent down to get his fallen toupee, which lay on the floor like a cat run over by a truck, and as he bent, a tuba blasted in his pants and the air turned blue and chartreuse. Nearby plants collapsed and died. Papers curled up and turned brown. The clock stopped. Two secretaries fell down in a faint as the cloud passed through. Firemen had to spray the school with milk of magnesia before they could bring in oxygen for the wounded.* I was safe from the Magendanzes because they got a big kick out of my work. "Write another one," they said. So I did. I could write as fast as they could read.

There was an epic about Coach Detwiler's cigar smoldering in the teachers' lounge and the school burning down and Miss Lewis's dress burning off and her icy tits, three of them, with hard blue nipples. And meanwhile, for Miss Schauendienst, I hewed to the ideal. *Rich green, bespecked with dew, / So beautiful it lies / around our house on summer day, / In the sprinkler's gentle spray, / Surrounding us with coolness too, / Beneath the baking skies.* "You have such a way with words," she said. "You will go far as a writer, I'm sure." She posted the poem on the corkboard, under a sign: EVERYBODY READ THIS!! Daryl Magendanz did. He told me I had written better stuff than that.

The summer before eighth grade, I found a skinny blue book in the library called *Improve Your Short-Story Writing in Thirty*

Days by a man named Will Crispin, a noted international authority on writers and writing. He was a studious man with big black glasses and holding a cigarette between his thumb and forefinger. I read Mr. Crispin with great interest and was intrigued by his "rock in the pond" theory of story-writing. The main character's life is all hunky-dory, the ducks lined up in a row, the house tidied up, the dog fed, the crumbs swept off the table, the savings account earning compound interest, the vacation trip to the Rockies all planned, and then the other shoe drops. Suddenly, it's a whole new ballgame.

"The art of the short story," said Mr. Crispin, "is to create a character who is believable and intelligent and good—a character whom *the reader himself would welcome into his home*—and then to poke that character hard with a sharp stick. This is the art of fiction in a nutshell. To have a story, you must have a truly admirable hero seeking to do good and you must have an immense bird with a sharp beak. You cannot make a story out of a nice guy and a canary."

I liked Mr. Crispin's emphasis on action and I tried to carry out his principles in a whole slew of stories I wrote that summer and fall, but unfortunately I was up against Miss Lewis, who was unnerved by action and preferred stories about admirable people period, no birds whatsoever. Rosemary Dahl wrote a story about a girl who sees the sun setting over the Pacific and is moved by this sight to dedicate her life to caring for the sick. That was a Miss Lewis type of story. It won the Writing Achievement Award in *The Literary Leaf,* and Rosemary stood up at the spring recognition assembly, and a gold medal was hung round her scrawny neck. I preferred the Crispin approach. A man is arranging paint cans in his garage, the whites and the grays and the pale blues and

71

greens, when a masked gunman bursts in, yelling, "Grab some sky!" and snatches the man's billfold and car keys and drives away, and in the car is a love letter to the man's girlfriend, and as the gunman races away the man realizes that he has no further interest in her, not really. The doorbell rings and Mrs. Anderson opens the door to a tiny girl on crutches who says, "I used to play Becky on *The Storm of Life*, remember? Now I'm in need of an operation." The child has no eyes. There are holes for eyes but no eyeballs. And the child is holding a small pistol. The Brethren gather around the bread and the wine on Sunday morning and Uncle Al prays, "Come quickly, Lord Jesus," and Jesus walks in and says, "What do you want?" They all fall face-down on the carpet weeping and exclaiming, and Jesus says, "What's going on? Why did you call me for no reason? I'm busy, you know."

A perfect example of the "rock in the pond" was Mother's story of the Lake Wobegon tornado of 1938. A peaceful Sunday in August, and the town was jam-packed with people on hand to attend a ballgame—Wally (Old Hard Hands) Bunsen's swansong as a Whippet—and many of the fans brought a picnic lunch and were eating on the lakeshore. A boatload of fishermen motored across the water. Mother and Grandpa and Ed and Doe were out for a Sunday stroll. Four fishermen in that boat putt-putt-putting along and one of them waved to her, a curly-headed man in a white undershirt. He shouted something she could not hear. Then she recognized him as Harold Ingqvist, who worked at the bank, and who she had danced with once at her girlfriend Dotty's wedding to Warren Bronson.

In some versions of the story she had a premonition that death was on his heels, and in other versions she did not.

In either case, a good time was being had by all, and then the sky began to turn dark and soon a black serpentine cloud could be seen on the western horizon, snaking its way across the countryside, slashing and thrashing, making a jagged circuit just south of town, turning this way and that, rising and falling, whacking the farms of the righteous and leaving the wicked to prosper. People dashed for their cars. Others ran to seek shelter in the Sons of Knute temple, but it was locked. It looked as if it would skip off to the east of town and then it came roaring toward them and the four of them hugged the ground. Miracles occurred left and right. Trees on the shore were knocked flat but the picnickers were not harmed. The scoreboard at the ballpark was carried away, lifted up, and smashed to earth, but the bleachers weren't touched. Blades of grass were impaled in a vanity mirror in the home of Mr. and Mrs. Hansen and could not be withdrawn. A teapot and cups and saucers were carried two miles on their teakwood tray and set down unscratched in a field of oats. A mother and infant were sucked out a kitchen window and deposited unharmed in the limb of a maple tree. Kernels of seed corn were embedded in the Ingebretsons' linoleum kitchen floor, and though the family sponge-mopped with a herbicide year after year, the corn always came up in the spring.

Mother told about the teacups and the grass in the mirror and the seed corn in the linoleum and the Stegers, who loved the Lord and lost their barn and the cattle, and meanwhile their wicked infidel neighbor escaped unscratched and celebrated his good luck by getting roaring drunk.

"We can't always understand why God does what He does, we have to take it as a test of our faith and accept that it is done for good," Mother said, sticking up for God as always.

All four of the fishermen were drowned, their boat was ripped to splinters. A black dog in the boat survived but the four men were doomed, including Harold Ingqvist, 22, who waved to the young woman in the white dress on shore and who, had he survived, would've married her, and I would've been Lutheran and better-looking, broader across the shoulders.

So I wrote a story for *The Literary Leaf*, incorporating the Crispin approach.

The Flaming Heart

Alfred L'Etoile and Jean du Nord, stars of stage and screen, toured the Midwest one sweltering summer in a hit play called *The Flaming Heart* and this particular Sunday found them in Willmar for a matinee performance. Their adopted son Roy stood in the wings and watched the curtain go up for Act One and decided to go for a walk. It was a typical Midwestern farming community. He walked to the edge of town and then along the railroad tracks and was so engrossed looking for snakes he didn't notice the sky turning dark until he heard a sound like a train coming and looked up and saw a dark cloud like an evil snake hooking into town and ripping houses to pieces. He tried to run to cover but tripped on the ties and suddenly was picked up screaming and kicking and carried bodily through

the air for several miles. It was terrifying. The loud
roar and a lot of junk flying past and several cows and a
cat that clawed at him and a 1948 Chevy, its horn honking.
He also noticed a Waring blender and a case of soda pop
and various farm implements. He fell to earth on freshly
plowed ground and stood up, unharmed. He was on a farm
where a family of Sanctified Brethren was just emerging
from their storm cellar.

"Where am I?" he asked.

The woman put her arms around Roy. "Praise the Lord,"
she said. There wasn't a bruise on him, his expensive New
York jacket and trousers were still clean and pressed, the
trousers creased, only a little debris in the cuffs. They
knelt and gave thanks to the Almighty for this safe de-
liverance in the storm. He was rather stunned from his
experience.

"The Lord has sent you to us in a miracle. It is His
Will that you're here," they said. He was about to tell
them about his actor parents and then their dog spoke up
and said, "Stay." He said it as clear as day: "Stay." So
Roy did. His New York jacket was hung in a closet and he
was given Brethren clothes. His parents never came looking
for him, they were too busy with the tour and interviews
and a new motion picture and all. So he became a Sanctified
Brethren boy but in his heart he knew that someday he
would return to New York and resume his true identity.

The big sister found an early draft of "The Flaming Heart" and
sneered at me for how dumb it was. She read a line aloud before I
could grab it away from her—" 'The old brown dog lay asleep in

the emerald light of afternoon like an old pair of pants somebody dropped on the grass.' *What?*" she shrieked, like it was the
worst sentence she had ever seen in her entire life. She couldn't
get over it. For days afterward, she'd say, "Lovely emerald light
we're having today, isn't it? By the way, is that a dog or a pair of
pants?"

I didn't care. I polished up "The Flaming Heart" and then got a
second big inspiration Sunday morning during Breaking of Bread,
when I felt something on my leg, and I came home and wrote:

Bad News

A man named Albert Fornay sits in the First Methodist
Church of Johnville, a small Midwestern farming community
indistinguishable from most such towns, on Sunday morning
and listens to small children play "Climb, Climb Up Sunshine Mountain" on the rims of water glasses and suddenly
he gets a very creepy feeling. Something is definitely
crawling up his leg. It feels like a spider. He tries to
press on it and crush it but the wily arachnid sneaks up
to a place he doesn't dare press on while others may be
watching. By the time the musical selection is over and he
can get to the men's room and pull his pants down, the
spider has bitten him twice and given him an incurable
blood disease. "How can this happen to me?" he thinks. He
is taken home and put in bed and given six or seven medi-
cines, but to no avail, he's dying, when his dog walks in
and says, "I could help you but I can't forget the way
you've treated me all these years." "What do you mean?" he

said. "I mean the two times you kicked me," the dog
replied. "Oh," he said. He was sorry but it came too late.
Mr. Fornay's wife and daughters prayed for a miracle, but
in his heart, he knew that the answer was no.

When I submitted "The Flaming Heart" and "Bad News" to
The Literary Leaf, Miss Lewis wrote at the top of the page, "Talking animals??? That's for children!" End of comment. Nothing
about the terrific sense of drama or the excellent writing style.
Just her prejudice about animals. If you ever allowed a dog to open
its mouth and say three words, she couldn't stand it.

She rejected everything of mine except "O maple tree with leaves
so bright," although my stuff was far better than Mary Jo
Samuelson's "Threnody d'Autumnale," which rhymed *autumn*
with *river bottom* and *leafy beauty* with *call of duty*, or Leonard's
"Planet XLN14," in which people of the Galaxy Dendron under
the leadership of El-Phar and Lord Grodna fought off a phalanx of
robots that went *bedebedebededumdum*, which Leonard insisted
was code for something. Or his sister Laura's pitiful "Homage to a
Lady" *(She is there at her desk every morning, wearing a bright
smile and a twinkle in her eye, encouraging me even on the darkest day, saying "You can do it, Laura! Try!" and instilling in me
the ideals of hard work, promptness, courtesy, and neatness that
she herself so beautifully exemplifies)* and of course the lady is
Miss Lewis herself. It was sickening.

* * *

Miss Lewis is a battle-ax of a woman with eyes like feed pellets and an aroma of disinfectant about her, as if she washed her hair in toilet-bowl cleanser. She is offended by any sudden sounds or movements, so if you drop a pencil she'll turn and give you her death glare—and if there is whispering or laughter (except at her own puny jokes) she goes berserk. It's strict decorum at all times with Miss Lewis. Obedience and intelligence are, to her, one and the same. She took a long prim look at my poem, "Rich green, be-specked with dew," and shook her head. She said, "Surely you meant to say 'so beautifully it lies,' not 'so beautiful.' This adverb describes the manner in which it lies. It lies beautifully." So I changed it to *beautifully*, though that was wrong and practically destroyed the effect I was going for, and then she thought it should be "how beautifully," so I changed it again. Then she didn't see how the grass could surround the house with coolness. Wasn't it the air that was cool? And it couldn't be any cooler around the house than it was next door, or down the block, could it?

I stood by her desk, smelling her prickly heat, her lozenge breath, and her toilet-bowl hair, as she systematically dismembered the poem and handed it back, a mutilated corpse, and said, "That's much better, don't you think? Do you see how it's clearer now?" I said not a word. There was no point in arguing. Miss Lewis was deaf to argu-ment. If she decided that grass doesn't cool off a house, then that was how it was, and the grass would simply have to stop doing it and also stop being beautiful. If you bothered to correct the old biddy, she would be mightily irked and give you the hairy eyeball and sigh about the *triviality* of the matter, though of course it wasn't at all trivial when she heated up the grass. So I nodded and took my poem with her angry scratches on it and said, "Thank you," and whispered *witch* and resumed my seat and scribbled her a poem of her own.

There is an old teacher named Lewis
Who tries to teach grammar to us
Which the poor lady can't
'Cause her mind's a houseplant
And you know what a houseplant's IQ is.

And I wrote a story for private circulation, "Miss Lewis & the Giant Turd," about a painful bowel movement that began in class, as she was drilling us on prepositions. Suddenly she emitted a low scraping sound like a box of rocks being dragged across concrete—like a glacier moving!—and she let out an *AIIIIEEEEEEE* and bent over double and hobbled to the girls' room, where she fell to the floor and cried pitifully for the janitor, who rushed in with a plunger and tried to extract the fecal mass from her, but it was too immense, and then the fire department arrived and laid her over the sink and attached a suction pump, two men on either side of her skinny butt, working a lever, and they managed to suction the poop out of her, and when they were done, she weighed forty-five pounds. And she couldn't teach anymore, she just sat on her front step waving to passing cars.

This title passed from pupil to pupil, two grimy sheets of paper folded to pocket-size. David Magendanz thought it was the best thing I ever wrote. He wrote "READ THIS. A++++!" at the top. He thought I was a genius. He was now my biggest fan. He let it be known that anyone who messed with me would answer to him personally. The story found its way to Laura, Miss Lewis's pet, who handed it over to her, and she read it, thin-lipped, and tore it into tiny pieces and dropped them into the wastebasket. "This is so childish it doesn't bear talking about," she said "It is beneath contempt."

8

Kissing

I took *High School Orgies* home and stashed it in my desk, in a manila folder marked *Misc. Keep Out*, intending to read it quickly and return it to Leonard. And then caught a glimpse of myself in the bureau-dresser mirror. What a geek I was! That dumb green plaid shirt, the blue pants with the inkstains on the pockets. And what better proof of geekhood than to be looking at pictures of naked women! I was scalded with shame. But this did not make the stories less fascinating.

Open the magazine and here is Miss Erickson, a demure young history teacher in blue jumper and white blouse, at the blackboard, her pointer aimed at a list of the causes of the Civil War *(Slavery, Western Expansion, Cotton, States Rights)*, and here she is on the next page in only her bra and panties, looking severely at a shy young man in horn-rimmed glasses. *Miss Erickson asked*

young Bill to stay after class. "You've done nothing but cause me
trouble all day," she said. "Now, for once, you're going to do what
I say." He offered no resistance as she unbuttoned his shirt. "Now
take off your pants," she whispered huskily. He did so, and as the
jeans dropped to the floor, his manhood rose like a ball-peen
hammer. "Now do as I tell you," she said. She unclasped her
brassiere to give him easy access to her gleaming orbs and
pressed her lips against his, her tongue playing in his mouth. "Fi-
nally I discover something you're good at," she murmured.

I dreamed of pressing my lips against Hers. Her tongue in my
mouth. Her gleaming orbs pressed against me. But imagination
failed me. The only girl I ever kissed was Cousin Kate, a wonderful girl but so plain that I may have been the first one she ever
kissed, too.

The kiss occurred right after we drank wine in Aunt Flo's
kitchen that Sunday morning after the Breaking of Bread, when
Kate and I were hiding from everybody. We had sat in the living
room, all us Brethren, and when Uncle Al stood and prayed a long
sonorous prayer in King James style with *surely*s and *doth*s sprin-
kled around and how the Lord was stricken, smitten, and afflicted
as *propitiation* for our perfidy and transgressions, out of the corner of my eye I saw Kate cock her right hand and loft a paper airplane toward him. It fluttered his way, a vexation with wings, then
swooped toward Daddy's bowed head, but swerved and bit the
older sister in the left tit, and she squealed aloud. Uncle Al kept
right on praying for succor against the temptation of temporal
things. I sat, eyes clenched tight, and made a couple of snarfling
sounds until Mother jabbed me. The sister of course held me responsible for everything. After the B of B, she glared at me and
stalked off. Kate and I were in the kitchen, recalling the tit-biting

airplane. The others had all gone to the backyard to take a family portrait beside Uncle Al's beautiful rosebushes. Kate and I had no reason to trust photography, it had betrayed us so often in the past. She looked out the window. Uncle LeRoy was posing my older sister so she appeared to be standing in the palm of his hand. There was great merriment outside and I said, "Don't go out there."

"I have no intention of going there," she said. "I don't want to be with those people any more than I have to."

We stood still for a minute, waiting to hear our names called—*Kate! Gary!*— and meanwhile Daddy was placing his camera on a stepladder, setting the timer, telling everyone to move in closer.

"Have you ever drunk wine?" she said. I said, "Of course. Lots of times." A bald-faced lie. And I reached up for the jug of Mogen David in the cupboard and poured some in a jelly glass and took a gulp and she did likewise. And then she said, "Lips that touch wine shall never touch mine." And I held her shoulders and leaned in and kissed her.

"You're very bad," she said. "You're as bad as everyone says."

"Who says?"

"Girls say."

"Ha!" I kissed her again. She gave me a dreamy look and sighed and clasped her hands to her bosom and then I realized we were playing the Movie Game.

—When do you return to your ship, Lieutenant? she said.

—At six A.M. We sail to the Mediterranean. Greece, North Africa, and then on from there, God only knows where.

—I suppose I may never see you again.

—Perhaps not.

—It is such a dreary little town without you.

We liked to make up movie scenes, but always they were espionage or detective movies. A body lay on the floor, someone like Mr. Halvorson, an ax buried in his skull, the room full of clues. I'd never kissed her in a movie before.

I moved in for another kiss, remembering to press lightly, lightly, not grind. I thought, *I'm doing this pretty well for someone with no experience.* It was only pretend kissing, but it was real to me. And then I felt her tongue between my lips. What was that about? Where did she learn it? From a book? It must mean she was enjoying herself.

And then the screen door slapped open, and we jumped apart, and the older sister slouched in and said, "You're wanted in the yard. Everybody's waiting for you." And she took a closer look at me and said, "You've been drinking wine."

—I haven't either.

—You did so, she said. What's that spilled on your shirt? It's wine.

I hesitated.

—It's the juice of the grape, said Kate.

—No, said the sister, it's wine from the glass.

—It didn't come from the glass! said Kate. It came from the bottle.

—Bottle or glass, it makes no difference. It's still the Blood of our Lord Jesus Christ. You were drinking the Blood that the Lord shed on Calvary's cross. You drank it. As a joke. Both of you.

I shook my head, but not convincingly.

She put her big flat face up to mine and told me that drinking the Lord's Blood for fun was blasphemy. She said, "That's the unforgivable sin. You want me to show you in Scripture? I will. You're going to hell. You know that? You're going to spend eternity in the everlasting lake of fire. Think about it." And she said to Kate, "You're to blame too. I'm going to tell. I'm not going to protect you." And she marched out the door.

We stood a long minute and waited for Aunt Flo or Uncle Al to come storming in, yelling, waving flaming swords, driving us from the house and out of town to wander the earth.

Nothing.

Then Mother called, in a pleasant voice, "Gary? Kate?" And we went outside and were photographed, the two of us, Miss Moon Face and Mr. Tree Toad.

Kate said that God knew that we were going to drink that wine, and so, if we hadn't, then what were we saying, that God is a dope? We drank the wine because that was what we were going to do and God knew it.

But I felt shaken afterward, as a person would, of course.

Because hell is a real place. We Sanctified Brethren knew that, we sang about the fiery pit, the reefs of woe. We sang, *Only one life, 'twill soon be past; / Only what's done for Christ will last.* Jesus is looking down from heaven, not missing a thing. Grandpa is at his side saying, "I don't know what happened. They took him to Sunday school and now look at him. Drinking the sacrament. Jesus, what a disappointment he's turned out to be!" And Jesus says, "I hope he straightens out soon, because in a couple minutes we're going to blast on down there for the Second Coming."

"I saw some of the heavenly host getting ready."

"It's coming up real soon."

Grandpa looks down and he's worried. In heaven, there are no worries, no tears, but Grandpa is Grandpa and he can't help wishing that I'd straighten out. How can a kid be so dumb? Eternal glory awaits, and a golden crown, and an eternity of love and rejoicing, and there I am, thinking about farts and naked librarians and my throbbing manhood and drinking the Sacred Wine for the thrill of it. Blasphemy!

Then Grandpa looks at Jesus, and he grasps the hem of Jesus's garment. "That is really beautiful raiment," says Grandpa. "Thanks," says Jesus. "I've been saving it for my return to earth. Now I just need to put on my golden shoes."

I was saved, I think, at a gospel revival at the Green Lake Bible camp two summers ago after a sermon by Brother Fred Rowley, who preached about the ship *Titanic* and the tycoons and society ladies on board who paid little heed to Spiritual Things and devoted themselves to Worldly Pleasures and suddenly, in the midst of their glittering evening of Glamour and Elegance, them in their tuxedos and evening gowns sipping their champagne and discussing the wonderful fun they'd have when they docked in New York City, the parties, the dinners—suddenly came a horrendous CRACKING and CRUNCHING and GROANING and SHRIEKING from the bowels of the "unsinkable" ship and the roar of seawater and a few hours later they plunged to their deaths in the frigid Atlantic, their souls sinking into an Eternity of Darkness without God. And I sat in my seat, trembling, thinking that if God could sink an ocean liner, He could easily drop a meteor on our house or blow up the furnace or poison the water or arrange for a gunman to come and murder us in our beds, as the choir sang, "I've wandered far away from God, now I'm coming home. The paths of sin too long I've trod. Lord, I'm coming home." And I said, "Come into my heart, Lord Jesus."

But was that enough?

Brother Rowley said anyone who wanted to accept Jesus Christ as Saviour should come forward—and I didn't go. I preferred to be saved sitting quietly in my seat. I didn't care to be a tree toad on his knees, bawling, for everyone to gawk at. So I sat in my seat and quietly invited Jesus into my heart. But did He come in? Or did He say, "If you're too scared to come down front, then why should I walk all the way back there?"

Condemned to eternal perdition because I was too shy to walk fifty feet! What a fool!

Just like the Flood! The rains were falling harder and harder and people started knock-knock-knocking on the door of the Ark. *Hey, Noah, the boat looks great. Nice job. I've been thinking about building one myself. Mind if I take a peek inside?* And Noah didn't open up. And the Flood came and the Ark floated free and those friends and neighbors were drowned like rats. The rainbow and the dove with the olive branch were all very nice, but they came too late for the drownees. God is love and God can also be rough on people. Ask the Midianites.

I sit every Sunday morning with the Sanctified Brethren in Aunt Flo and Uncle Al's living room, the Body and Blood of our Lord Jesus Christ on a card table in our midst, and listen to the men pray their long expository prayers ("O Thou Who didst pass over the dwelling places of the children of Israel, so too watch over us, Thy Church, Thy Faithful Remnant, as we seek to uphold Thy Word in the midst of great spiritual darkness"), and we sing mournful dirges to the risen Christ and read all the owliest and crankiest passages of Scripture, and I think, *If these are the Lord's people, then who am I? Not one of them.* Though I'm related to most of them.

Maybe I am adopted from an orphanage in New York City.

Maybe my parents were interrupted by a phone call as they made love and were a few minutes late and got someone else's child. God has all the souls lined up in the chute, and if your timing is off and you miss your turn—surprise!—you get a tree toad.

God knows. God knows who you are and what's in your heart, what you really believe. He knows whether you are His or not.

So there I sit on Sunday morning, listening to the Word of God, legs dangling, on the edge of eternity, a sheer drop down to hell, and I can't keep from thinking about the story in *High School Orgies* about the young Chip, who goes to the school nurse because his stomach hurts, so she has him take off his pants. She presses on his belly and his groin and tells him to cough, and he does, and she puts her hand between his legs and says, "How does this feel?" It feels good. She puts his hand inside her blouse. "How does that feel?" That feels good, too.

I can imagine some woman doing this to me someday in the dark. Someone like my cousin Kate.

9

Eleanor of Aquitaine

The very beautiful 17-year-old Eleanor of Aquitaine, of noble degree, is enjoying a fine summer on her parents' palatial estate when one day both of them die of a rare blood disease and she is sent by her evil stepsister to work in the scullery, where she spends the day drying pots and pans. One day, a woman in a white satin robe comes in bearing a fiery torch and sings "Stand Up, Stand Up for Jesus" in a loud voice, and this startles Eleanor and she drops a cast-iron skillet on her dog. He bites her and she goes to her room, weeping, and the next day doctors tell her that she has the same rare incurable blood disease that felled her mother and dad. She is given two weeks to live. The evil stepsister is exultant and planning what she will do with her gold shekels once Eleanor is out of the way. The next day, a tornado comes up suddenly and destroys the palace and estate and it drives a blade of grass into Eleanor's left foot. Amazingly, her incurable disease is cured, and she takes shelter in a nearby church. That night, the dog creeps into the church and finds the pew where she is sleeping and says, "Would you like to know what it was on the grass that cured you? A little chemical formula known as K9P, that's what." The next night, a Bible salesman knocks on the church door. He is selling Bibles bound in black leather, with gold edging, study guide and reference helps, maps of the Holy Land, and when he sees that she is alone, he says, "I'll give you this one free, darlin, in exchange for some of your sweet lovin," and she screams and he chases her around the church. As it turns out, she is not alone. A handsome toad is sitting on a window ledge and sees her predicament and leaps onto the Bible salesman's neck and down his shirt collar and terrifies him so that he runs away screaming, and the toad drops out of his shirttails and lands, semi-conscious, on the stone church floor, where he is suddenly transformed into a comely young man. This often happens to toads who perform heroic deeds with no thought of reward. She is so grateful, she takes him upstairs, and in no time she is pregnant.

He knew her upstairs in the bedroom. She didn't know it but he had wanted to know her for months, and right away he said, "Oh, darling, let's know." She said no and he took this to mean yes and he took her clothes off, which greatly surprised her. "What?" she said. And then, before she knew it, they were knowing. They knew and knew until they were exhausted and kept knowing until all was known. "This has been the strangest day of my life," she said. And yet in some way she was rather happy. She had always felt it was likely to happen sooner or later and now it had.

The comely young man is terribly confused. One minute ago he was an amphibian and now, in a few minutes, he's become a human and had sex for the first time. The evil stepsister takes Eleanor away to live with relatives, and as they decide what to do with her, they eat a very rich supper. "I'm about to explode," says an uncle, and then he cuts loose with a salvo of silent rippers, and so do three of the others. The air is very curly. The relatives sit very straight in their chairs, trying to keep the gas from escaping, but anytime they lean even slightly one way, there is hissing and fizzing and then the dog walks in the room and says, "I wish you people knew what you smell like to me," and they jump up to brain him one and the lady in the white satin robe walks in with the fiery torch and there is blue flame everywhere. And meanwhile, in a room upstairs, the young Eleanor Aquitaine powders herself after her bath, drying her breasts like small friendly rabbits, and preparing to run away with the comely young man and marry him and live happily ever after, she guesses. Why shouldn't she, after all she's been through?

10

In the Boys' Toilet

Kate is way older than I, she's seventeen, but she is a rebel and a writer like me, though we've both been rejected for *The Literary Leaf*, her stuff for being too scary and mine for being dumb ("JUVENILE!!" Miss Lewis wrote at the top of two of my stories. "Talking animals??? Really! And why is there a fatal blood disease in every story??"). Kate was not a tree toad—more of a muskrat, with big hips and narrow sloping shoulders and somewhat flat-chested, a big beak inherited from Uncle Sugar, not sweet or demure at all, as her mother was hoping for, but she dwelt on a plane of sophistication extremely rare for Lake Wobegon, Minnesota. She was a devotee of *The New Yorker* and shared copies with me and pointed out the good stuff like Liebling and Perelman and explained the cartoons. She wore her dark hair short with bangs in homage to the great Audrey Hepburn and she acted in school plays, but of course a big-hipped girl with a moon face usually got to be the mother, or the maid, in blackface, dusting the drawing room as the curtain came up. She didn't care, she loved to perform. She liked to say things to make people's jaws drop *(I am incredibly horny today)*, and then be nonchalant about it, *What's the big deal?*, and walk away, cool. It was a show. She told a girl from Youth for Christ that she had seen boys naked lots of times and had once held a boy's penis in her hand, just for the heck of it. She said she thought it was okay if people had sex, so long as they loved each other. The other girl told everybody and Miss Lewis got wind of it and sat Kate down for a talk and Kate denied the whole thing. That was her way. It was all a big show. If you dared her to show her underpants, she would. If you dared her to kiss you, she'd be there. If Miss Falconer needed someone to sing a solo at the Christmas choir concert, Kate's arm was high in the air, her hand fluttering.

I could no more stand up and sing in front of other people than I could flap my arms and fly. My one venture into the realm of entertainment was seventh-grade choir, when we traipsed around to nursing homes singing Christmas carols to slack-jawed people who were no longer mobile and had no choice about their entertainment and were liable to pee in their pants. When you stand and sing "Silent night, holy night, / All is calm, all is bright," and see a big pool of urine spreading on the floor around the wheelchairs, and hear an old lady cry "Go get the ponies!" it does not inspire a person to want to perform again.

Kate knew sophisticated songs. She read Tolstoy and Dostoyevsky. She smoked. When she was in the mood, she spoke in a Hepburn glissando, cool and thrilling—she'd say, "Darling, what a day I have had, I'm in an absolute *state*, the things I put up with, don't ask me about it"—definitely not a Lake Wobegon way of talking, and she'd reach into her coat pocket and pull out her Herbert Tareytons and plant a cigarette between her lips and say, "Darling, I have been *dying* for this since noon," and light it and let the smoke trickle out her mouth and draw it up her nose. She learned to smoke at Bible camp, from some unsaved kids the Brethren brought in for conversion, and she also learned from them how to swear and dance the shimmy. "Sweet pea," she said, "it is awfully hard to be in absolute top form when you're surrounded by Lutherans."

That spring, her poem "soliloquy" was rejected by Miss Lewis for *The Literary Leaf*—

> death is easy like taking a bath
> with an electric fan and waving hello to god
> you could die like walking in front of a bus
> or jumping into the big blue air
> or into the lake
> or doing almost anything
> you could die by living in minnesota
> and forgetting your scarf
> or remembering your scarf
> and it catches on the axle and strangles you
> god is love but
> he doesn't necessarily drop
> everything and go save you
> does he

Miss Lewis was horrified. She told Kate she was a very sick girl. She sent the poem home to my Aunt Ruth and Uncle Sugar, and it scared them silly. How could Kate say such crazy things? And putting an electric fan in the bath? Where did she come up with something so grisly? And why wasn't *god* capitalized?

"It's only a poem," said Kate. She pointed out that a soliloquy is a speech to one's self and that it wasn't her talking, it was the person in the poem. Nonetheless, Sugar hustled around and locked up all the knives and razor blades and small electric appliances, and hid the rope and the garden hose.

She kept Ruth and Sugar in a constant uproar, wondering what she would do next. She announced that she planned to attend Athena College in Melisma, Iowa, where, on May Day every year, the students run naked as jaybirds across the quad and through the fountain and into the arboretum (*Prof Doffs Duds at May Day Do*, was the headline in the Minneapolis *Star*). Uncle Sugar said he would rather eat a can of Dutch cleanser than have her attend a school like Athena. But Kate just laughed. "Darling," she said to me, "I don't intend to spend my life baking cookies and waxing the kitchen floor. These poor women! They think that, if they're very quiet and smiley and keep their floors clean, everybody will like them. I am not a scrubwoman. I am an artist, my darling. So are you. Artists are put here to paint big strokes of color in a dull, gray world—and if some people prefer the dull, gray world, too bad for them. Don't be a bump on a log. Wake up and die right."

A few days after the "soliloquy" scandal, Kate waltzed into school in a blue angora sweater unbuttoned three buttons from the top, a dramatic slutty touch. She seemed even more coltish and *Oh darling*–ish than usual, flying around the halls, crying out *Woo-*

hoo and blowing kisses and striking a come-hither pose and hugging people. It was the day of the spring talent show. The whole student body packed into the auditorium, and the lights dimmed, and the spotlight focused on the microphone in front of the blue and gold *L.W.H.S.* curtain. I ached to walk out on that stage in a shiny white suit and a Stetson, twanging on a guitar, singing a Doo Dads song like "I'm Weird," but it wasn't in me, not with my nursing-home background.

A girls' sextet sang "Green Cathedral" and a boy in a red-striped suit lip-synched to a Spike Jones song and a sweaty girl in a pink formal played "Deep Purple" at the piano in a studious way. Leonard Larsen recited "Stopping by Woods on a Snowy Evening." Painful. The boy took himself quite seriously. The sextet returned and sang "To Know Him Is to Love Him." Kate hated them because they wouldn't let her join, even though she sang better than any of them. They rejected her because she wasn't cute and perky enough. They sang a third song about wanting to be loved by you, boop-boop-a-doop, in which Cathy Tollerud did a stutter-step rag-doll dance that showed flashes of white panties, and boys around me whooped and whistled, and right after that came Kate, determined to show them up. She danced to the Doo Dads' recording of "Dance Me"—

> Baby, baby, I'm your man.
> Kiss me, squeeze me, hold my hand.
> Kiss me sweet and kiss me strong.
> And dance me, dance me, all night long.

As she danced, she pulled her sweater down so you could see her bare shoulders. Then she turned her back and showed off more of her shoulders. She didn't seem to be wearing anything under-neath. She stood with her hands on the sweater as if she might take the whole thing off, and boys whistled and yelled, "Yes! Yes! Do it!" and Mr. Halvorson sidled toward the stage and she smiled at him and winked and flounced off to whoops and yells, and came back for a deep bow that revealed a little more. After the show, Daryl Magendanz saw her in the hall and grabbed for her bra strap and didn't find one and threw back his big flat head and hollered, "She ain't wearin no UN-der-wear!"

Kate was sent to the school nurse, Mrs. Dahlberg, for inspec-tion. Kate refused to cooperate. She told Mrs. Dahlberg to sit on it and spin. The nurse lunged at Kate and threw her up against the wall and was about to put her hand up Kate's sweater when Kate squirmed loose and raced out the door and down the hall past the English classrooms and came pedaling for dear life around the corner by home economics as I was opening the door to the boys' can.

I had gotten out of Miss Lewis's class to go to the library and look up the Globe Theatre in the encyclopedia so I could make a model of it out of balsa wood.

Kate yelped at me and slid into the can ahead of me and we hustled into the far stall and latched the door and I sat on the throne and she sat on my lap with her legs braced against the door.

"I don't know as this is a good idea," I said, but actually it was a lovely idea, her sitting on my lap. She put one hand on the toilet-paper roll and lay back against me, her legs slightly bent, her brown shoes on the green door, and then she said, "You better pull down your pants so it looks like you're taking a dump." She hoisted herself up an inch and I slid my trousers and underpants down, and she sat on my naked lap. She told me what happened in the nurse's office. I put my arms around her. I could feel her ribcage, breathing, her back against me. I put my face in her hair. She was a little heavy but it didn't matter.

A door slammed open and the nurse yelled, "Who's in here?"

I jumped and felt my innards clench and there were two little splashes in the toilet. Kate bent over to keep from laughing. She clapped both hands over her mouth.

"I said, who's in here?"

"Me," I said. Kate snorted.

"Are you alone?"

"Yes."

"Did a girl come in here?"

"No, of course not, Mrs. Dahlberg."

"Come out here and let's have a look at you."

Kate shook from the effort of not laughing out loud. She scootched up and I slid out from under and opened the stall door and looked out and there was Mrs. Dahlberg breathing fire. Her hair had come loose and she was grinding her teeth. "Step out of there, young man," she said. She was so ticked off she didn't even recognize me as Kate's cousin. I stepped out, Mr. Tree Toad, pants around my ankles, shirttails out, my hand over my pecker, and she looked at me with pure loathing. "What do you think you're doing out of class? You came in here to smoke, didn't you."

"I had to go to the toilet."

She snorted. "Let's see your hall pass."

I dug the pass out of my pants pocket, which entailed letting go of my pecker, which dangled free. "Oh, for pity's sake," she said. She looked at the pass. "This says you're supposed to be in the library."

"It was an emergency. I had to go real bad."

She shook her head. "If I don't see you in the library in five minutes, young man, there better be a reason why." She wheeled around and out the door and lit out down the hall.

The door slammed and Kate almost split a gut. "Boy, she scared the poop right out of you." Then she saw I was blushing and she hoisted herself up and I slid under her, on the throne. "Good you had your pants down."

I asked her what we should do now.

She said, "Sit tight, darling, and wait for the coast to clear."

I sat, half naked, with my arms around her middle and my pecker getting hard, and I poked it down and closed my legs over it. I could feel the tip touch the cold porcelain. It was big. I was scared to think she might be aware of this. Also, I was wondering what to do if, when I pulled my pants up, it stuck out in front like a porch. How could I conceal this? I had no books to hold in front of me.

She said, "You know, they just might kick me out of school for pushing Mrs. Dahlberg." She chuckled. "Oh well. If they kick me out, I'll run away from home. Two can play that game." She said she'd go up to Roger's dad's hunting shack in the woods near Bemidji and stay there for a while.

"Roger Guppy?" I said. She nodded. I had seen her with Roger at various times lately and chose to believe it was mere coincidence. Roger Guppy was two years older than she and nobody you'd ever expect her to be interested in. He was not an artist. He dug septic tanks with his dad. He had a big hank of blond hair that he slicked back in a ducktail. He was a ballplayer. He hung out with the ballplayer crowd. He was somebody who had probably never heard of *The New Yorker*.

"I could come visit you up in the woods," I said. She said that'd be nice.

That'd be nice. Her exact words.

"I wouldn't want you to be alone up there," I said.

"That's very thoughtful of you, sweet pea."

I assumed that her *That'd be nice* meant that Roger Guppy would not be at the hunting shack with her.

Two boys came in and unzipped and a moment later two powerful streams hit the steel urinal like horses pissing. I sat and imagined living with Kate in a shack in the woods. Swimming in the Mississippi. Talking late into the night. Talking about everything. Lying around writing stories for *The New Yorker* and reading them to her. Pure heaven.

When the boys left, she said she had to go straight home and put on a bra.

I said, "You don't have a bra on?"

And she took my hands and put them over her sweater, over her breasts, small and soft and unholstered, the soft nipples. I didn't squeeze or stroke, just let my hands rest there. It was sweet that she trusted me. A tender moment.

"Why didn't you wear one?"

"I didn't feel like it."

Grandpa was looking down and saying, "I don't believe it." Jesus saying, "Yeah, there's more and more of this sort of thing going on nowadays." I took a deep breath and Kate stood up. "I'll see if the coast is clear," she said. I stuffed my pecker down one trouser leg. It hung there like a garden implement. She pretended not to notice. We went skittering down the back stairs and out the door by the metalworking shops—a boy in welding mask glanced up as we passed—and then we were on McKinley Street and heading downtown. Fugitives.

I was scared of what Mr. Halvorson might do to us, but Kate was cool as a cucumber. "May as well enjoy your freedom once you got it," she said. It was a poetic spring day. Two cats lay on the sidewalk, soaking up the sun; meadow larks sang in a vacant lot. The steeple of the Lutheran church rose up before us. Inside a soprano was practicing. Praise to the Lord, the Almighty, the King of Creation.

We went down the hill and across Main Street, which was almost deserted, and headed toward the trees by the swimming beach.

I was scared somebody would see us and call up the school, but she just laughed—"Don't be such a gloomy Gus," she said. She sat down and leaned against a pair of birch trees. I sat next to her.

"This is what I call a good day," she said. "You ever worry that you might turn out to have a really really boring life? I do. I worry about it all the time. I look at my mother, ironing sheets, putting her spice rack in order; I think I could end up like that."

I said I doubted that very much.

She said, "Only way to avoid it is to move away, darling. A person needs stimulation. It's the oxygen of the spirit. Here, you're practically dead by the time you're thirty."

I said I was worried I'd wind up going to hell.

She gave me a pitying look. "Either you're going or you're not, and God knows which it is, so there's not much to be done about it, is there?"

I knew her reasoning was faulty, and yet it appealed to me, in a way.

I walked her home, and there in the front hall was Aunt Ruth, her eyes red from weeping. She had been watching for us out the window. The school nurse had called. Ruth sat on the couch and took a deep breath and asked Kate if she honestly felt that pulling your sweater half off your body was the sort of behavior that glorified the name of Jesus Christ. And how in the world could you go around without underwear? What must people be thinking?

"My bra broke," said Kate. "So I took it off."

"As Christians we are to glorify the Lord in everything we do. How does this glorify Him, to do a striptease?"

"It was only for fun," said Kate.

"Fun!!"

"Yes, darling Mother. Fun. And it was loads of fun!" And she flounced up the stairs to her room.

My aunt gave me a haunted look. What could a person do with such a girl?

That night, the sky turned dark after suppertime. Black thunderheads floated in from the west like a range of mountains; the streetlights came on. People emerged from their homes to stand out on the sidewalk and watch the storm's approach, admire the purplish light, the stillness, and then the bolts of lightning ripping the sky, thunder booming. I sat on the porch, the older sister sitting next to Daddy on the daybed, Mother pouring him a glass of iced tea, and I expected one of those bolts to come straight into my chest. My toasted black body crumpled on the porch swing, and Mother weeping over me and Kate running in and blurting out the terrible truth: *We were in the boys' toilet together and he took his pants down and touched my breasts.*

And they carry my body away to finish the job of cremation, and an angel descends, holding a flaming sword, and speaks in a loud voice to the people gathered in the street:

He took his pants down and touched her breasts. And the Lord God dealt with him. Let it be a lesson unto the children of Lake Wobegon. Lo, saith the Lord God, keep thy hearts pure and thy minds centered on that which is edifying and let not thy pants be taken down except that thou washeth thyself and changeth to other garments or emptieth thy bowels thereof.

The missing bra, the dance, the disobedience in school—these things did not escape the eye of our watchful family. Mother heard about them. Sugar and Ruth were horrified. Aunt Flo knew all about it. She knew everything. Once Kate and I ran into Aunt Flo downtown and Kate quickly hid her cigarette behind her back and said, "Hi, Aunt Flo," and when Flo passed, Kate smiled at me and exhaled smoke, cool as could be. But Aunt Flo knew. She didn't miss a trick.

11

Underwood

The lawn is a thing of beauty. Anytime I'm out working on it, I get compliments. People stop and say, "What'd you do to get that lawn so nice!" Mr. Stenstrom came over once and said I should go into the lawn business. No comment from the Andersons: the line of demarcation between their property and ours is quite clear, like the Iron Curtain.

I lie on the big porch swing, looking at *Look* magazine. Mother is perusing the *Star* and Daddy lies on the daybed, eyes closed, mouth open, snoring. Directly beneath Daddy, a man and a blonde babe embrace, and under the picture it says: *He pulled the lacy black bra from her twin mounds and pushed hard against her, his manhood hard as a judge's gavel. She shivered as his tongue caressed her hot mouth.*

It's tucked inside *Look*, next to an article entitled "The World in the Year 2000," with a picture of the Family of Tomorrow in their bubble-top home, their rocket-backpacks stacked by the airlock door, talking over a picturephone as they eat their little food capsules. The man is bending to kiss the blonde babe's breasts. God knows I am staring at this. God knows if tonight the sky over Lake Wobegon will be filled with angels singing and Jesus will descend to call up to heaven all of the Sanctified Brethren except the ones looking at dirty pictures.

Mother is reading the latest about Ricky and Dede. They abandoned the station wagon in Billings and stole another car and evaded a sheriff's blockade near Missoula and fled west. Authorities believe they are stealing money from newspaper boxes. Ricky wrote a poem and sent it to the *Star*, which has turned it over to the FBI.

Uncle Sugar comes ambling up the walk in his white pants and a palm-frond sportshirt, trailing a cloud of cologne. He is carrying a black Underwood typewriter.

"What a beautiful lawn," he says.

White shoes and pink socks.

In his youth, Sugar sang with the Eldon Miller Orchestra, and then he met Ruth and got saved. Booze had kept his wheels greased, and then Jesus straightened him out and brought him into the Sanctified Brethren. Thank you, Jesus. But he still dresses like a singer and has long singer-hair. It is swept back on the sides like fenders and some is swooped up over the top to cover the bald spot. Hairpins hold the swoop in place.

Sugar sets the typewriter gently on the floor and eases himself into a wicker rocker, a tight squeeze for a wide butt. "'Maybe I ought to hire Gary to do our lawn. I sure can't keep up with it," he says.

I smile. I am looking at the typewriter.

"Have you heard about this boy who attacked his mother?" says Mother. Yes, he has. "Gary knew him in school."

"I didn't know him well," I say.

"They were in class together," says Mother.

"What sort of kid was he?" says Sugar.

I would rather not talk about Ricky Guppy, a person I knew briefly from rope climbing, nobody you could call a friend, but here is my uncle with an Underwood typewriter, and I don't wish to offend him either.

"He was extremely quiet and pretty much kept to himself. Nobody knew him that well. He was a bus kid."

Uncle Sugar nods. This all fits the pattern all right. The silent loner. "What I don't understand is why he'd kidnap his girlfriend. Why get her mixed up in it?"

I would like to examine the Underwood closely and press on its keys, but it's never wise to show too much eagerness around these people. They're apt to yank the rug out from under you.

"I'm not sure he kidnapped her," says Mother.

"Of course he did," says Sugar. "Why would a girl want to drive off with a crazy person and get into all that trouble?"

"I wonder if she didn't go of her own free will."

"But why?"

Daddy hoists himself up from the daybed. He says it is not a fit subject to discuss in front of children.

"What is your secret of lawn care?" says Uncle Sugar, putting Ricky on the shelf. "You got some secret elixir you pump into it at night?"

Daddy mutters something about it being a good summer for lawns.

Mother offers Sugar a slice of rhubarb pie, but he is feeling a little gassy, so he'll take a rain check, thank you.

"That's a beautiful typewriter," says Mother.

"Bought it a year ago, thinking I'd write a history of my family," says Uncle Sugar, "and of course I didn't have the time or the talent. Wrote two pages and that was it. Of course, with my family, nobody wanted a history anyway. Too many horse thieves in the closet." He chuckles. "It's just been gathering dust." He turns to me, beaming. "So I thought Gary here might as well have it. Thought he'd put it to better use."

I am stunned. I had no idea. *God.* A typewriter.

"Doesn't Kate want it?" asks Mother.

"Kate has a typewriter already."

"This is awfully generous of you," says Mother. And to me: "What do you say?"

I murmur thank you. The enormity of this gift is truly staggering; it's as if he gave me the keys to a new car. I promise myself that I will never think snotty things about Uncle Sugar's hair and his balloon butt ever again. I have lusted for a typewriter for so long.

I kneel on the floor beside it. It is practically brand-new. An Underwood, jet black, with leafy gold lettering, a solid steel frame, the type bars nested in a semicircle, ready to be flung at the page. I press lightly on the round keys, flexing the bar. I rub the frame.

"You better oil that and keep it in good condition," says Daddy. "And don't be leaving it down the basement and letting it rust."

Uncle Sugar says he's sure I will take very good care of it.

"Well, that'll be a first," says Daddy.

Uncle Sugar beams at me. "I know you'll make good use of it,"

he says. I could almost walk over and hug him, but we're not hug-
gers in this family. I smile back at him my warmest and sincerest
smile. He always was my favorite uncle and now he has locked up
first place for many years to come.

"You don't know the first thing about typing," says Daddy.

"But I do. We had two weeks of it in Miss Lewis's English
class." I fetch a sheet of paper from the kitchen and place it in the
roller and crank the carriage return and type on the field of white,
whap-whap-whap—*For God so loved the world, that he gave his
only begotten Son, that whosoever believeth in him should not
perish, but have everlasting life.* The action is stiff, and I like that;
you have to strike with force and give the key a snap with your
finger and bang bang bang at the page.

I take out the page and pass it around. "An excellent job," says
Sugar. "Not a single mistake."

Daddy examines it. A perfect job of typing John 3:16 but he
can't bring himself to say so. Daddy doesn't believe in compliments. Earlier this evening he was rumbling around woofing
about who left the lights on in the bathroom and *what do you
think we are, movie stars? It's all I can do to pay the bills around
here. If you kids don't wise up, we're going to wind up in the poor-
house, and don't think I'm kidding. Do you know what a foster
home is? Do you?*—maintaining his drumbeat of disapproval to
keep us on our toes. The older sister was the one who left the
lights on, and she burst into tears and went to her room and hasn't
been seen since, poor thing.

I put the page back in and crank the carriage return a few more
times and am strongly tempted to type *Pecker. Dong. Horseshit.*
And pass that to Daddy and see how he likes it. But I type, *The*

quick brown fox jumped over the lazy sleeping dog. Now is the time for all good men to come to the aid of their party. Fast and accurate. As Miss Lewis taught us.

"I don't want to see that thing kicking around on the floor, or I'll take it away from you," says Daddy, sternly. "If you can't take care of it, then you don't deserve to have it."

"He'll take care of it," says Mother.

"Sure, and how many times have I heard that before?" he sighs and lies back on the daybed. He has fought the good fight for conservation of electricity, for regular maintenance and economy, sensible living, hard work, all the Republican virtues, and nobody listens to a word he says, it goes in one ear and out the other.

"Let me show you a little trick," says Sugar. He kneels down beside me and taps a *t* and then backspaces and taps an *f* over it. The superimposed letters make the symbol for the English pound. "Somebody showed me that once," he says. He smiles at me. "So what do you say? You going to write a book?" He gives me one of those fake chuckles. "If you do, don't put me in it!" He chortles. "I've got enough trouble as it is!"

The fake chuckling of grown-ups is embarrassing. Why laugh when there's nothing to laugh at?

"Have you been seeing much of Kate this summer?" asks Uncle Sugar.

I say, No, not much, she's been busy.

He gets back in his chair. He leans forward, his elbows on his knees. "You know this boy named Roger Guppy?"

Not really. He's quite a bit older. Graduated last year.

"I hear he's a little wild."

I wouldn't know about that. He pitches for the Whippets, that's all I know.

"He's the brother of the kid who attacked his mother and stole her car," says Daddy. "And I believe another brother is that rock-and-roll singer named Jim Dandy. His group got kicked off the radio for singing dirty songs."

"That's what has us worried," says Sugar. "I wish Kate wouldn't run around with that crowd."

"And the other brother is in prison," says Daddy. "And the dad is a heavy drinker, from what I hear." This is according to Aunt Flo, who gets her news at the Bon Marché Beauty Salon every Saturday morning and is in the know. Luanne at the Bon Marché knows where the bodies are buried. "Someone told me Kate goes to beer parties with this Roger Guppy person," says Sugar, looking at me.

I shrug my shoulders. I wouldn't know the first thing about beer parties.

"Somebody buys a trunkload of beer and they drive off to a rock quarry or some deserted cornfield and stand around and drink and smoke and kids go off in the bushes and neck and goodness knows what," he says. "I'm worried about her."

Mother makes a reassuring sound but he shakes his head. "We spoiled her rotten. Gave her everything. Took her on trips. Bought her clothes, a phonograph. She has no idea what it's like to work for something. And then she goes and does a striptease in school and writes poems about suicide and runs around with this ballplayer from a family of criminals."

Poor Uncle Sugar's voice is quavering. He chokes back his tears. "She's my little girl," he says to me. "If you knew something bad was happening, you'd tell, wouldn't you?"

I nod. I have no idea what I'm agreeing to, but I nod because I don't want him to cry and I want the Underwood typewriter.

Clearly it is a token of goodwill, given in hopes that I will keep my eyes open and report back to Uncle Sugar whether Kate is running around to beer parties with Roger Guppy.

I crawl back onto the swing and pick up the copy of *Look*.

"You like Kate, don't you? You wouldn't want to see her get into trouble like that girl Dede, would you?"

He pulls out a hanky and honks into it. Daddy sits in mute agony, looking out toward the streetlights, wishing he were hoofing it toward the Chatterbox Café.

"Kate thinks she knows it all, but she doesn't. She's just a small-town girl. It's so easy to put your trust in some big shot and run off with him and get married—I don't know what I'd do if she ran off with him. Or died in a car crash because he was drunk. You think about these things when you have a daughter. You think about having to go to the county morgue and identify her body. I don't see how I could go on living if that happened. I really don't."

And now his shoulders shake and he bows his head and sobs and Daddy almost levitates from the daybed. "I'll go see if the coffee's ready," he says, though nobody said a word about wanting coffee. He scoots toward the kitchen. Mother puts a hand on Sugar's shoulder. "We're praying for Kate," she says.

Uncle Sugar is crying for all he's worth, he sounds like an old badger moaning for its dead. *"Let me explain about fractions, Melanie," said Mr. Britton, reaching for the workbook on the desk in front of her, brushing against her luscious young breasts.—*"It's a terrible thing to fail your own child," Sugar says. "Where did we go wrong?"—*Melanie offered no resistance as he unbuttoned her blouse.—*Mother tells me to go see where Daddy went to and bring Sugar a cup of coffee. "Just a minute," I say. "Go. Now," she says. "Okay. I'm going." *She was hot as a furnace,* *moaning, as his manhood pressed against her.*—"Go see about the coffee," says Mother. "I'm okay," says Sugar. "Don't worry about me. I'm just being a big baby. It's time I should be heading home."—*She pulled him into the closet and began to thrust against him violently.*—"What are you reading?" says Mother. "Nothing," I say.—*She cried, "Oh, Mr. Britton! Oh my gosh!" as waves of pleasure rolled over her young body.*—"Well, it must be something," she says. "What is it? Look at me when I'm talking to you."—*"Oh God!" she screamed, as the first of several orgasms struck her.*—"It's only a story," I say. I close *Look* over the naked algebra student and go into the kitchen. The coffee is boiling on the stove. Daddy is nowhere to be seen. I pour a cup and take it out to the porch, and Sugar says, "I should be going," but he doesn't move. Mother sits still. I sit on the swing, with *Look*. The neighborhood is peaceful. The Stenstroms' is dark, they're in Duluth at a Lutheran Ushers' Convention. Somewhere nearby a car rolls over gravel and stops and the motor shuts off and a door opens. Even the Andersons are at peace in their little house. Perhaps they all killed each other.

And now the piano plays the old theme and the Trojan Troubadour speaks to us of hybrid seed corn and sings—

> *Let's go dancing in Lansing,*
> *Let's have a ball in St. Paul.*
> *Love is torrid in Fargo-Moorhead,*
> *There's euphoria and joy in Peoria, Illinois.*
> *Whenever you ask a girl from Nebraska,*
> *You know she'll always say yes.*
> *Forget Paris and Rome, let's just stay home*
> *And find love in the Midwest.*

Out there in the dark, Kate sits in a car with Roger Guppy, perhaps on his lap, his face buried in her hair, his hands fiddling with her breasts. Daddy is hiding upstairs. "Good night," says Uncle Sugar, still distraught, and gets up and heads home. The sprinkler goes around and around and there is the smell of fresh-boiled coffee in the air. Nothing moves on Green Street once Sugar's footsteps die out around the corner. Mother and her tree-toad boy sitting on the porch, and above us, Grandpa looking out the window of heaven, and Jesus standing beside him.

Grandpa says, "Jesus, why did you give an Underwood typewriter to a boy who thinks dirty thoughts all the time? All he's going to do is create filth."

Jesus says, "Well, we'll see what he does with it."

"We brought him up right and he's no different from those Guppy boys."

"Yeah, that sort of thing happens sometimes."

I go inside and turn the sprinkler off, and when I come back, Mother asks if I remember when we lived on the farm and she went away to New York to see Daddy. Of course I do.

—Did you ever feel I abandoned you?

—No.

—Aunt Eva took good care of you, didn't she.

—Yes.

—She was always wonderful to you.

—She was.

—I was jealous of her. All the things she was good at. Baking and gardening and doing fieldwork and butchering chickens and carpentry and the whole shootin match. She and Grandma were awfully nice to us, taking us in like that. And I was so glad to get into our own house. It just doesn't work, living with relatives.

I wait for some further revelations. It feels like Mother is on the verge of blurting out something more about Eva. I can feel information in the air, the barometric pressure rising, a rock about to drop in the pond, a brain tumor, an unrequited love, a fall from a horse—and then Mother thinks better of it.

"I remember how crowded New York was that time I went. You walked down the street and you were always in a big crowd. Threading your way through the mob. People on the street at all hours. Standing around and eating pretzels and hot dogs and smoking. Women smoking cigarettes. That shocked me. I'd seen it in movies but not right out in the open like that."

Mother has now confessed that she once attended movies. Wonderful. Amazing. I'd like to hear more things like this. (Who did she go to movies with?)

"And people bumping into you and not saying, I'm sorry. That was really something. But I suppose if you did you'd be apologizing all day. We went to Chinatown and saw a butcher shop with live chickens and ducks in the window and piles of fish on ice. Crab and octopus. Daddy and I had the chow mein. The restaurant was full of Chinese people speaking Chinese. It was ten o'clock at night but it was too hot to sleep so we went to Coney Island and rode the roller coaster—it was scary—we sat behind six girls who were screaming their heads off and standing up waving their arms in the air. I remember their hair was in curlers. They wanted Daddy to take their picture when the car was going down the steep drop, but by the time he understood what they wanted, the ride was over. So we went on it again and we took their picture and they took ours. We went on the carousel and stood in line for the parachute drop and we ran into an Army buddy of his, Don, and his girlfriend. They were trying to cool off, too. We rode the subway which was like a steambath so we walked around Brooklyn with them. Walked for miles. It was after midnight but it was too hot to sleep, so we kept walking."

Mother stops, flushed from the memory of that hot night long ago. She left behind her three little kids on the farm with Grandma and Eva and rode the train to New York City and stayed out until all hours walking around on the streets. She who had gone to a movie, too. This is not a story you'd stand up and tell on Sunday morning to Sanctified Brethren.

"What did you see in Brooklyn?"

"There was a candy store open on the corner and people buying ice-cream sodas, so we got sodas and we sat on the curb, and across the street there was a park and thousands of people lying on blankets spread out on the grass. Thousands of them. Some men sitting on park benches smoking, and some women sitting and talking on the grass, and all the others lay sleeping, whole families, men and women and little kids, on blankets they spread out on the grass. I couldn't hear what they were saying but just the sound of voices, like birds, it made me think of the children of Israel in the desert. God watching over them and not slumbering. All those people."

I don't know where this story is going—if she's about to tell me that Daddy pulled out a Lucky Strike and lit up? And they ducked into a corner tavern and ordered highballs? No, probably not, but it is almost as amazing to think of them out on the town, taking it easy, Daddy not grouching about how crowded and hot it is and how expensive the sodas are. It is after midnight but there he is with Mother, enjoying himself and hang the expense. Hard to believe.

"What did you do then?"

"We sat there on the curb and drank our sodas and then we said good night to Don and his girlfriend because she had to go home to the Bronx and get up and go to work in the morning. We took the subway back to Manhattan, to our hotel on Broadway, the Broadmoor, and a man was selling flowers from a pushcart and Daddy bought me a bouquet of violets, and we went up in the elevator and it was hot in the room, so Daddy took the mattress off the bed and we slept outdoors, on the fire escape. On an open grate, nineteen stories in the air. You could look right over the edge and see people walking on the sidewalks below. But we went right to sleep and didn't wake up until eight in the morning, and it was raining."

She glances at her watch. "Goodness gracious. Look at the time."

"You really slept on a fire escape?"

"Yes, it was cooler out there."

I wish she would talk more about New York and the fun they had but she stands up. "Well," she says. "Time for decent people to be in bed."

"Weren't you afraid you'd fall off?"

"No, we were asleep."

She slips into the kitchen and clinks around in the cupboard for a minute or two and runs water in the sink, and I sit and wait, wishing she'd come back and tell more. I don't know what I want to know. Everything. Everything they did and said and everything they thought about life and what they were hoping for.

12

At Joe's Bar

Uncle Sugar has a pool table in the cool of his basement, a
souvenir of his old life, and on the knotty-pine paneling
hang pictures of the Eldon Miller Orchestra, Sugar in a
white tux looking young and moody. Kate and I shoot eight-
ball on a hot afternoon, listening to Jelly Roll Morton on the Vic-
trola, and Lars Hinkley singing, *Honolulu Mama, how she could
dance / In her little pink nightie when she took off her—Oahu!
Oahu! Oahu!* It's hard to imagine Uncle Sugar's life before
he found the Lord, but it included "Hyena Stomp" and "Panama"
and the Famous Del Ray Ballroom on Lake Elmo—here's the Eldon Miller Orchestra on the bandstand, saxophones poised, Sugar
at the microphone, the handsome maestro holding the long white
baton, and women in skimpy dresses with the hemline above their
knees dancing, knees in, heels up, arms akimbo, on the long
veranda. Kate twitches her butt in time to the music as she lines

up a shot and—*whack!*—she bangs her four-ball into the corner pocket, and as she angles for the three, she says, "What did your parents tell you about sexual intercourse?"

Sexual intercourse! I have always wanted to say the words out loud, so I do. "What did my parents tell me about sexual intercourse?" I say.

"Yes," she says.

"They pretty much let me figure sexual intercourse out for myself." I was in Minneapolis once to go to the library and walked down Hennepin Avenue with its marquees blinking and neon arrows pointing and neon women kicking their legs up and down and up and down and neon champagne glasses with bubbles rising and a bookstore, Shinder's, where I found a book called *Sexual Hygiene* where I first saw the words *coitus* and *vagina* and *penis.* I read it, wrapped in a *National Geographic,* standing in the aisle. I couldn't afford the $1.50, and anyway the clerk was a woman.

—Did it have pictures?

—More like maps.

—What did they show?

—It showed how the penis goes into the vagina.

My heart pounds to hear myself say this delicious thing. I would also like to say *coitus* but I'm not 100% sure about the pronunciation.

—So it told you how to have sex?

—It gave you a pretty good idea how it goes.

—Did it sound like fun?

—Sort of.

Sort of!!! Sort of?? It sounded like the greatest thing in the world. Even saying the words for it is utterly thrilling and naming the parts of the body.

It's my shot, the ten-ball, a long shot, lots of green.

—Sex is a lot better than what those books say, she says.

"Oh?" How does she know?

I poke the cueball and the ten-ball skews off into nowhere.

"My mother gave me a book that made sex sound painful, like having your appendix out. That's what they don't want us to know, darling. How much fun it is."

And she switches into her Southern accent.—"Oh, Randolph. It's so hard to send you back to the front. I can't bear the thought! I hate this war! Do you hear me! I hate it!" She lights a cigarette and comes around the pool table to me and touches my arm. And kisses me on the lips. "That's so you'll have something to remember me by, soldier," she says.

We shoot pool, listen to jazz, Kate gives me a smoking lesson. She passes me a Herbert Tareyton. I hold it and she corrects my technique. The right arm should be cocked, the wrist bent, the fingers relaxed, the cigarette between the first and second fingers. I light it off her match and inhale, it burns, but not too bad. "Breathe it out." I do and notice a certain light-headedness. Not nausea, not a prelude to vomiting. But I don't feel like making any sudden moves.

It's a New York bar called Joe's and she's sitting at a table in the corner and I walk in, a stranger in a black suit, black hat, and I ask her for a light and she says, "You come here often?"

—Now that I know you're here, I'll be coming much more often, I'm sure.

—You look like a writer.

—I am. You're very beautiful. But I suppose you know that.

—Beauty isn't that important to me. Physical beauty. It's only a way to get to meet people. Who do you write for?

—*The New Yorker* magazine. Ever hear of it?

—I've seen it around here and there. What sort of stuff do you write?

—Write about jazz, theater, that sort of thing. Baseball, movies. From now on, I may be writing a little bit about you.

—Ha! You don't even know me! You don't know one thing about me.

—Give me time. I'm a good learner, sister.

And we kiss a movie kiss. So light, so sweet. We kiss twice. And then she pulls back and says it's time to go. We open the windows and wave wet towels and put away the 78s. "I really shouldn't do that anymore," she says. "Roger asked me if I ever kissed other boys and I said I didn't. I don't want to be a liar."

"I don't think this counts. It's only pretend," I say. "It doesn't really mean anything." Lie, lie, lie. It means everything and I know it.

—I don't want to hurt his feelings.

—He'll never know.

—You always know if someone you love is lying to you.

A scary thought. Very scary. Love as a lie detector. A tree toad has to tell a hundred lies before anybody would dream of loving him.

—Do you love Roger? I say.

—I do. We have a lot of fun together.

—Someone said you and he go to beer parties.

—We do a lot of different things. Mostly we talk.

—What about?

She makes a face.

—Wouldn't you like to know?

Yes, I would. But apparently I'm not going to. So I rack up the billiard balls and set the cue sticks in their clips and I brush the green felt and pick bits of lint off it. Kate waits at the light switch at the foot of the stairs. I am sad to think that Joe's Bar is going to close. It was a cool joint to hang out and shoot pool in and listen to jazz and do some kissing. I am going to miss the kissing. I wish there would be one last kiss, but she turns and climbs the stairs ahead of me and says goodbye without turning around or waiting and I go out the door, into the Kateless world.

13

A Quiet Pond

That night on Weegee, Big Daddy was about to devour Cheeseburger No. 9 and he rang the Ding-a-Ling Bell and told all the duck butts and skinny minnies to listen up, here's the latest from the Doo Dads, and in came the bass bip-bip-bip-bumming and a falsetto *ooooooooweeeeeee-we-we-ooooo* and it was called "The Ballad of Ricky and Dede"—

> *He was the nicest kid*
> *That you ever saw.*
> *How did he become—a*
> *Fugitive from the law?*
>
> *He lost his cool and*
> *Slapped around his ma,*
> *Stole her car and drove west,*
> *A fugitive from the law.*

In the song, Ricky and Dede try to run a roadblock in Wichita and are gunned down by Sheriff Shaw *(He had a shotgun and was quick on the draw)* and are laid down on a bed of straw and covered with a mackinaw, and though he was shot in the jaw Ricky reached out a finger *(like a twisted claw)* and managed to draw in the dirt—

> *Forgive me, Mama,*
> *For my wicked past,*
> *And now your fugitive*
> *Is going home at last. Amen.*

It was not one of the Doo Dads' best efforts and seemed an odd song for a guy to write about his own brother.

So I tried a couple versions of my own.

The Fugitive

The Guppy family sat around the kitchen table eating fish sticks and hash browns, and their dog Rex walked in and said, "I wish you people knew what you smell like to me, I think you'd find it informative."

There they were, eating, talking about the upcoming Boy Scout Rope Climb in Littleville and their visit to Ray at the reformatory, and a still, small voice spoke and they looked down and Rex's little black lips were moving.

But it couldn't be true. Dogs can't talk.

But Rex just did.

"Why's everybody staring at me?" said Rex. "Did I say something wrong?"

Nobody let out a peep. To reply to Rex would mean that you believe he just spoke to you, and of course dogs can't talk.

"What's the matter?" says Rex. "Cat got your tongue?"

The mother looked at the father, Roger looked at Jim, who looked at Ricky, who said to Rex, "What do we smell like?"

Rex said, "Very pungent. A bad combination of smells. Like kerosene, hair oil, beer, cigars, and that blue slop you put in the toilet. I go to get a drink of water and it makes me gag."

The father opened the door and told Rex to go outside.

"Gladly," said Rex.

And the next day there was no more Rex. Ricky came home from rope-climbing practice and Rex was gone and his water dish too. The boy searched all over Littleville, from the schoolyard to the junkyard, but the old dog was gone. "Daddy took him to live on a farm. He'll be happier there," explained Mom.

A despicable lie and the boy knew it. And the next day Daddy didn't return home from work at the gas plant. Daddy, poor Daddy. People at the gas plant said he seemed normal and everything when he left. The police said maybe he stopped at a roadside tavern for a libation. But Daddy doesn't drink. "I guess he went to live on the farm with Rex," said Ricky. "Maybe what we do unto others eventually is done unto us. This happens sometimes."

But the next day Rex came back. Mom was cooking up a burger and was so shocked she almost dropped the skillet.

"Your hubby is lying in a ditch with stars in his eyes from getting clobbered by a two-by-four. Ricky did it. And then he stole your car and headed west with that sweet girl with the luscious orbs."

Mom was distraught but what could she do? The coppers fetched Daddy from the ditch but he was never the same after that pasting he got, and the FBI hightailed it after Ricky and Dede, but the West is a big place and the desert tells no tales. Nothing would ever be the same again. The Scouts climb the rope and the crowd waits and the Scouts don't come down. We are all fugitives but from what? We may never know.

To Hell With It

The big sister is washing dishes in the kitchen and the dog walks in and barks, "Glory be to God in the highest!" and suddenly a fat lady in a white satin robe appears, holding a flaming torch and singing, "Stand up, stand up for Jesus, ye soldiers of the cross," and suddenly the big sister is with Jesus and Grandpa in heaven. The streets are copper, not gold, and people don't play harps (thank goodness), but otherwise heaven looks much as you'd expect from the pictures you've seen, very peaceful and shiny.

"Good to see you, kiddo," says Grandpa. "Say hello to our Lord and Saviour."

"Pleased to make your acquaintance," says Jesus. "How was your trip up?"

"It was real quick."

They stand around chewing the fat and then she says, "Would you do me a big favor? I know you're very busy, but this'll only take a sec. Would you give somebody a painful

disease that would make him a helpless cripple in a wheel-
chair? I think it'd be good for him to learn a lesson."

"Who?" says Jesus.

"You know."

Jesus gives her his Good Shepherd look and tells her
that she can't stay in heaven if she is harboring anger in
her heart.

The big sister looks down at me on earth reading my
filthy books and getting away with murder and she feels a
big hot lump of lead in her left ventricle. Should she
love me or should she wait until Jesus is in a better
mood? She decides to wait.

"He's a friend of that kid who knocked his mother down
and stole the car and took his girlfriend to Montana. He
and that boy are peas in a pod. Practically brothers. Both
of them willful and rebellious and heedless of Your Holy
Word and—what's worse, Lord—*they're getting away with murder!*" There are no tears in heaven but the big sister's
eyes are full of them. *"Just look down there! Look at what
he's reading! And look at that kid in the motel in Montana! Take a gander! How can you let this go on?"* She
pulls a sheaf of papers from her radiant white robe.

"I've made a list of 493 different infractions of Your
Holy Word that Gary and Ricky have committed—*just in the
past four days that I've been in heavenly paradise and
have been able to conduct surveillance.* Here. If you
really are omnipotent, now is the time to show it."

It's the wrong thing to say, and even she knows it and
is about to say she's sorry, but heaven is no place for
apologies.

Suddenly she's smack-dab in the middle of a burning lake, flames licking her legs, her hair and eyebrows gone, clothes burned up, and Satan is sitting on a rock nearby and laughing his big hairy ass off.

"You're a dumb shit, you know that?" he yells. "You were in paradise and it wasn't good enough for you, bitch! Hope you enjoy suffering, 'cause you're in for a whole train-load of it! You are going to suffer your butt off!"

And she says, "Would you do me a favor and go and get my brother and his buddy Ricky Guppy and bring both of them down here?"

"He's not scheduled for here. Not yet."

The big sister brightens. "You mean he's coming eventually?"

"Wait and see. Maybe. Who knows?" Satan laughs again. "Meanwhile, here's some piss to drink and a big dogshit sandwich for lunch."

I didn't show that story to Miss Lewis or anyone else, I kept it in a shoebox in my closet, where later *High School Orgies* and other sensitive materials joined it, such as my story about Kate. I couldn't stop thinking about her blue angora sweater and that day in the boys' toilet when I said I could run away with her and she said *That'd be nice* and she put my hands on her breasts. I thought about it every day. I wanted to write letters to her saying how sweet it was, but they were too corny.

Dancing at the Del Ray

My favorite Doo Dad song is "My Girl" and Kate and I are dancing to it at the fashionable Del Ray Ballroom ("The

Dance Hall for Folks on the Ball") and she tells me what cool dance moves I have, as the Doo Dads sing,

> *Her eyes so blue and pale*
> *Could make a good man go to jail*
> *I once was lost and now I'm blind*
> *Because I got her on my mind*
> *My Girl*
>
> *What a success I could have been*
> *I'll never dream of it again*
> *I would murder, I would steal*
> *Because of all she makes me feel*
> *My Girl*

And after the dance, we step out on the long tiled veranda to cool off among the potted plants and she dabs at her temples with a hanky I have given her, not knowing it is soaked in secret cologne.

We stand at the railing and look at Lake Elmo bathed in moonlight and she whispers, "Wouldn't it be nice to have a cool swim right now?"

The Doo Dads are singing the next song,

> *Saturday night and time to be gone,*
> *Slipping and sliding with my new shoes on,*
> *Heading downtown to the old dance hall,*
> *Baby, we'll have a ball.*

But she leads me by the hand behind a potted palm and gives me a Herbert Tareyton and lights it and we share a smoke and she says, "I want to be naked with you."

I got my hepcat threads and a gold watch chain,
And with you in hand, I'm feeling no pain.
Hold me close, baby, don't let go,
And we'll dance all the way down to Mexico.

A few minutes later we stand in the shadows beside the bathhouse. Dim figures swing and sway in the lighted windows of the ballroom.

"Too bad we don't have swimsuits," I say.

"You don't need swimsuits to go in the water," she says. And she pulls her dress up over her head and walks toward the water in her bra and panties.

I strip to my shorts and follow her. We swim out to the diving dock and float there for a minute, her proud young breasts clearly outlined under the taut wet cloth.

"I admire your lack of inhibition," I say. She says, "I love being naked. I love it more than anything."

My heart pounds at the thought. I have long hoped for this. She slips off her bra and panties and flings them into deep water and motions to me to do likewise.

"God created our bodies, why shouldn't we enjoy them?" she says. I don't know what she means exactly but I can see her breasts underwater. Then, suddenly, she dives, her trim young buttocks rise, and I feel her grab my shorts and pull, and they're off! She comes bubbling to the surface, grinning.

"What if someone sees us?" I say. I can feel my manhood thickening.

Her beautiful buttocks rise again and under she goes and gropes for me underwater and I dive and she holds my arms tight, pulls me close, and we kiss a bubbly kiss, eyes open, her breasts like two small friendly otters. I struggle to rise to the surface but she won't let me go. She holds my hardness in her hand until I can bear it no longer. With a powerful thrust, I propel us both to the surface and hoist her onto the dock and rise dripping from the water—

It was an unfinished story.

14

Sportswriter

An ordinary Wednesday in the middle of June and then a large rock fell in my pond, a phone call from Uncle Sugar: "Are you otherwise occupied today?" he said in his slow trombone voice. Rodney Starr at the *Lake Wobegon Herald Star* needed a sportswriter to fill in for Slim Swanson and cover Whippets games until Slim recovered from a broken hand suffered in a mishap involving a wall. Slim had gone to recuperate at his sister's in Bemidji and wasn't expected back for a month or so. I would take his seat in the press box for the games and file my stories by noon the following day for $3.50 a week (expenses included), use of office, typewriter, telephone, etc., *not* included, but Rodney would provide ten (10) sheets of standard-quality white paper per week and two (2) No. 2 pencils. It would be a temporary position, termination at employer's absolute discretion. Not liable for injury from batted balls, thrown bats, irate readers, acts of God, or any other cause. Uncle Sugar was pleased as punch to have arranged this. "I know Rodney from Kiwanis. He's a great fellow. I told him you have a real flair with words," he said.

I said, "What happened with Mr. Swanson and that wall?" I'd been reading "Slim's Slants on Sports" since I was a little bitty guy. The thumbnail picture at the top of the column was of a youngish man in a porkpie hat, but actually Slim was a liverish old guy with a ropy neck, and the hat was to hide his bald spot.

Sugar said, "Between you and me, he was drunk as a boiled owl and got ornery and started yelling at Rodney, who wasn't even there at the time, and he took out his frustrations on Rodney's office wall. It was a misunderstanding about money. Can you come over for practice after supper and I'll introduce you to Ding Schoenecker."

Mother didn't like the idea of me sportswriting and being around all the swearing and tobacco-chewing and beer-drinking that go on at a ballpark, but she could see it was my big chance to gain journalistic experience, and of course I'd be up in the press box, observing the game from a safe distance. And Uncle Sugar would be around.

So, at 6 P.M. sharp, I reported to Wally ("Old Hard Hands") Bunsen Memorial Ballpark, down the street from the creamery and the county gravel pile, wearing Grandpa's old tweed snap-brim hat and carrying his battered brown briefcase with a Webster's dictionary inside, as befitted a serious journalist.

It was a sweet old ballpark on a summer evening, a cool breeze fluttering the flag in center field. The old green wooden grandstand was freshly painted, the chicken-wire backstop in good repair, the pigeon dung scrubbed from the façade with the gold lettering, W. (O.H.H.) B., under the pennant poles where no pennants flew. Sugar had told me about the golden era back in the Thirties, the era of the Schmidts, the Schrupps, the Battling Bauer Boys, when the team was a powerhouse feared in every town across central Minnesota, the ballpark packed with diehard fans, cheerleaders (the Whippettes) dancing on the dugout roof, chanting:

> WOBEGON
> We said it once, we'll say it again.
> WHIPPET
> Just as proud as proud can be.
> Woof woof woof woof woof woof woof woof
> Whippets!

Uncle Sugar knew the cheer, complete with arm movements spelling out the letters and a low crouch for the woofing. He remembered those championship days fondly and now those days were gone and the team was a perennial cellar-dweller in the New Soo League, a bunch of stumblers famous for choking in clutch situations. The called third strike with the bases loaded, the wild pitch, the muffed throw, the missed sign. The easy pop fly to short left and our shortstop pedaling back, glove in the air, waving, calling for the ball, our third-baseman lumbering back, back, back, our left-fielder galloping in, everyone shouting, "I got it! I got it!" and then, at the last moment, all three Whippets pull up short and duck their heads and the ball drops in for a double as the home fans writhe in shame and the visiting team whoops and guffaws and the shortstop snatches up the ball in cold fury and whips it to second, though the runner is already there, safe, standing up, and the ball skips under the second-baseman's glove and rolls all the way to the fence beyond first and the runner trots to third as the first-baseman retrieves the ball and (why does he do this? why?) heaves it home, ten feet over the catcher's head, and the runner trots in with an unearned run as easy as a walk around the block for an ice-cream cone. And Ding hauls his big belly out to the mound to settle down the pitcher, who is kicking big holes in the turf, and the teenagers in the stands yell, "Hey, when's the baby due?" And he marches back to the dugout and they chant, "Left, right, left, right, left, right." Our Whippets.

The players were on the field in gray sweatpants and T-shirts doing calisthenics in front of the blue concrete-block dugout with the red *L.W. Whippets* across the back and the letters *T P P T T P*. Thorough Preparation Produces Tip-Top Performance. Ding Schoenecker loved mottoes: "Winners never quit and quitters never win." "It's not the size of the dog in the fight, it's the size of the fight in the dog." (Not necessarily true for older dogs, however.) Four players were taking a break from calisthenics, resting in the dugout shade, enjoying a smoke. Two of them seemed to be nursing hangovers and were avoiding any sort of sudden movement. The rest of the team was attempting push-ups on the infield grass: some players looked as if more than fifteen would be a death sentence. I recognized Milkman Boreen in his catcher pads and Ronnie Piggott and Boots Merkel, and Leonard (The Perfesser) Hoerschgen, the old second-sacker, and Mr. Schoenecker, all well-known figures in town, regulars at the Sidetrack Tap. And when I scanned the outfield, where several Whippets were warming up, arcing long lazy throws back and forth, I spotted Kate perched on the scoreboard bridge, under the VISITORS and WHIPPETS, where the scoreboard boy hangs the zeros (us) and the 2 or 3 or 4 (them). She wore short green shorts and a black cowboy hat and dark glasses and was smoking in public. An outfielder leaned against the fence, talking to her. From his gestures, it looked like he was describing how he shot a couple of guys in a fracas over a kite and it was no big deal. If Uncle Sugar noticed her, he showed no sign, he was parked in the first row of bleachers behind home plate, gassing with Mr. Schoenecker, his ample gut with a WHIP PETS jersey stretched tight over it. It appeared to have grown some since the summer before. Not the biggest in town, by any means, but it did make you think: twins.

He bowed his head and squirted brown juice on the grass and stuck out his hairy paw and said, "Hey, sportswriter, the hell you doing here?"

My uncle winced at the profanity. "This is my nephew Gary, who's taking Slim's place while his hand heals up."

Ding Schoenecker looked me up and down and saw that I never had been and never would be a ballplayer. "Hope we can give you something to write about, Gary." He smiled a yellowish tobacco-stained smile. His nose was crimson and his face was the color of dry crusted mud under the gray heinie, his rheumy blue eyes squinched by the bags underneath. I knew him a little, everybody did. He liked to show kids a trick with a cigarette: light it, take it in his mouth, pinch his nose, grimace, and make smoke come out his ears. He could also, if you pulled his pinkie, let out a small but stately fart, which was pretty hilarious if you appreciate that sort of thing.

Uncle Sugar said, "We gotta have a writer who can make this team look like the champions we all know they can be, isn't that right, Gary?"

"A bunch of drunks with sawdust for brains. That's what we got here, frankly. Not to gild a silk purse or anything," said Ding.

"I hear you got a rookie pitcher with great stuff."

"Green as grass," said Ding, and spat again. "You never can tell about pitchers. They impress you for three or four games and then suddenly they get the yips and lose their touch."

"I hear he's got a good breaking pitch to go with his fastball."

Ding considered this for a moment and grimaced. "Meanness is what you need in a pitcher, more than anything. Never was a great pitcher or a great anybody who didn't have a lot of pure meanness in him. You have to want to humiliate that batter. Throw the ball right at his head and scare the piss out of him and then a fastball at the knees and then throw him the change-up and he takes a big cut and rips his pants and hits one back to the mound, one bounce, and you hold on to the ball and make him run with his hinder hanging out before you toss the ball to first. *Meanness*." Ding chuckled at the thought. "I'd trade the family jewels for a mean *hombre* like that, but I don't believe we grow them around here."

"It sure would do a lot for this town to have a championship ballclub," said Sugar.

"It would do a lot for this town if a spaceship landed and little green men got out. Maybe we should clear a landing area and paint a big white X so they can see it from outer space."

He took a few steps onto the field, clapping his big hands, and hollered, "Gentlemen! Take your batting practice!" and hobbled back to us and leaned against the fence, as a shambling galoot with a hound-dog face and slope shoulders took the mound and started grooming it with the toe of his shoe, smoothing out little imperfections, kicking bits of stone into the grass, where they wouldn't throw off his rhythm. "Ernie's gonna be 47 years old in September," he said. "Why a man that age would want to keep pitching, I couldn't honestly tell you. Some people crave punishment, I guess."

He lit a cigarette. Uncle Sugar leaned back to avoid a cloud of smoke drifting by. "Guess he must love the pastime," said Sugar.

"Has nothing to do with baseball," muttered Ding. "Has to do with the pastime of meeting young women under favorable circumstances. Ernie'd like to get himself a girlfriend. Don't ask me why. He's had two wives, one Polish, one German, you'd think that'd satisfy anybody's curiosity. But hope dies hard. So he wants to get out on the mound, show how limber and hardy he is, and hope to get lucky. There used to be such a thing as team loyalty, but these fellows got no more loyalty to Lake Wobegon than they do to the tree in my front yard. It's all about women. Baseball is just biology with a bat and ball."

Ernie kept grooming the mound, raking it with his foot, filling in hollows, as if the slightest irregularity would undermine him, then dug fresh grooves in the dirt to assist the delicate calculations by which he navigated. Meanwhile, the batter, Boots Merkel, did similar preparation of the dirt around home plate.

"Boots is Fred Merkel's brother. I went to school with Fred," said Sugar.

"He got the nickname 'Boots' from a little idiosyncrasy of his. He'd sometimes field a ground ball using his foot."

I could see the saliva turning in Ernie's mouth as he got set to throw. He bent to tie a shoelace, he juggled the resin bag, then turned his back to the plate and parked a large gob of spit on the ball. It was a mouthful. It glittered like the Hope diamond. "Don't bean him with it, he might drown!" yelled somebody. Ernie turned and threw the pitch with hardly a windup, and the spray flew up as the ball came fluttering in letter-high and Boots swung and missed by a mile and the ball slapped in Milkman's mitt like a wet towel on a bathroom floor. There was great merriment in the on-deck circle. "By God, the old man's still got the touch!" "Lucky for us he doesn't have a cold—that phlegm ball of his can turn you inside out."

Ernie threw ten pitches to Boots and ten to Orville Tollefson and ten to a fattycakes who Ding said was a friend of somebody's and was trying out for the team. Ernie was feeling his oats. He fished in his back pocket and got a white thumbtack and stuck it in the stitching and threw a big looby-loo curve, and the fat man waved the bat at it and laughed.

A tall man with a ducktail cupped his hands and yelled, "Hey, Milkman, yer crack is showin!" Milkman reached back to check, and the guy yelled, "Hey, lookit that! Milkman knows where his butt is!" It was Ronnie the center-fielder. He strode to the plate and stood twitching the bat like a cat's tail. Ernie threw and Ronnie drove the pitches into deep left and center, and two over the fence. The players whooped it up. "Take her downtown! Send that dog home! Lookin good, Mr. P.! Hooo-eeee! Give her a ride!" An amiable bunch. You'd never know they'd been dead last in the standings all these years.

Ding pointed to a lanky youth in the dugout, lacing up his spikes. "That's the pitcher you were asking about. Roger Guppy. Had a footrace with Ronnie and got himself a little knee-strain, so he sat out most of last week and the week before, and I believe I'll start him on Sunday." He shifted his wad to the other cheek. "Not what you call a snake stomper, but he's got a decent fastball and a nice curve and a pretty sneaky change-up. Nineteen years old. Hope he can do something for us. Other than him, there ain't much to choose from."

Uncle Sugar's gaze was locked on to Roger as if he were some specimen of animal never seen before in these parts, a one-horned gazelle or three-legged wombat.

"What sort of person is Roger?" said Sugar. "I've been reading some about his family in the papers. The Guppy family. I take it he's one of those Guppys—" Ding nodded. Yep. Roger was one of those Guppys. There might be Guppys somewhere who were climbing the upper slopes of Goodness, Truth, and Beauty, bound for the summit, but Roger wasn't one of them, he was one of the Millet Guppys.

"You know if he drinks?" asked Sugar.

"No more than necessary, I'm sure." Ding winked at me with his big gray bags, but Sugar was on the case.

"He's living with his folks, then?"

"I believe so. They're over in Millet. His dad is Alvin Guppy. Quite a fellow. Played ball in the Forties."

"But this is the family with the kid who sings rock and roll and the other stole the car and lit out for Montana."

Ding said, "I don't see to their personal lives. I just hope they make it to the ballpark by game time and remember to bring a glove." He winked at me again and yelled over to the dugout, "Hey, kid! Get up and throw! Let's see what you got."

Roger Guppy unwound himself from the bench and loped out to the mound and Ernie slapped the ball into Roger's mitt. His long dirty-blond hair poked out from under his cap. His shoes looked to be about size fifteens. He turned his back to home plate and blew his nose, one nostril at a time, onto the grass, two toots of snot, and wiped his hand on the ball. It was not the sort of thing a man should do in front of his girlfriend's father who is studying him as closely as Sugar was. "Oh, for pity sake," murmured Sugar, and he clucked and shook his head. I felt sorry for Roger. There he was with a noseful and he cleared his nostrils the best way he knew how and how could he know he was being judged for it? At the same time, I couldn't imagine Kate being in love with someone who did that. It was almost as bad as seeing an old drunk piss in the alley behind the Sidetrack. On the other hand, it interested me. I thought maybe it was something I should try when I got home.

"The kid has got a notion he's going to the big leagues in a couple years," said Ding. "I got my doubts but then I always did."

Out on the scoreboard, Kate leaned forward with her arms crossed, watching Roger on the mound. The Perfesser came up to take his cuts, a runty, dog-faced man who stood at the plate with his wrists up above his head and the bat cocked way back, like a man waiting to pound a rat. Roger gripped the ball, lifted his right knee almost up to his chin, kicked, and fell to his left as his arm snaked around, and the ball hummed into the glove hard. "Hey!" said the Perfesser. "It's only batting practice, rook!"

Roger laughed. The next pitch came in low and slow and Milkman stuck his glove down and the ball hit him in the chest. "That's his breaking pitch," said Ding. "It's got a nice hop to it." The Perfesser stepped out of the box and looked over Ding's way. "What am I supposed to do?" he said. "I thought this was practice."

"Try to hit the damn thing," said Ding. "With the bat."

Roger threw a slow change-up. The Perfesser swung and missed. Topped the next pitch and sent a slow roller to the mound. He called time and asked someone nearby if he was dropping his back shoulder or not. The Perfesser was a great student of the science of hitting, Ding said. "The guy's got a whole system of planes and angles of force figured out. It's too bad he's such a lousy hitter and doesn't get to use most of what he knows." The Perfesser swung at the ball like he was waving a wet towel and lofted a fly ball that almost made it out of the infield. He stepped out of the box and adjusted his crotch as if the problem might be down there and did six practice swings to realign himself and stepped back and Roger grooved a fat one down the middle and the Perfesser slapped a little grandma grounder back to the mound. Roger picked it up with his bare hand and flipped the ball over his shoulder and caught it behind his back. In disgust the Perfesser tossed his bat aside and hoisted up his belly and trotted out to second base, scowling at Roger on the way. "Showboat," he said.

Milkman Boreen was next up and Roger served him up five strikes in a row and the Milkman hit five high flies, dead center, Ronnie picking them off—one, two, three, four, five—almost without moving his feet. And then Roger threw his fastball and Milkman swung a full second late and the ball whacked into the catcher's mitt like a black-snake whip.

"Nice," said Ding. "Gimme nine innings of that and we almost got us a ballclub."

I heard a faint fluttering sound and looked out to center and Kate was applauding. Uncle Sugar sat back in the seat beside me.

He said, "What's she doing here? I thought she was with her friends swimming."

I said that it was too hot to sit on the beach, you'd get all sunburned.

"I read about the Guppy boy in the paper, too," said Ding, "and I felt bad for his daddy. He was a natural ballplayer, Alvin. Prettiest swing you ever saw. Quick wrists, everything in synch. Went to Iowa when he was seventeen, batted .450 for the Davenport Romeos and discovered girls and his batting average dropped to .185—he was holding his head wrong, thinking about who might be in the stands watching him—but he got himself a girlfriend and that helped settle him down. Had a respectable season and then lost his temper the last game and said something to the ump about his mother and the ump stomped on Alvin's instep and broke his big toe and he had to hitchhike home and it was a rainy fall and nobody cares to pick up a wet hitchhiker, so he had to walk two hundred miles and the broken toe swoll up like a balloon and Alvin stopped in St. Paul and somebody bet him he couldn't throw a baseball across the Mississippi and like a fool he tried to do it and he strained his arm. Got home, limping, with a crippled wing, and got in a bar fight over some dumb thing and twisted his back. That winter he found out he'd become a father without being aware of it at the time, so he married the girlfriend and settled down and she had that baby and then three more of them nine months and ten minutes apart, all boys. Alvin was farming, which he hated, and when Pearl Harbor came along and we got in the war, it was like a dream come true. He joined the Navy, thinking he could play ball on a Navy team, and they assigned him to the USS *Lexington* as a gunnery mate and he was in the Battle of Midway with Jap Zeros coming out of the clouds like cars out of a parking lot and machine guns rattling and he managed to get a shell in his gun and was about to fire when a kamikaze hit the *Lexington* amidships and the next thing he knows he's in the drink and trying to teach himself to swim. Came home a hero in August 1945 and celebrated for three months, thought about becoming the town drunk, but there already was one and he didn't want to go into partnership, and one night he threw a gin bottle at Alvin, hit him in the back of the head, the part of the brain where your hand-eye coordination is, and the next summer Alvin hit .400 for us. This is a true story. There is such a thing as a *good concussion*. Bob Bauer was on that team, and Fred and Frank Schrupp, and Alvin was the star. Last championship we had in this town—1946. Whatever good that gin bottle did was temporary, though. The next year he dropped to .200 and he never got above .200 the next four years, and when he hit .150 he quit. I read about his boy Ricky and I thought, Yeah, that's Alvin's boy, headstrong, like the dad. Seems like each of his boys had some of their old man's qualities—he could sing, he liked to get in fights, he liked girls, and he could play baseball."

Ding motioned toward an old blue mud-spattered Buick parked by the right-field fence, a man inside, his chin on the door, watching the game. It was Alvin Guppy, war hero and the only Whippet ever to bat .400.

"If I'd had a life like his, I'd sure want a son like Roger," said Ding. "Someone who was trying to make me proud, by God." He blew his nose. He was close to tears. Uncle Sugar was unmoved. He sat up in his seat and crossed his legs and looked straight ahead. He sighed. Then he leaned over to me and said, "I'm trusting you to look after her, you know."

I mentioned that Kate was someone who does pretty much what she wants.

"Just while you're at the ballpark. You'll be sitting up there in the press box"—he gestured with his thumb back over his shoulder—"you can make sure there's no hanky-panky in the parking lot." He patted my knee. "You're my right-hand man, you know."

15

Ravine

From the ballpark I walked across the gravel parking lot and into the ravine where I spent so many afternoons back in 1950, when we first moved to town. A creek bed that wound along the south side of town, cornfields and pasture on one side, backyards on the other, and in the spring a creek ran through it for a couple weeks, and then it was dry all summer. We boys used the creek bed for a trail, and about a quarter-mile east of the ballpark, it went under the highway through a culvert you could crawl through, and into a narrower and rockier ravine that led to the lake. The ravine was not so deep, maybe fifteen feet, no more than twenty-five, but the moment you descended into it, you were safe from adult supervision and correction. Nobody went down there except boys. Grown-ups lived for years within a stone's throw of it who knew nothing about the gorgeous goings-on that boys were privy to. We conducted our wars here, Indian wars and World War II and skirmishes between crooks and G-men, and our favorite, the Civil War, the Confederate cavalry chasing after the boys in blue, the shouts of a lone sentry, figures darting behind trees and dashing from the brush, charging the artillery behind the breastworks, and rifle fire, and a brave boy writhing in the grass and lying crumpled and still, and the quiet on the battlefield, smoke drifting east, the valiant dead, the ground torn by hoof and shell. A short and glorious life. I hadn't gone in the ravine for two whole years. I set down the briefcase with the dictionary and took off the snap-brim hat and walked down the slope through the sumac to where the main camp was, at a bend, on a bed of rocks around a sycamore tree, and the camp wasn't there anymore, there was just the rocks and tree.

16

Human Events

That night, on the porch, Daddy is concerned about army caterpillars. He saw two of them on the sidewalk, and where there are two, there likely are ten thousand, he says. He wonders if we should spray. An infestation of army caterpillars and the yard will look like ground zero at Hiroshima. "Those guys'll eat your eyebrows if you let em get out of hand." He was lying on the daybed, relaxing, trying to forget about Hjalmar and some hullabaloo at the bank, but now the prospect of devastation by insects has aroused Daddy, and he pads over to the screen door in his stocking feet and peers out into the dark, as if he might sense caterpillar movements in the underbrush and could attack with a bug bomb.

Mother says, "I wish you'd take a summer vacation like everybody else in the world. You need the rest."

"When I lose my job at the bank, I'll have all the vacation I can handle. Years of it. We'll be vacationing at the county poor farm."

Hjalmar is hiring his nephew Lars, fresh out of St. Olaf College, as assistant cashier starting in September. The boy majored in English. His experience with banking is limited to having had his own savings account and having filled out the withdrawal slips— Daddy shudders to contemplate what lies ahead.

Mother says she has always wanted to see the Gunflint Trail and the North Woods and cross the Canadian border. The North Woods holds no allure for Daddy. It's nothing but miles and miles of trees. A lake, then more trees. "We can't go off willy-nilly and leave the house, the garden—" He is envisioning busted plumbing, the basement filling with water, the furnace exploding. He has always taken a dim view of traveling, period. Why not see it in the *National Geographic* and save the wear and tear? Mother showed him a brochure with color photos of log cabins nestled in the pines, each two-bedroom unit with fully equipped kitchen, but he isn't buying it. Something in him rebels against the very idea. He says he could never sleep in motel beds and would be a nervous wreck inside of three days. She points out that in Greenland he slept on bunks for three years. "That was an experience I don't care to repeat," he says. "I have yet to get over it."

But with the danger of army caterpillars looming over us, there is no point in discussing a vacation. "Put it out of your mind," he says. He lies listening to the night crickets, a car passing, the electric meter turning, turning, on the wall of the garage, money leaking away. The tide's running against us. Hope dwindling. The precariousness of the situation. Danger and decay, funds evaporating, prices rising, bankruptcy beckoning. The auction sign on a stake in the front yard, creditors coming to seize furniture and silverware, china, clothing, the sheriff ushering us to a squad car to be driven to the poor farm and given blue coveralls and put to work picking potatoes.

Mother is absorbed in the latest *Star* story about Ricky and Dede. They eluded a sheriff's posse that tracked them to the Overlook Tourist Cabins outside Butte, Montana, and banged on the door at 2 A.M. but it wasn't their cabin, it was the cabin of a minister and his wife from Des Moines, and by the time the posse established the fact that the man was a minister and married to the woman, the two fugitives had crawled out the bathroom window of the cabin next door and snuck away to the highway and thumbed a ride, leaving behind some socks and underwear. Meanwhile, the FBI has released Ricky's poem:

> To live in peace is our desire.
> We love each other. Hold your fire.
> Why is love believed so wrong
> That we are hunted all day long?
> You can chase us 'til we drop,
> But our love you cannot stop.
> Your machinations only show
> We have a love you'll never know.
> Because you live in emptiness,
> You seek to cause us great distress.
> But soon will come the tragic news:
> Your sons and daughters you will lose.
> Remember this, for it's a fact:
> The pain you cause always comes back.

Mother reads it out loud from the paper and Daddy groans: "I don't think Robert Frost needs to worry much." Mother thinks it's sweet. So do I.

"Did you know he wrote poetry?" she asks.

"I think I saw some of it. I can't remember." But I do remember. It was one morning before first hour, beside Leonard's locker, and Ricky Guppy was there with Leonard and another boy, looking at a poem of Ricky's that Miss Lewis had written *Rather sophomoric!!* at the top of. Which we, being in the eighth grade, at first thought was high praise indeed until Leonard set us straight. Ricky was embarrassed to have us see his poem, entitled "Her Eyes of Brown," a sonnet, I could see, in which *Dede* was rhymed with *sweetie,* and he took it away from Leonard before Leonard could give it his full attention. "Maybe you could rewrite it," said Leonard, but Ricky didn't seem interested in discussing the matter. He wanted to collect the 50 cents the other boy owed him and get the heck out of there. The other boy rooted around in his pockets as Ricky fidgeted. And then I noticed how he was facing us, head down, his back to the mob coursing down the hall, and it was obvious he was sheepish about being seen with us. With me and Leonard, the class intellect. The same boy who two months later swiped his folks' car and absconded to Montana with his girlfriend. The boy whose face is now (according to Leonard) on a Wanted poster in the Lake Wobegon post office. He was afraid of being publicly identified as a friend of the toad.

Mother reads the story again, soaking up the small details. The Overlook Tourist Cabins were owned by a Mormon family with eleven kids. The minister was Dutch Reformed and he and his wife were celebrating their silver wedding anniversary and he got his feathers ruffled plenty by that posse, which (according to him) treated him like a common criminal and threw him down on the bed and stripped him. The minister thought the police should be able to tell the difference between a 17-year-old kid and a 52-year-old man. "Maybe it was dark," says Mother. "Maybe he looks young." What offends her is the FBI agent saying that more manpower is being brought in for the dragnet, highway patrol, G-men, sheriff's deputies, town constables, and an Idaho man who trains bloodhounds.

"I say it's time to forgive and forget and bring those kids home," she says. "What is the point of a posse of grown men chasing around after a couple of teenagers? Let them go and they'll come home, wagging their tails behind them."

Daddy says that Ricky, like any other felon fleeing the arm of the law, must be brought to justice, otherwise it'd be every man for himself and the devil take the hindmost, which unfortunately we already have in this country, thanks to the Democrats, but there's no sense in letting it get even worse than it is.

"Bring them home, and when they finish high school, give them a nice wedding."

Daddy snorts. "I wouldn't have my daughter marry somebody who beats up his mother and steals her car."

Daddy is busy over there on the daybed. He turned off the Millers game long ago and got out a tablet and started writing, and now he is reading it to Mother, though she still has her head in the *Star*—it's a letter to the editor of the *Herald Star* complaining about the upcoming Fourth of July celebration. Daddy has gotten wind of an appearance by the Doo Dads at the celebration. I am thrilled to hear this. *The Doo Dads! I'll actually get to see them sing in person and finally figure out how they do all those great sound effects they do.*—Daddy is outraged. Someone at the American Legion Post must have a screw loose to even consider inviting this gang of delinquents to entertain us on the birthday of American independence.

"Delinquents?" says Mother.

"Loan delinquent. The guy can't pay his bills. What sort of example is this? To put them on a stage in front of families, small children, everybody, and the American flag, and there they are cavorting around and singing suggestive songs."

Mother suggests that he speak to someone in the Legion and hear their side of it.

"I've heard it! Heard them talking about it in the café yesterday over lunch! Couldn't believe my ears!"

Daddy says the Legion wants the Doo Dads because they're popular and draw a young crowd and the Fourth of July program hasn't been drawing well in recent years. The ballgame and the fireworks and the picnic and the Living Flag get a good crowd, but the *program*—the heart of the whole thing, where the Legion guys lead the Pledge of Allegiance and somebody reads the Declaration of Independence (not all of it, the highlights, the *When in the Course of human Events* and the self-evident Truths and unalienable rights of Life, Liberty and the Pursuit of Happiness and the actual declaration at the end and the pledging of *Our lives, our Fortunes, and our sacred Honor,* and skipping the long whiny part in the middle about what the King did)—the program is lagging, only about eighty people turned out for it last year, which is pitiful. And so some genius at the Legion, some guy who probably was in his cups at the time, thought, "Doo Dads," and mentioned it to the other geniuses, and everybody went along with it like a herd of sheep.

Daddy is good and steamed. He reads his letter:

I take up my pen reluctantly, believing as I do in the virtues of patience and forbearance and not wanting to stir up a "hornets' nest," but when it comes to the Fourth of July and what it means to us as Americans, I'm afraid I must take a firm stand, unpopular though it may be. Perhaps freedom is not of interest to everyone in this community. As it says in the old song, "You don't miss the water till the well runs dry." Nevertheless, someone must make sure that deadly poisons are not seeping into our drinking water. And that is what is happening with Lake Wobegon's upcoming observance of the "Glorious Fourth." I'm sure that the planners of our Independence Day festivities have worked hard, and I do not question their dedication or their loyalty to our nation and its principles. But they are making a tragic mistake when they sully the Fourth of July tradition by inviting a so-called "rock-and-roll" group to appear as featured performers. If the adherents of such music wish to enjoy its cacophony and wild gyrations in the confines of a nightclub, such is their privilege in the "Land of the Free," but when this Godless music is thrust upon an entire community, forcing us to choose between endorsing said music and its lascivious excesses or turning our back on the beloved Fourth, then you are abrogating the very freedom that the day is meant to celebrate. I beg the planners

GARRISON KEILLOR

to reconsider this decision in the light of principle. The Declaration of Independence, adopted in Philadelphia on that auspicious July 4 so many years ago, pays reverence to "Nature's God" and to the "Creator" and to "Divine Providence." Does anyone believe that "rock and roll" does likewise? Or does this decision mark the end of the Fourth as we know it and its descent into mere sensuality and drunkenness until it becomes the sort of heathen carnival that no God-fearing family could support? Are we nearing a time in this country when patriots must celebrate in secret? Does this augur the approach of some greater, all-encompassing darkness that will require the "Lovers of Liberty" to take the same determined steps and make the same terrible sacrifices that our Founding Fathers made one hundred and eighty years ago? I call on all citizens who love their country to ponder these questions.

"Oh dear," says Mother. "You're going to send it to the paper?"

Daddy is worn out from the effort of composition. "Is it too long?" he asks.

"It may be."

He hands her the pages, four of them, dense scribbling with a lot of cross-outs and insertions and squiggly arrows. She glances at it.

"Remember what Lincoln said about writing angry letters," she says. Daddy says he didn't know Lincoln had expressed himself on the subject.

"Lincoln said that you should write them and then put them away and not send them."

He lies back on the daybed. "Somebody has to take a stand," he says, forlornly.

"You can catch more flies with honey than you can with vinegar," she observes. He says that catching flies isn't the point, he wants to make people think.

"You'll make them think, all right, but they may not think what you think they should think. They may just think that you're grumpy and trying to cause a big ruckus."

Daddy lies in silence, eyes closed, his hands folded on his chest. He knows she's right. Mother knows the score. You have to toe the line and keep your mouth shut in this town. These are stubborn people and the rules are chiseled in stone and one of them is *Don't swim upstream. Don't piss into the wind. Get along by going along.* The commander of the Legion Post is Florian Krebsbach. He got the job as part of the deal when the Catholic War Veterans merged with the Legion. Probably the Doo Dads idea came from his son Carl. Florian doesn't care about rock and roll. Wouldn't know it if it came up and bit him. Makes no difference to him. But maybe Carl put the bug in his ear, and so they'll have the Doo Dads get up and sing something. No big deal to Florian. But you send this letter to the paper and they print it and Florian is going to feel this is an attack on the Roman Catholic Church, his family, and his own honor. He will never say one word to you about it, but he'll have plenty to say to a lot of others, and for the next twenty years you'll be walking around in a shadow with a stone in your shoe, all because of one letter.

Mother folds the letter and puts it under the cushion of her chair. It's gone. I don't think Daddy is going to see it again.

"We could go away for the Fourth," she says, hopefully.

"It's one of the worst times of the year to drive anywhere. You ever see the death toll in the paper? It's in the hundreds. That doesn't count the maimed and injured."

"How about Chicago? We could go stay at the Blackstone."

"The traffic jams are unbelievable. Unbelievable. Somebody told me it now takes you the better part of a day just to get into the Loop and find a place to park. It's ten times worse than it was when we were there two years ago and it was bad then!"

"Then you choose. Where would you like to go?"

"It doesn't matter to me."

Mother suggests the Black Hills. Mount Rushmore.

"Anywhere but out west. I read that the danger of forest fires is at a twenty-year high. Montana is like a powder keg waiting to explode. I was reading an article about forest fires that said they can travel at a hundred miles an hour—a wall of flame—a hundred miles an hour! You could be driving top speed and not be able to escape it!"

The truth is, Daddy hates to go anywhere and both of them know it. He is a nervous driver, one foot on the gas, one on the brake, speed up, slow down, speed up, slow down, it makes you green around the gills, but when Mother mentions it to him, he says, "I'm doing the best I can!" This is probably true.

—Well, I'm not going to drag you someplace if you don't want to go, says Mother.

—It's up to you. I can't sleep on mushy beds, that's all.

—We could go to a resort.

—To do what? Play golf?

—To do whatever we want.

—You can do that at home.

—You won't even think about going to a resort?

—Find one that doesn't cost an arm and a leg and I'll consider it.

The ebb and flow of my parents' conversation is so familiar to me, Mother's voice and Daddy's voice, it is like summer music, with the sprinkler whispering and the radio turned low and cars humming by on the soft asphalt and the chittering of birds and dog barks and distant thumping of boat motors and women laughing and someone playing piano scales, up and down, and the tinkling of the glass-bead contraption, Mother suggesting the North Shore of Lake Superior and Daddy saying it's too crowded there in the summer, Gooseberry Falls, Split Rock lighthouse, Grand Marais, it's like a madhouse, packed with people from Chicago.

"I got a letter from Doe today," Mother says. "She may visit in July. She's all over the trots." Daddy looks at the ceiling. This is the price of not taking a vacation: your relatives come and take a vacation with you.

17

Flo

A lovely summer night, almost ten o'clock, the Stenstroms' house dark, the Andersons growling around in
their smoky cave, and up the street comes a shadowy
woman clicking along in a pair of flats with cleats on the heels. She
sees us on the porch, Daddy inert, Mother paging through the paper, and a comely young man reclining on the porch swing and
reading a book. A fine family indeed. *And what a handsome lawn!*
The big sister has gone to bed, miffed about a boy she met at a
Youth for Christ party. It was a Shoe Mixer. All the girls took off
one shoe and put them in a pile, and each boy was brought in
blindfolded, and whoever's shoe he chose, she was the girl he sat
with for cocoa and cookies. The sister was picked last (because her
shoe was so big, presumably) and the poor boy plopped down next
to her and she tried to testify to him. She told him that, in Christ,
the last shall be first. And in contravention of the rules of Shoe
Mixing, he went off and sat in a corner by himself for the rest of

the evening. She was hurt. Hurt feelings run in the family. Daddy is hurt about the Doo Dads singing on the Fourth, and Mother is hoping that Aunt Doe doesn't think we don't *want* her to visit, and I am feeling guilty about *High School Orgies* even as I sit and pore over it.

One story left to go, that of Julie and her drama teacher, Mr. Peters, with a picture of a young girl spread-eagled on a desk with a gray-haired gent leering down at her. *Mr. Peters gazed at the front of her blouse and her pert young buds barely visible between the buttons. "Oh, Mr. Peters," she said. "Do you really think I could be Juliet in the class play?" He had taken the precaution of locking the classroom door. "You certainly have the talent for it, Julie," he whispered. "It's only a question of being able to lose your inhibitions onstage."*

I have a dirty mind and this is a fact. I know it, Grandpa knows it. Someday it will be general knowledge. *Be sure your sin will find you out.* That's Aunt Flo's motto. Never do in secret what you wouldn't want the world to see, because time brings all things to light. People steal and lie and scheme and do all manner of surreptitious deeds in the dark, but don't kid yourself, the lights will come on someday. It's only a matter of time before the ladies in the Bon Marché Beauty Salon find out about Kate and me drinking the wine and sitting in the stall in the boys' toilet, her on my lap, and my pants pulled down.

"Is that right?" says Myrtle Krebsbach under the hair dryer. "Somehow that doesn't surprise me. That family always acted like it was a cut above the rest of us. Now we know. Fair on the outside, false on the inside. In silk and scarlet walks many a harlot."

"And her without a brassiere on," says Luanne. "According to what I heard. No bra whatsoever. Pulled her sweater off in front of the whole school and she was naked as the day she was born."

"Doesn't that take the cake."

"Heard it from two different people."

"Those Brethren kids always were wild."

"They don't dance, they don't drink, they just go off and hump each other in the bushes."

The Lake Wobegon *Herald Star* prints official stories like "Road Repairs Under Way, Says County" and "Awards Banquet Termed Big Success by All," but the ladies of the Bon Marché have the inside dope on all the hanky-panky in town, they know who's been fighting like wild banshees and their voices were heard at two A.M. screeching something about wishing they had never met, and them with three little kids, poor lambs, and who fell off the wagon and wound up drunk in a cornfield last week and singing at the top of his lungs and his poor mother had to come get him, his wife wouldn't, she was ready to shoot him, and who is drinking heavily who you probably think never touched a drop but she's hitting the vodka and orange juice soon as the kids are out the door in the morning, and whose daughter got in a family way with a man in Duluth (married) and the family is trying to hush it up, as if everybody wasn't wise to her years ago, and whose husband turned out to be carrying on with the church secretary, whose son is suspected of stealing money at work, who is moving away, who is acting funny, who is on her high horse and needs to be taken down a notch, who is spending money hand over fist, who is skipping church . . . Aunt Flo brings us this news every Saturday after her hair appointment. We are Sanctified Brethren and we believe in forgiveness, but we do like to know exactly what it is we are forgiving people for. And are they going to stop doing it or are they going to make it a new way of life?

Julie offered no resistance as Mr. Peters unbuttoned her blouse. "You see, an actress has to learn how to free herself from self-consciousness and release her innate passions," he said. "That's what I look for in an audition. That sense of freedom." She unclasped her brassiere to afford him access to her delectable young breasts. "Every performance means making love to an audience," he whispered. His fingers slipped into her panties; she was hot as a furnace.

Mother is listening to Cedric Adams and the news, shushing Daddy when Ricky and Dede are mentioned, but there's no news, just that the manhunt continues and authorities are following up all leads. Daddy says he is heading for bed but he doesn't go. And on comes our old friend the Troubadour singing for Trojan Seed Corn:

> Put on your hat and put your pajamas on,
> And let's take a trip down the Amazon,
> Have tamales and corn tortillas
> Served by señoritas—Si!Si! Buenos dias!
> Fly away to Paraguay and Peru
> For a year and a day, me and you.

The Troubadour is a nice man and a friend of the family and all, but I wish we had a TV so we could watch Jack Paar and the *Tonight* show, which I saw at Leonard's the one time he invited me to sleep overnight. But if I told Daddy I wanted a television set, he'd say, "People in hell want ice water." His philosophy in a nutshell: *You want it, forget it.* Desire makes the object of desire recede in the distance—this is the curse of common life. Spring comes late because we want it too much.

If we had TV, I could watch *American Bandstand* and learn to dance and become popular. A delicious word: *pop-u-lar. He is extremely popular. He is such a good dancer. So smooth. No need to use X-ray binoculars ever again or employ secret colognes. Just be yourself!*

BEFORE: a tree toad, squinting, spasmo face, arms hanging like ropes, goofy clothes. *Ay caramba*, what a percy!

AFTER: neat clothes, nice smile, great hair, a real smooth article, and, Lordy, can he dance!

The Troubadour sends a howdy to Myrtle in Elbow Lake and wishes the Gustafsons of Onamia a happy fiftieth anniversary from their kids in Minneapolis and he sings a request for John, the best hubby a gal could hope for, with love from Marcy—*You're the peak of the Machu Picchu. You're unique and it's great to micchu.* And the new me is motivating around the dance floor with a little heartthrob who looks up with dreamboat eyes and says, "Spin me, Daddy-o," and we spin, we swing, I toss her up like a bag of potatoes and slide her between my legs—*You're a Broadway song played along the Great White Way. / You're a four-leaf clover, the cliffs of Dover, you're Doris Day.* "You are such a good dancer," she whispers, and we dance close, round and round, sparkling lights play over our bodies, magical moonbeams, fairy dust. *You're a goddess, you're an Aphrodite. / You're as hot as Mae West's nightie.*

Mother is tapping her toe to this. Daddy says, "Do you need to play it so loud? The neighbors'll think we're throwing a party and serving free champagne."

The neighbors would never imagine any such thing. They

know us too well. We are Sanctified Brethren. We can never have a good time if other people are watching. God only knows what we do behind closed doors, but in public we are pills. Walk around like birch trees, grimace, look down at your shoes, mumble hello. *Julie was an apt pupil indeed, responding to his every caress, kissing him with a depth of passion seldom found in one so young, and before he could remove his shoes and socks, she was clawing at his trousers, trying to get at his lovestick, and before he knew it, he was buck naked, flat on his back, and she was riding him for all she was worth and moaning like a truck on an uphill grade—*

And Mother turns up the radio—the Troubadour is dedicating a song to Ricky and Dede. "This goes out to a couple of confused kids in Montana who may be picking up our signal in their car on some lonely backroad—Ricky, Dede—two kids who've been on the run a bit and maybe are looking for a way to come back home. God bless both of you, and keep you safe and bring you back to us, and if you're listening and you want to talk to somebody, give the old Troubadour a call, okay?" And he sang to a throbbing accordion—

> *Come live with me and be my love*
> *Midst valleys, woods, and fields,*
> *And we will all the pleasures prove*
> *That this brief summer yields.*
> *And we will sit upon the rocks*
> *By shallow waterfalls,*
> *And listen to melodious flocks*
> *Of birds sing madrigals.*

"That's sweet," says Mother. "I hope they call." Daddy says he plans to write to the Trojan Seed Corn Company and ask whether the dedication of a song to an escaped felon would be a regular feature on the show or just an occasional treat. And while they're at it, perhaps they could play a few obscene songs by the felon's brother. After all, he will be performing for the Fourth of July, so what harm could it do? And finally Daddy is done with us and lumbers up to bed and it's Mother and me. The street is dark except for our porch, bathed in light, like the bridge of a great ship plying the dark ocean waters.

She's a nightowl, like me, she understands: we don't all have to sleep the same hours, we're not dairy cattle.

—Would you care for a glass of ginger ale? she says.

—That would be nice, thank you.

It's just like Tony Flambeau and his mom, Eileen, on *The Flambeaus* on the radio every Monday night: when the detective dad is off solving a case in Las Palmas or Guadalajara or Ushibuka, Eileen (the real-life star of *Lucky Lady* and *Whoopsido!* on Broadway) and Tony sit around in the family's penthouse suite with their pals Joan Bennett and Bennett Cerf and Jack Benny and have a few laughs and Tony serves drinks.

For one shining moment I can imagine myself an only child. The older sister is a foster child rescued from her natural parents, two convicted con artists serving time in Sing Sing, and the poor thing is no prize herself, having been shut up in a root cellar for the past two years, but we took her in as an act of Christian charity and are doing the best we can with her, given her limitations. The older brother, the genius, is actually an uncle, Grandpa's love child by the cleaning girl, and frankly we don't expect to see much of him anymore. Daddy is gone, in Minnesota, doing his business, whatever that may be. Mother and I are in New York City, our penthouse at the Chadwick Arms. The Lake Wobegon water tower is the Empire State Building. I'm a writer for *The New Yorker*. A close personal friend of A. J. Liebling. He and mother and I went to a Broadway play last night and it was very disappointing, not funny at all, though the rest of the audience hee-hawed throughout, and afterward the Rainbow Room was mobbed with tourists and we turned on our heels and went to a tiny restaurant, L'Etoile du Nord, that A.J. knew about and we stayed until 3 A.M., laughing, reminiscing about Paris, talking about our magazine pals, Audax Minor, Elwyn Brooks White, James Thurber, George Price, the long-winded lady, Genêt, the whole crowd. Wonderful. Glorious.

And then Mother breaks the mood.

—I don't understand why you and Kate always have to be so different.

—Everybody's different.

—She used to be so sweet. You all were. It's so sad when children grow up and have to rebel against everything and make their parents worry. I remember you kids tearing around the farm and playing in the haymow. You seemed so happy. And now—

Mother is lost in thought for a moment.

I ask her why Aunt Eva is so different.

—Who told you that?

—Nobody has to tell me. I can see it for myself. Our whole family is odd, but she takes the cake.

Mother looks into her glass of ginger ale and shakes it a little so the ice clinks.

—I don't know that we're all so odd. Are we?

—To ourselves we're not, but compared with other people we are.

One odd thing about us is how we are devoted to keeping secrets. Everything that doesn't belong in the picture, we shove behind the picture. Conversation at the dinner table can be like a walk in a minefield. "Some things are better not talked about" is our motto. Mother gets up, still clinking her drink, and stands at the screen door, listening.

—Eva is a little odd, but that's because she's not right in the head. I thought you knew that. Grandma was sick when she was carrying Eva, and she was just born that way, and that's all there is to it. It's just one of those things. She can't help it and neither can anybody else. We just have to make the best of it.

I wish I didn't know this about Eva. I wish it didn't make any difference to me, but it does.

—Is she crazy?

—She has spells when she needs to be left alone. You knew that, didn't you?

I can remember Eva going to her room. I didn't know it was because she was crazy.

—It's nothing terrible. It only lasts for a day or so. She has to be alone, without anybody looking at her or talking to her and especially nobody touching her. It's something she has to live with, there's nothing anybody can do. That's why she never married and had children.

—Does she hear voices?

—I don't know. I don't talk to her about it.

—Has she seen a doctor?

—She won't go and Grandma won't tell her to. They're afraid she might be put in an institution.

And then there are sharp clicks on the walk and in comes Aunt Flo in her yellow housedress and slippers, carrying a big black umbrella. "I saw your light was on," she says. It's late, eleven-thirty. "They say it may rain tonight," she says. She plops down on Daddy's daybed. She is his favorite sister, two years older, the one who mothered him. Mother goes to get her a glass of ginger ale. Aunt Flo asks what I'm up to this summer. She already knows but I tell her. Not much. Taking care of the yard. Writing for the paper.

"Well, the yard sure looks nice," she says. "A person has to keep up with a yard. You let it get away from you and it's gone for good. You'll never catch up."

Aunt Flo knows everything about Eva, I'm sure, and could tell me Eva's whole story, but she won't, so there's no point in bringing up the subject.

Mother brings the ginger ale. Aunt Flo says that the Andersons' youngest child, Willmar, had to be taken to the St. Cloud hospital because he swallowed paper clips. This morning. The boy puts everything into his mouth. Cigarette butts, clods of dirt. And he won't vomit. He'll gag until he turns inside out but he won't bring it up. All they can do is pour Listerine down him and hope for the best. And then, today, it was paper clips. They fed him a slice of bread and off to the hospital he went and the nurse did something and out it came from both ends. Mr. Anderson has been hitting the bottle more than usual, that's why he was home at the time: he quit work at the feed mill, he couldn't remember what day it was and they were afraid he'd fall into the machinery and wind up as flavoring in the cornmeal.

"Luckily they came into some money when her father died. He hung himself with an extension cord, you know." No, we didn't know, we had no idea. The Andersons live next door to us and we know nothing, because Mrs. A. and Mother are no longer on speaking terms on account of something Mother said to an Anderson child about torturing a cat. "Yes, he came up from the basement one night looking for an extension cord and of course his wife had no idea what he wanted it for. He was down in the dumps over something or other. She gave him the cord and she went off to bed and when she went down the next day to do laundry, there he was hanging from a water pipe. Anyway, the Andersons got fifteen thousand dollars from the will. No need for him to work for years! They're sitting pretty."

Aunt Flo knows everyone's story and she doesn't mince words. People try to cover up their sins, they lie like rugs, but Aunt Flo knows what time it is. *Poppycock*, she says. *Horsefeathers. Balloon juice.* What's His Face and Miss Coles, the two English teachers—those two are shacking up and anybody with eyes in his head can see it. Remember the Lutheran pastor who went guest-preaching to Granite Falls and came home with a love note *in his Bible?* Remember that? Aunt Flo had him figured out from the git-go. That man was a secret only to himself and an open book to anyone who looked him straight in the eye. You can tell by the eyes. Flo can.

I try not to look Aunt Flo in the eye as she sips her ginger ale. She might look me in the eye and see young Julie losing her inhibitions and moaning like a truck in low gear.

Aunt Flo is flying high tonight. She is going a mile a minute. She gets up from the daybed and walks the length of the porch, past me, past Mother, to the screens facing the Stenstroms, and then paces back to the Anderson side. She reminisces about that pastor and his nice manners and his three-piece suits and all those women who came to him for spiritual guidance. "Guidance!" she snorts. "The man only knew one direction and that was toward the bedroom!"

This is her great theme. All the Lake Wobegon men who got caught in adultery and never expected to. One after another, caught at the old game like a weasel in the moonlight, held up, dangling from the leg trap, and people cry *Shame! Shame!* and among the shamers is a man thinking, "Lucky for me that I covered my tracks. Nobody'll ever find out." And they sniff him out two weeks later, and tar and feather him and ride him around on a rail, and of the men carrying the rail, one thinks, "Good I burned those letters when I did." Two weeks later, they find two unburnt letters addressed to Angel Eyes, and put him in stocks, and people throw dead fish and used fruit at him and buckets of slime and entrails, and one of the main hurlers thinks, "If I'm ever caught, which I won't be, I'll deny everything," and two weeks later, he's caught. He denies it, but they have found the pink garter, the hotel-room key, and he is made to walk around with a deceased pelican hanging around his neck, and the man who ties the pelican to him thinks, "I'll call her and tell her I can't meet her again until after this all blows over." And two weeks later, he meets her, and when they are at a high pitch of excitement, suddenly red lights flash and two cops arrest him for gross indecency and drag him downtown, and one cop thinks, "I am the last person anyone would ever suspect of misdeeds." And two weeks later, he stands up in the HiDeHo, wearing his fake beard and glasses, and he inserts the $10 bill in the dancer's bodice, and feels the hand on his shoulder, and it's his wife's brother, who drags him home, where he sits in the dark basement and weeps for all the pain he has caused, and the wife's brother is thinking, "I'll meet Trixie tonight, as planned. Nothing to fear. We'll go to Sauk Centre, where nobody knows us."

And so it goes. One after another. Each one dumber than the one ahead of him in the parade. Ping-Pong balls for brains! Pudding heads! She sits on the daybed and snorts. Mr. Hansen, that gilded idiot, who fell for the size 38-DD waitress at the Chatterbox and bought her a dozen tubes of crimson lipstick and promised her the moon and stars and inveigled her to accompany him to a truckers' motel on Highway 10, and who should be parked in a booth at that very same motel coffeeshop but Hansen's brother-in-law, eating a hot pork sandwich! He rose and collared the old goat before he could get his paws on the room key, and oh how the pitiful miscreant begged the brother-in-law to please look the other way. Oh, he was ten yards short of glory—oh, please please please, but no, he was hauled home and there was hell to pay and women yelling at him, *How could you be so dirt stupid?* He was in the doghouse for *years!* And yet—did that keep Clint Bunsen from flirting with the very same waitress? Sitting there drinking coffee and suggesting he show her Chicago. *Show her Chicago! What is that supposed to mean?* And him a former mayor and deacon of the Lutheran church. Didn't stop him for one minute. And Mr. Hansen's brother-in-law? He of the hot pork sandwich? Six months later, he was pulled over by the Benton County sheriff for speeding; and sitting next to him was the reason for his haste, a married woman from Kimball in a pink negligee with little fur puffs on the sleeves. The man returned home with his tail between his legs and had to sleep on the couch for six months and was made to take his dinner and go sit in the garage. And for what? A roll in the hay. A ride on the Ferris wheel. Wham bam, thank you, ma'am. For this they're willing to give up everything? But that's men. Men believe in their hearts that God will make an exception in their case and look the other way.

I sit listening to Aunt Flo as she paces, like a captain walking the bridge of his ship, looking out ahead past the lawn and the street and the distant red light to some stormy seas ahead in the stilly night, and it slowly dawns on me that *I* am being preached to, not Mother, and that all of this is not about adultery, it's about *High School Orgies* and Kate and me in the boys' toilet and the Sunday-morning wine and everything else. Men prefer darkness to light because their hearts are evil, and in the dark the truth is less troublesome, you can invent beautiful illusions. Don't grow up to be like them, young man.

The county extension agent was a smart young man with a bright future. He'd gone to ag school and knew everything there was to know about soil conservation, and yet he could not keep himself from visiting the Weiss farm when the mister was off at the cattle auction in Melrose and the extension agent and Mrs. Weiss did some dancing between the sheets and made the bedsprings squeak and this went on for three months and did the smart young man ever stop to think that in open country on flat terrain a car can be seen for half a mile and it's no big mystery whose car it is? No, he just kept on taking his pants off. And finally the news reached Mr. Weiss, who didn't take it well and marched straight to the extension office, next to the post office, and spattered the young man's brains all over the soil-conservation map he had been studying that very morning. A St. Cloud jury found the husband not guilty by reason of temporary insanity and the young man was laid out in a box with his head half reconstructed of molded rubber so his grieving mother could view the remains. A gruesome tale—and yet did it make Jim the barber stop tomcatting around at night with Mrs. You Know Who of the lavender toreador pants? Did the mechanic at the Chevy garage stop tiptoeing through the tulips with his daughter's best friend's mom? Not on your Prince Albert, he didn't. Because men have no more self-control than a dog in a bratwurst factory, and so it is up to women to lay down the law.

She is so right. I have no self-control at all. If Julie said, "Come outside and let's neck in the backseat of my car," I'd be out the door in a minute.

18

In the Press Box

I got to the ballpark an hour early for the Sunday game so I'd have time to write some possible leads—*The resurgent Lake Wobegon Whippets, coming off a nifty win last week against Bowlus, nearly made it two in a row Sunday but alas fell short against the Bards of Avon*—and strolled up the battered wood stairs and into the grandstand and stopped, struck by the beauty of a diamond on a summer day. So green, and the infield dirt raked smooth and watered to a deeper shade of brown. And at the top of the stands, the seat of privilege and royalty, the press box, fifteen feet long, with four big windows behind the foul net that swooped up from the top of the backstop to the press-box roof.

"I don't have the key to that up there," said Mike the groundskeeper. He was rolling and raking the third-base line so that bunts would roll foul. "I wash my hands of it. That's Jim Dandy's bailiwick. He installed the locks on the door. Those aren't my locks."

"When does he arrive?"

"Who knows? They bring in this two-bit skirt-chaser in tight pants and a duck butt hairdo to handle the PA announcing, who by the way doesn't know a sacrifice bunt from his sacroiliac—he mispronounces names, gets the score wrong, you name it; meanwhile, he and his dipshit friends are having a party up there and getting high on snake smoke from their funny cigarettes—all I can say is, don't come to me about it, okay?"

"I have to get into the press box."

"Climb in the window."

So I stood on the seats below and raised the window and crawled inside.

Inside was a splintered plywood table with thousands of cigarette-butt burns and numerous dark rings from old beer bottles. An old silver microphone and amplifier and a child's phonograph sat on it with *Prop. of J. Dandy* written on them, on strips of masking tape. On the back wall were scrawled hundreds of insults and salacious messages and desperate dirty thoughts, phone numbers for Donna and Tina and LaVerne and Dolores, some with a word or two about each one's specialty. There were two chairs, an easy chair covered with an Army blanket and an old busted folding chair. I figured that one was for me.

As one-thirty approached, the fans filed in, like men taking their places at a urinal, nobody getting too close to his neighbors. The gloomy old diehards in the plaid shirts and feed caps camped behind the home dugout; the teenagers sat behind the visitors' dugout, where they could rag on them; the fathers and sons were directly back of home plate; and the gamblers sat at the very top of the stands along with the drunks. I busied myself making descriptive notes on the pre-game spectacle—*The crowd trickled in like rivulets of muddy water on a hillside of seats*—*The crowd fluttered in like birds of many feathers settling down on a bank of phone wires*—*The little white spheroids made expressive arcs in the air, higher or lower, as if the throwers were speaking a geometrical language.* I made a list of words to work into the story, to give it tone—*auspicious, harry, thwart, drowse, entreaty, pliant, incipient, plaintive, sortie*—and then I heard the key in the padlocks, and the bolt opened, and there stood Mr. Jim Dandy, in a seersucker suit and straw boater and white bucks, mirror shades, his curly black hair slicked back on the sides. He was carrying two brown paper sacks that clinked when he set them down.

Mr. Dandy took off the shades and gave me the hairy eyeball. "What in the hell are you doing in here?" he said. "There better not be anything missing."

"I'm writing up the game for the *Herald Star*." My voice came out a little squeakier than I was hoping for. What I wanted to say was, *I listen to the Doo Dads almost every night on Wonderful Weegee and you are my favorite group.*

"Next time ask permission before you go barging in."

It was already one-thirty when Mr. Dandy appeared. Game time. The ump behind home plate turned and looked up toward us and waved. Jim Dandy eased down in his easy chair and switched on the microphone and blew into it—people jumped as if a bomb had gone off—and he said in his six-foot-deep voice, "Ladies and gentlemen, welcome to Wally (Old Hard Hands) Bunsen Memorial Ballpark, home of your Lake Wobegon WHIPPETS! Let's honor America and rise and salute the Stars and Stripes and join together in our national anthem," and he held the mike up to the phonograph and put the needle down and a scratchy version of "The Star-Spangled Banner" blasted out. I wondered how many of the fans were aware of his eminence, a man whose records were heard in thousands of homes and cars across the Upper Midwest every night on the radio. Meanwhile, he fetched from his sack a bottle of vodka and a bottle of tomato juice and sploshed equal parts of each into a paper cup and tossed it down before *the home of the brave* and shouted into the mike, "Let's play ball!" and the crowd below let out a sickly cheer as the Whippets trotted onto the field and Roger Guppy strode to the mound and picked up the resin bag and threw his warm-ups.

"That's my brother pitching," said Jim Dandy. "You be sure to treat him right. I don't want to be reading snide comments just because he throws a gopher ball or two."

Jim Dandy had a little black mustache that suffered from a hair shortage. It was raggedy in a couple of places and he kept fussing with it. He had doused himself in a syrup-sweet cologne, but his breath smelled like he'd been eating dead raccoons. It was rank. He removed his jacket and hung it on a nail. "When my buddies come, we're going to have to ask you to make room," he said. He freshened up his drink with more vodka. He asked, "What's your name?" and I told him, hoping he wouldn't associate me with the man from the bank who repossessed his car.

"I gotta keep the place locked up because we store product up here." He nodded toward a stack of cardboard boxes in the corner, marked DANGEROUS/DO NOT OPEN/THIS MEANS YOU!

"You've heard of my singing group. right? The Doo Dads?" I nodded. "Yes, sir," I said. I was about to say more about this, but he wasn't looking at me, he was scanning the crowd for hot babes. And then he picked up a pair of binoculars for a closer look. "Nice set of maracas over behind first base," he said. "Boy, I wouldn't mind doing the cha-cha with those bazoongies! And look at that honey in the blue cap. Oh, baby. Mr. Jim Dandy would sure like to spend a few hours doing some bed dancing with you, darling."

Roger set the Bards down in order, and when the first Whippet came up to bat, Mr. Dandy cried out his name—"RIGHT FIELDER—WAYNE *TOMMERDAHL!*"—and let out a wolf howl as if to arouse fan fervor, but it was like trying to make whipped cream from skim milk. The fans made no more noise than if they were at a plowing contest.

"Norwegians," said Mr. Dandy. "I'll tell you, when God created Norwegians, he was still learning. He used what he knew about sheep and gave them hands to drive a tractor and jerk off, and there you have it. The dumbest of the dumb. Men who go fishing for fun. Imagine it! Sitting in boats and staring at the water! You want to know what's fun, kid? Walking across the parking lot with a 19-year-old babe to get in your car and take her to the beach. That is what makes for a happy man.

"Norwegians!

"Kid, if Elvis Presley had grown up among Norwegians, he'd still be driving a truck for a living. These people cannot be *entertained* in any way, shape, or form! I'd rather do a show for a herd of *Holsteins*! I'd rather sing for a bunch of brook trout!"

He got friendlier and more confidential as he got deeper into the vodka. He told me the story of his career. How the Doo Dads started out as the Coral Kings—him and Mitch and Donnie and

Dutch—the first rock 'n' roll group in the Midwest—1954! before Elvis!—and they got an offer to go to New York and work for Alan Freed—Moondog!—and Dutch wouldn't go on account of his dad needed him at the linoleum store. The Coral Kings stayed up all night pleading with Dutch and plying him with strong drink. It was their big chance, man. Give us two months! Give us two weeks! If we don't hit big in two weeks, we'll come home, no hard feelings. But Dutch wouldn't budge, so they gave him the ax and found Richie and taught him the ropes, and now they were called the Hot Rods, and they came out with "Mama Mama" on the Band Box label—he sang a little for me—

> Two and two is four,
> And two and three is five.
> My little mama mama gonna smile when I arrive.
> Three and two is five,
> And three and three is six.
> There ain't no kind of blues that a woman cannot fix.
> Three and four is seven,
> And four and five is nine.
> I'm ridin up to heaven on the Mama Mama Line.

The song shot to No. 6 in the Midwest with no publicity or anything, and they went on a six-week package tour headlined by Carl Perkins and Roy Orbison, both of whom said the Hot Rods were the real thing, but now it was Donnie's turn to chicken out—his girlfriend wanted him back home or else—so they came back home, Donnie being the high tenor, not easily replaced, and the Hot Rods pleaded with Bonnie to marry Donnie and move to Memphis and in two years' time we'll all have fourteen-room mansions with white pillars and fifty-foot swimming pools and be driving pink Cadillacs, and Bonnie said she could never leave her family and if Donnie wanted to go, fine, he could go by his own self and have his ring back too. There was no pleasing Bonnie. (Two years later, she broke up with him anyway.) So they wasted six months shopping around for a high tenor. Got Earl the Girl. Got him from the Cowlicks when that group broke up. He could go high and keep going higher. But he and Mitch didn't get along. Fought like dogs from day one. Mitch quit. He was the lead singer, not so hard to replace. They stole Stevie John from the Diddly-bops. Then he wanted to change the name from the Hot Rods to the Blue Jays. Jim Dandy begged and pleaded—man, they had *four hot records* as the Hot Rods, "Mama Mama" and "Please, Baby, Let It Be Tonight" and "Home Base Man" and "Out in the Corn-field," let's not give away the franchise—but the three new guys outvoted him, thinking that the Hot Rods' name was holding them back. So they did a record for Band Box, "It's Summer, It's Midnight, and It's You," but as the Blue Jays they were lost in the confusion of bird groups—the Robins, the Lovebirds, the Flamin-goes, the Flickers, the Swallows, the Thrashers, the Starlings, the Warblers, the Woodcocks—and "It's Summer" languished on the charts, so did "I Don't Need the World If I Have You" and "Zsa Zsa Zsa," so in April they became the Doo Dads, and now Band Box is talking about doing a long-play album of car songs with their "Hot Rod Alley" as side 1, band 1.

Meanwhile, it was the bottom of the second inning, the Whippets were down 1–0, and I couldn't remember exactly how or why. I tried not to listen to him, but he was hard to not listen to. When he wasn't yakking, he was singing to himself, going *bip-m-bip-m-bip-a-bomp-bomp, hmmm-ba-dee-ba-dee-mmm-ba-dee, mmm-ba-dee-mmm-bomp-bomp*. After the second inning, he dug into one of the cardboard boxes and got out a 45 and played it over the PA—

> *You got a Ford, you're on board.*
> *A Chevrolet, you're okay.*

I told him I heard that song on Weegee and he nodded. "It was Number One there for three weeks in a row."

Most of the crowd took the song as a minor annoyance, no cause for alarm, but a few heads turned to gaze our way, and one of them was Leonard Larsen, sitting next to his dad. Leonard peered up at me, trying to catch my eye, his hand raised, ready to wave, a tentative smile on his face. He was hoping I'd invite him up to sit in the press box with me and Jim Dandy. No way, José. He shielded his eyes with his hand and waved with the other and I ignored him. *Plead all you want, pal. I'm here, you're down there. That's just how things are. No hitchhikers. And if you think it's so great up here, guess again.*

Jim Dandy put the 45 back in the paper sleeve and scribbled on it and handed it to me. It said, "To Larry, All the best in life, Your friend Jim Dandy." *Jim Dandy* was an illegible squiggle with a fancy scrollwork tail under it. "Someday this'll be a keepsake. After you see us on *Ed Sullivan* you can tell your girlfriend, you knew that guy when he worked at the ballpark." He grinned and shook his head at the wonderful irony of it. Then he said, "What are those words, kid?" He was looking at my word list, *auspicious, entreaty, incipient,* and so forth. "You don't want to use words like that, kid. People're gonna think you went to college, they won't believe a thing you say."

There was a knock on the door. It was the bratwurst man. Mr. Dandy bought four with onions and mustard and ate them fast, a brat in two bites, and chewed with his mouth wide open and chased them with vodka and tomato juice, and then reached down for a coffee can and took out his whanger and peed into the can; meanwhile, he had the binoculars trained on the maracas below. "This is the life, isn't it, kid?"

It seemed to be the life for him all right. Up high in the press box, getting a royal perspective on things, the green field of manly combat and the motley crowd of peons below. He snorted at them. "Norwegians! They don't even *contemplate* sex unless they're too drunk to go fishing. Then they marry the ugliest woman in town so they won't have to think about it too often. Or marry a pregnant woman to save themselves the time and trouble. A Norskie spends his life looking at the rear ends of Holsteins, shoveling the feed in one end, shoveling the shit out the other, pumping the milk out the bottom, twice a day, 365 days a year, a prisoner of lactation. Couple times a year, he nails the old lady, and a couple times he slips off to the ballpark with a roll of cash in hand, looking to make a wager, and that's when I like to make the acquaintance of Mr. Dairy Farmer—yes, sir! When he's ready to roll—oh yes!—you let him win a few, and then you lift that roll of fifties from his pocket like you were taking sugar from a bowl." Then he spotted another woman in the crowd. "Oh boy, oh boy, oh boy, honey in the dish!" he cried. "Coupla mangoes on that babe! Oh, buttercups! Have mercy!" He had examined every female chest in the grandstand and had yet to see one he didn't like. They were all good, there were no bad ones in the bunch.

"You ever hear 'Gambling Man' on Weegee?"

I hadn't. So he played it after the second inning.

> I'm here to tell you people
> I'm doing all right.
> I am a rambler and gambler,
> I play cards every night.
> I have a porterhouse steak
> Every night for my board.
> That's more than any loafer
> In this town can afford.
> Got a beautiful mattress
> That's a couple feet deep.
> An electric blanket
> Keeps me warm when I sleep.
> And I earned it with poker
> And craps every night.
> I tell you folks,
> I'm doing all right.

He was halfway into the vodka now and getting more expansive by the minute and it wasn't even the fourth inning yet. He leaned back with his feet up on the table and the microphone on his chest and I told him who was next up to bat and he switched on the mike and announced it. A couple times I had to reach over and switch off the mike because he started commenting on the mangoes and maracas.

"Some people go into music for the money. Ha! In two years, kid, I'll have a million bucks, bet you anything, but it can't make you happy like a woman can. No, sir. Money is something to throw off the back of a train. Women are the reason to go into rock 'n' roll. All the babes flock to the band. Hit bands mean hot babes. You do your set and a coupla encores and you come off backstage and they're standing there by the back door, the babe auction, holding out the paper for the autograph, and their eyes are saying, *Take me, Jim Dandy.* Yes, sir. And they come back next day saying, 'Jim Dandy, do that thing again!' I got more young honeys than I personally know how to handle. A bass singer like myself has more capacity than the average man, but five women a day is physically taxing to me, and the backlog of womanhood seeking my attention—I have to tell them, 'Get in line. One man can only do so much!' "

He grabbed another 45 from the box and slapped it on the phonograph, but before he got the needle down, in came the other Doo Dads, Richie and Earl the Girl and Stevie John, all in white Bermudas and peppermint-striped shirts and sneakers and none of them happy to be here. I shoved over into the corner, squished between the boxes of product and the table, and tried to get my mind on the game, but it was hard to ignore the Doo Dads up close, they had large personalities, like Jim Dandy but not so well lubricated.

—What a bunch of pumpkin-rollers and nose-pickers we got before us today. Oh my. Rednecks as far as the eye can see.

—You on bush patrol, J.D.? Who's yer little pal?

—Shut yer yap.

—My, somebody's flying high.

—C'mon, you lovebirds, stop the goosing.

—Gimme some of that rope, my good man.

—You got hash?

One of them opened up a brown bag and pulled out a cigar, and when he lit it, it smelled like burning tires.

—He's got the real shishi, the black Russian.

—Hang it on me, scout.

—Oh, Nelly, let those temple bells ring.

Thick smoke rolled out the windows.

—Don't breathe, kid.

I was trying not to. Meanwhile, the Whippets had leaped into the lead on the strength of Roger shutting down Avon and also hitting himself a nice triple, scoring the Perfesser and Boots. Mr. Dandy shared the Doo Dads' cigar and announced the batters— "Leading off for Avon, second-baseman Fred Lederer!"—and down below Leonard kept glancing up, trying to catch my eye, and the bratwurst man returned with four more dogs, slathered with mustard, and the vodka dwindled, and finally came the seventh-inning stretch, and Jim Dandy announced, "Ladies and gentlemen, please welcome . . . the Doo Dads!" and they gathered in close to the microphone and sang—

> HOME BASE! (That's the place!)
> HOME BASE! (You win the race!)
> I got to first when she gave me a kiss,
> I got to second when I squeezed her like this!
> I rounded second, I was going hard,
> Slid into third and caught her off-guard,

> *I got a glimpse of nylon and lace*
> *And I headed for HOME BASE!*

And they started in growling and howling and squealing and
moaning in rhythm, and Jim Dandy grunting and grinding like a
slide trombone and Earl the Girl up high squeedling and whining and Stevie John singing, *Here it comes here it comes here it
comes closer closer*, and Richie panting and sighing and then they
stopped and sang two big chords with Earl going up through the
ceiling, *HOME . . . BASE!!!!*

There was not big applause at the end, but Jim Dandy hollered
into the microphone, "How about a big hand for the Doo Dads,
ladies and gentlemen? They came all the way over from Millet for
the game and to entertain you folks today, let's give them a big
hand!" And a few more hands clapped.

And then the Avon batter came to the plate and Roger looked in
for the sign.

Jim Dandy shoved the microphone down toward me. "Here,
kid, have yourself a ball," he said. And the Doo Dads piled out of
the press box and loped down the stairs, waving to the crowd that
sat ignoring them. There was so much I wanted to ask him—Did
he ever hear from Ricky? Has the FBI talked to him about Ricky?
What do FBI agents look like? Where do the Doo Dads record
their music? Is it heard all over America or only in Minnesota?
Has he ever met Elvis Presley?—but they were gone, disappeared
into a passageway and out to the parking lot, and I heard their cars
start up, one by one, four big mufflers snarling, and the rear tires
kicking up gravel, and out of the lot they roared, and four pairs of
rear tires caught the asphalt, one after another, four long screams

of rubber, as they raced out of Lake Wobegon, heading for the HiDeHo, where they would sing that night to a crowd that really truly loved them, and afterward there would be a line of brand-new girls backstage. Nobody announced the players over the PA and the crowd did not seem perturbed at the lack of this information. Leonard sidled into the press box after the eighth and tried to make chitchat. I told him I was busy. I said, "I'm on deadline."

19

The Freshman
Fireballer

The Whippets won the game, and I worked Sunday night and Monday morning polishing my story, and made Roger Guppy a hero of the first order, a *rookie hooker*, a *blazing young southpaw*, a *Whippet rifleman*, a *freshman fireballer*, and Ronnie Piggott was a *fleet-footed shagger* who *patrolled the garden* and *garnered flies*, and the Perfesser became *the veteran speedster* and he came up to the dish and *got a ticket to first*, whereupon he *purloined second* and was in position to *waltz home* when Roger Guppy *larruped a mighty sacrifice fly deep in the garden*. The next inning, Roger *snagged a scorcher at shoelace level* and *tossed the pill* to shortstop Rasmussen to set up a 1-6-3 DP, erasing an Avon rally. The old spitballer Ernie *(mound mainstay Ernie Sauer)* came in for Roger in the eighth and *toyed with the Avon stickman before giving him his walking papers*. Backstopper Milkman Boreen became a *slugger*, a *cloutsman*, a *lumberman*: he applied the lumber to the ball, powering a homer and sending the Avon twirler to the showers. Our boys drilled the ball, they hammered the ivory, kissed the apple, aired the orb, pummeled the pill, pasted the pellet, rammed the radish, tore into the tomato, slammed the spheroid, overpowered the oval, bounced a beaut into the bleachers, sent one by airmail. They donned their spikes and crossed bats with the foe and brought home the bacon. They rang the bell, stole the show, and took the verdict. They jolted the Bards, squelched their rally, settled their hash, and wowed the fans.

The big sister was steamed over me breaking into print in the *Herald Star* and complained bitterly to Daddy that she was pulling more than her fair share of the load, dishwashing-wise. She watched my yardwork like a hawk for any sign of slackery and was overjoyed to point out a few incipient dandelions by the birdbath. She told Mother that there definitely was smoke on my breath. And she snatched up the paper on Wednesday and opened it to the sports page ("Whippets Limn Avon, 5–4, As Guppy Pitches 9-hitter") and read it out loud, my first story, shrieking at every poetic turn of phrase. *Portside flinger Roger Guppy twirled a nifty nine-hitter—"Twirled!* Did he have a baton? Were there tassels on his hat? Why don't you just say pitched?" I liked *twirled* because it lent some artfulness to the pitching. But there was no explaining that to her. *Local baseballites were treated to a thrilling sixth-stanza swatfest by sticksmiths Piggott and Tommerdahl, who larruped the leather for back-to-back round-trippers, hoisting the home nine from the cellar to sixth rung in the New Soo circuit.*

It was a small story, six paragraphs and box score, sandwiched between a column of Cards of Thanks ("The Joseph Schrunk family wishes to thank everyone at Our Lady of Perpetual Responsibility Church for their kindness and prayers during our father's recent illness") and an article from the state home-extension service about how to liven up your summer dinner table with colorful centerpieces made from milk cartons, and it was a real bell-ringer, including the line *an auspicious sortie behooving incipient contenders as the Whippets thwarted the pliant Bards, to plaintive entreaties from the drowsy crowd.*

I dropped by the ballpark Wednesday evening for practice and there was Roger in the dugout, rubbing oil into his glove. He offered me a cold beer from under the bench. I declined. He said, "Nice story about the game. I like your style, man. You really know your onions." He finished with the glove and started oiling his shoes.

I would've gladly oiled them for him. My face burned from the compliment. I sat at the end of the bench. "Yeah," I said. "It was a good game."

He said, "Kate said you write other stuff."

"Yes," I said. "Poems. Stories. Different things. Whatever I think of."

"I really envy somebody who can do that. Just make things up."

"It's not that hard once you get going."

To the great surprise of all, the Whippets won their first three games, with Roger on the mound every time. He was a stomper. The opposition was accustomed to feasting on the big meatballs served up by the Whippets' knuckleballer, Ernie Sauer, and instead, here was a barn-burning aces-high pitcher who tossed his hair back and wound up, his right knee tucked under his chin, and kicked and threw a hard one under your chin and one across the plate, low and slow, and a third one breaking up and in, and the umpire pointed you to the dugout and off you went, carrying the bat like you had never seen one before.

I sat in the press box game after game and tried not to breathe too much of Jim Dandy's cigar smoke and gave Roger a nice write-up and also Ronnie and Milkman and Fred Schue and even the Perfesser if he didn't mess up too bad. The others, like Boots Merkel and Orville Tollefson, there wasn't much to say about. They were dead weight in the batting order, and in the field they were obstructions, like trees or boulders. Hit a ball at any of them, it bounced off.

Uncle Sugar waited for me after Roger won his third game *(Lakeside Nine Brands Bulls, 7–4; Ragin' Roger Fans 6)* and asked, "What do you think of him?" I said I thought Roger had a fast-ball, a curve, and a change-up and was the best ballplayer on the team. And he was a good guy, with an appreciation of the English language.

"I wish I knew he were a Christian," said Sugar.

20

Tomatoes

I t was a little envelope, the stamp slightly askew, the flap taped shut, and inside was half an index card, and on the back, in her small precise hand:

Gary,

The tomatoes are ripe and awaiting harvest. Where have you been keeping yourself? Are you anticipating a visit to your old aunt and grandmother in the near future or must we be patient and wait until the snow flies and your social obligations lighten?

Aunt Eva

The next Sunday morning, at the Breaking of Bread, sitting in the circle in Aunt Flo's living room, I try not to look at Aunt Eva in her Sunday outfit for fear she is looking at me. I look at Kate instead, then Sugar, then Flo. If Mother is willing to tell me Eva is "not right in the head," I wonder how much she isn't willing to say. Last Sunday, Eva brought a rhubarb pie for Mother, and when Mother served it after dinner I declined a slice. The thought of poison entered my head. A crazy idea, yes, but maybe that's how a crazy person thinks. Uncle Al stands, hands clasped behind his back, head bowed, raising up and down on his toes, and prays, thanking the Lord for His Precious Word that sufficeth for all our needs, surely. Maybe it sufficeth for them. But it doth not suffice for me. I want more. I want to kiss girls, just to name one.

Sit in a car with a girl, my arm across the back of the seat, my right hand stroking her hair, and kiss her on the lips, our lips parted, my tongue in her mouth.

Go to the University of Minnesota and study writing and meet girls who are also interested in writing and kiss them.

Have my own ideas about things, especially about girls.

But the Sanctified are hard on independent thinkers. Thinking is something that is simply not supposed to happen. You're supposed to read Paul's epistles and conform your life to them, like you'd read a book about how to play the violin and then, by George, sit down and play the thing. Just do it. A writer in the Brethren is like a fish wanting to sing, you have to leave the lake and be eaten by a singer.

Eva corners me afterward, when Grandma is talking to Mother. She leans close and I smell that smell so beloved to me when I was little.

—You seem to be avoiding us.

I pretend not to know what she means.

—I brought you up from a pup. I know when you're being sneaky. You can't fool me.

I say that I have been extremely busy with my yardwork and writing for the newspaper.

—We don't get the newspaper. I never found anything in it that was worth my time. Maybe you should send me a copy.

Eva and I stand in the doorway to Aunt Flo's kitchen and the others drift away from us. Uncle Al leads some of them to the backyard to look at his roses and Aunt Flo pours the wine back in the jug and puts it on the shelf. The remains of the bread she drops into the wastebasket! A revelation. The Body of Christ, thrown out with the garbage—I can't wait to bring this to the attention of the big sister.

—Well, I suppose Mother is anxious to get going, says Eva. She tells me to come and collect some tomatoes before they get mealy.

—I'll see you soon.

—I'll believe that when I see it, she says.

I feel bad about her, thinking how lonely it must be on the farm with only Grandma to talk to and how good to me Eva always was and how close we were in that bed with Mother gone to New York to ride the roller coaster and walk around Brooklyn at midnight. The people slept on blankets in the park and I lay curled up against my Aunt Eva.

I get out clean paper after dinner and write a poem to her, which I type up cleanly on the Underwood, double-spaced, on my best white vellum.

On August days when I was young
My aunt and I in bright sunshine

Took the pail from where it hung
And walked among the leafy vines.
And reaching down, she quickly drew
One red tomato from its nest,
The finest one that ever grew,
And wiping it across her breast
She gave it to me to enjoy—
And O the juices hot and sweet—
And on that day the happy boy
Tastes where earth and heaven meet.
    Of food or love, if ever I should be in want—
    I'll think of that bright day and you, dear aunt.

I sent it to her on Rural Route 1, Lake Wobegon, and a few days later received a note saying, "Thank you very much and I hope we get to see you in person before the summer is too far gone."

21

The Glorious Fourth

On the Fourth of July, Roger drove Kate and me in his pink Pontiac in the parade, pulling a haywagon with other Whippets riding on it, and throwing taffy to kids in the crowd. The parade started at the grain elevator and went down Main Street all the way to the end of the bathing beach and turned around and came back, three marching bands and six floats and contingents of Scouts and a Scout fife-and-drum corps that didn't play their fifes at all and a haywagon full of 4-Hers with their dogs on leashes and the American Legion honor guard, a bunch of old barflies in campaign hats slumping along shouldering white ornamental rifles and Florian Krebsbach slumped in the back seat of a brand-new Chevy convertible with *Grand Marshal* on the side and little flags flying from the fenders. The Knights of the Holy Nimbus came behind him, the Catholic fraternal lodge, men so decrepit and footsore it was painful to look at them. They wore admiral hats with floofy white plumes and crimson tailcoats and knee breeches and pink sashes with swords hanging down. You would think it was Halloween.

The Sons of Knute rode on a hayrack, drawn by four white horses. There were thirty or so, waving little Norwegian flags and wearing all their medals and ribbons and odds and ends of uniforms, and marching alongside, holding bright-blue ribbons tied to the hayrack, members of Luther League, classmates of mine, trying to be as inconspicuous as possible.

They were followed by the Doo Dads.

The Doo Dads were late arriving and the parade was held up for their benefit. They were six or seven units behind our car and we didn't see them until we'd made the turn at the end of Main Street and were headed back. The four Doo Dads wore dazzling white jackets and white Bermuda shorts and pink shirts and socks and white shoes, and of course dark glasses. They stood arm in arm in the back seat of a white Ford convertible with two loudspeakers on the hood playing "My Girl" at very high volume and they waved and waved, even to upper-story windows where nobody was. Their hair was slicked back and they were grinning like this was all in their honor, Doo Dad Day.

"My brother," said Roger. "What a character." He pulled the wire under the dashboard that honked the horn, a special horn that made a low mooing sound. And Jim Dandy grinned at us and did a little dance, making milking motions with his hands. I was in the front seat, by the window, Kate between me and Roger. She wore a tiara, pink, the color of cotton candy. He had won this for her by breaking plates at a carnival booth in Holdingford until the booth operator gave him the tiara and $5 to go away and not come back. His right arm was around her, his big hand, the little black moons of dirt under his nails. He drove with his left, except when he swept back his long blond hair or freshened his breath with a mint. His sleeveless T-shirt revealed a tattoo of a dragon on his left shoulder. He smelled fresh and happy.

We were poking along behind the DeMolay drum corps and a big-butt kid thumping *boomboomboom* on a bass drum, following the Knights of the Holy Nimbus, and Roger said, out of the blue, "When we go off to New York next spring, I think I'll have Gar take care of the car for me."

Gar. That was me.

"Need somebody to start the engine every day and take her for a spin. Can't leave a car sit all summer or they go to pieces on you. Gar could keep it in shape, and then you and me'd come back after the World Series and drive it out to California."

Nobody ever called me Gar in my life. I would remember it if someone had. Someone called me Specs once, and I was Doc, and someone called me Foxfart until Daryl Magendanz beat him up, but *Gar* was new to me.

The parade made the U-turn and then came back past the Chatterbox and Skoglund's Five & Dime and the Mercantile and Lucky's Hardware and the Sidetrack Tap. Daddy stood on the steps of the bank in his dark-blue suit, behind Hjalmar, his snowy locks fluttering in the breeze, and Uncle Sugar was there, and Miss Lewis. The Pontiac crawled along behind the bass drummer, who was perspiring heavily now and losing the beat.

"Next February, when everybody's freezing their butts off, I'll be in training in Florida," said Roger. "I'll practice in the morning and the afternoon and then we'll head for the beach, Katie, you and me. And in April we'll take the train up to New York City." He said *New York City* like it was the name of a favorite song of his. "All these other guys, they've gone about as far in baseball as

they're going to, but I've got a lot left in me. A lot. The best is yet
to be, Katie. Next spring I'm walking into that locker room and
there's Mickey Mantle and Whitey Ford and Yogi Berra . . ." and
his voice trailed off at the very thought of it, the audacity.

The Legion's Fourth of July program took place on a haywagon
parked on the grass by the swimming beach. The schedule said it'd
begin at one o'clock *sharp*, and around one-fifteen the crowd began to gather. They knew about Legion events. No matter how
well organized an event was, with committees and assignments
and lists of things and regular meetings and official badges for
everyone and the coordination of watches, the moment the event
was about to get under way, it was plunged into darkness and
chaos, thanks to the Legion guys' penchant for standing around
and discussing the pros and cons of things. You couldn't tack up a
three-foot swatch of red-and-blue bunting without three Legion
guys stepping in to wonder if maybe this was a middle swatch or
an end swatch and wanting to compare it with other swatches in
the box, and one of them worrying about the wind tearing the
bunting loose, and another thinking about whether carpet tacks
might serve the purpose better than these little roofing nails, and
another reminiscing about the time in St. Joe when the bunting
flapped so hard on a float that one of the horses bolted and hauled
six Benedictine nuns at a terrific rate of speed for three blocks
straight into the millpond, horse and nuns and wagon, a lovely
story, but now a ten-minute job has stretched into half an hour
and no bunting has been hung. This happened at the Fourth of
July program—knots of Legion guys here and there pondered
where to put the microphones and where the Gold Star Mothers

should stand and how to chock the wheels of the haywagon to se-cure it and whether the mayor would speak before Commander Krebsbach and if the honor guard should stand in front of, beside, behind, or on the wagon. And then someone figured out that the microphones didn't work because the electric cord wouldn't reach all the way to the warming house, so they'd have to get Bud down here to hook it up directly to a power pole, and it took up another twenty minutes to comb the neighborhood for Bud and not find him, and finally the Doo Dads parked their Ford convertible in front of the haywagon and Jim Dandy hooked up one microphone to the loudspeakers on the hood, which were powered by the car's battery, and a Legion guy stood and blew into the microphone, and we seemed to be almost ready to start at 2 P.M.

I had staked out an excellent position on the grass in the shade. I was holding a spot next to me for Kate, but she had disappeared. As time wore on, however, my shade moved to the east and I was left in scorching sunlight, behind two old men and an old lady in green-striped canvas camp chairs.

"You want to go or you want to stay?" one man said, around 2 P.M.

"Whatever you want," the woman said.

"Well, what do *you* want?" he cried.

She didn't know.

The second man said that anything they wanted was fine with him, he could go either way, stay or go. The woman said she hated to come all this way and then miss the show, that's all. "But what if the damn thing doesn't start for another forty-five minutes?" said the first man.

"If you want to scoot along," she said, "that's fine, but you know that the moment we get up and leave, that's when they're going to start the show. Same as what happened in Bemidji with the Paul Bunyan Pageant."

"I suppose I'll be hearing about that damn Paul Bunyan Pageant for the rest of my born days," said the first man in disgust. He turned his head and looked in the opposite direction. He wore a blue denim jacket with HAPPY HOOFERS embroidered on the back.

The second man said that maybe she should stay and wait for the show and he and Bob could go get a beer or something. No, she didn't think they should split up and then have to wander around trying to find each other: "I've spent half my life looking around for people." Man No. 1 was irked. "Forget it. Forget that I ever mentioned it. It's not worth the aggravation," he grumped. "I'm sorry I brought it up. We'll just sit here in the sun and roast and wait for the damn show to start—anything to keep you happy."

"Oh, now you're mad at me," she said. "I knew this would happen! I knew it! Now I've gone and ruined the whole day!"

The No. 2 man said, "Let's not get all worked up over it."

The first man sat with his arms folded. "I'm not worked up over anything. Have it her way. We'll just sit here until we burn up."

"Okay, I give up," she said. "We'll forget the whole thing. I'm sorry I ever suggested we come. It's the last suggestion I'll ever make. Let's go and you can have your beer and I'll sit and wait in the car." She looked around as if searching for allies. "Doesn't make sense to me, drive all the way from St. Cloud to see the Doo Dads and then miss them. But whatever you want."

The No. 1 man threw up his hands. "I give up!" he yelled. "Let's get the hell out of here. I've had about all I can take."

"If you are going to curse and cause a public scene, then I'll just go sit in the car," she said.

I guessed No. 1 was her husband and No. 2 was her brother. He said to the husband, "Let's discuss this like reasonable people."

"Oh, go stuff it," said the husband. His face was red. He was steaming. He glared at his wife, who was now folding up her camp chair. "I came to your show, so the least you can do is sit your fat butt down and we'll wait for the stupid thing to start."

She said, "I'm going to go sit in the car. You can stay as long as you like. I'll be in the car waiting whenever you want to go home." She headed toward Main Street. She didn't stop and neither of them tried to stop her. She disappeared beyond the trees. No. 2 said, "She's upset. She'll get over it."

The husband glared at him as if he'd like to stuff him in a corn chopper. The brother turned around and said, to nobody in particular, "Looks like it's starting."

And then the Gold Star Mothers traipsed out, and the Pledge was said, the honor guard horsed around for a few minutes, the mayor and Florian took turns honking about our town and our country, a little girl read part of the Declaration at a painful deliberate pace, word by word, and finally the Doo Dads came bounding out in their same white Bermudas but with bright-pink sportcoats.

After the long wait, the applause was not as warm as it would have been an hour and fifteen minutes earlier, but it was warm enough. "Thank you," said Jim Dandy. He said it was a great honor to be chosen to sing at the Fourth of July and he hoped we'd all sing along with them, and then Earl the Girl sang *Mine eyes have seen the glory* in his high tremulous tenor, hanging on the *glory*, pulling it like taffy, and then the four of them did *of the coming of the Lord* and the *Lord* came out foursquare with falsetto icing on it, and then the grapes of wrath, and the lightning was loosed of the terrible quick sword, and the Doo Dads let loose a big gorgeous *Glory, glory hallelujah*, slow and sweet, with Easter and Christmas in it and Washington's Birthday too, every syllable hung with lights and covered with gravy and when *His truth went marching on*, Jim Dandy's voice descended to the ocean depths and Earl the Girl flew into the stratosphere, and they held on to that last big chord and then *modulated up to the next key*—and if the crowd had not been so Scandinavian, they would've leaped up and screamed and gone to pieces, but being the sensible folk they were, they clapped lightly for the principle of modulation, and they waited for the Doo Dads to finish the song, and then they clapped again, it being the end and the time to applaud.

The "Battle Hymn" wore the Doo Dads out. You could tell it. They were all dripping wet and mopping their brows, and those nice pink sportcoats had big dark spots under the arms. It was time to say thank you and goodbye and get off the stage and let the Legion guys come up and read about *Life, Liberty, and the Pursuit of Happiness*. But when Jim Dandy heard that tepid Scandinavian applause for their killer-diller "Battle Hymn," it got his back up.

"You're a great audience," he yelled. "It's great to be here with you." More tepid applause. "You make us want to sing you another song!" Even more tepid applause. "Okay, darn it, we will!" And the Doo Dads swung into "My Girl." It was an okay performance but not after the "Battle Hymn," even this crowd could tell that.

> *My baby holds my hand*
> *I feel so doggone happy and*
> *When I hold her close and tight*
> *The moon and stars come out tonight,*
> *My Girl*

After you have lived to make men holy and died to make men free
and been transfigured by a glory in Christ's bosom and all, it does
not feel right to right away start mooning over a girl. This is just a
fact known to most in show business, surely, and the Doo Dads
finished "My Girl" to very light applause indeed.

Jim Dandy grabbed the microphone. "How many of you here
from Millet?" he hollered. Not that many. About five. "How
many of you here who went to Lake Wobegon High?" More
whistles and whoops and applause, but still no big hullabaloo.
"Well, so did I, and let me tell you something. I'm darned proud
that I went to Lake Wobegon High. Proud to be a Leonard!" A little more light applause. "I don't care what happens with us Doo
Dads. If we wind up digging ditches or we go on to national fame
and someday find ourselves singing on *The Ed Sullivan Show*—
how many of you here watch *Ed Sullivan* on Sunday night?"
Light, dutiful clapping. "—If we sing on *Ed Sullivan*, and if Ed
asks us, 'Boys, where you from?' I personally will be very proud
to say, '*Lake Wobegon!!!!*' "

The problem now was sunlight. The sun had been beating down
on the crowd for an hour while the Legion guys decided who
should stand and say what and where to seat the Gold Star Mothers and the disabled vets and the kiddie choir and got the honor
guard straightened out and the flags and buglers and the Youth
Citizenship Award winners and so forth, and it was a Scandinavian

and German crowd and these folks do not take to sunshine. Exposure to the sun's rays makes them dopy and sullen and eventually turns them toward violence. If the sky had darkened and rain fallen and turned to sleet, the crowd would've perked up and felt refreshed, but the onslaught of sunshine deadened them. The Doo Dads did not seem to realize this. Because Jim Dandy announced that, since the crowd had been so warm and generous to them, the Doo Dads would like to sing one more song. The crowd slumped down at the very thought; if he had called for a vote, the additional song would've gone down like Wendell Willkie. And then Earl the Girl hummed a high note, and the Doo Dads filled in the chord, and off they went into "The Star-Spangled Banner"—well, it was too weird for words. No other way to describe it. Our national anthem is supposed to be sung the very first thing, and if it's tacked on later in the program, it doesn't feel right at all. Some people jumped to their feet and others didn't. And the way the Doo Dads sang it—the *broad stripes and bright stars* sounded like a neon sign, and then Jim Dandy tried to get the crowd to clap along in time—*and you do not clap along to the national anthem*—it simply is not done—and they came to *the rockets' red glare* and *the bombs bursting in air* and you could feel what was coming—they got very warbly and loud and grabbed the mikes and leaned way back and gave *the land of the free and the home of the brave* everything they had, 150%, a big purplish splay-footed chord, and the chord died out, and there was dead silence as far as the eye could see, nothing, not a clap, not even one person waving a hanky. They'd never heard the national anthem sung so freely and didn't know what to think and didn't want to clap until the others clapped, which nobody was doing, so nobody did.

Jim Dandy looked out at the crowd, the other Doo Dads lurking behind him, sweaty, grinning their big stage grins, and I wanted in the worst way for him just to say thank you so much and get off the stage, but he didn't do it. He stared out over the sea of heads. *Walk off, walk off,* I thought. I was feeling pretty agitated. I liked the Doo Dads and this was not a good place for them to be right now, standing in front of five hundred sun-dazed Scandinavians, and it was not going to get any better. I knew this. I knew it.

"It means an awful lot for us Doo Dads to sing for you folks today and I hope you know that," said Jim Dandy. "You're wonderful hardworking God-fearing people. Salt of the earth! I look out across all these faces and I see so many folks who have meant so much to me and my family all the years we've lived here." This was dreadful humbug and everybody knew it and it didn't improve the crowd's disposition. "I know that many of you have been concerned about my family and about my beloved younger brother Ricky, who left us a few weeks ago and went west. I know that you've had Ricky and me and my mom and dad and my brother Roger in your prayers." The crowd was now sullen and resentful. It wanted him to go away and the show to end and everybody go find some shade and a cool drink. "And I want to thank you for your prayers and your good wishes. I think that families are the most important natural resource we have in America today."

He left this sentence hanging for the crowd to contemplate, while he bent over and whispered to Earl, and then he said, "And what would a family be without love?

"That's where it all starts, doesn't it."

The crowd was dreading what was to come. And sure enough, it was "Let Me Call You Sweetheart," and with the first notes of that moldy old song, the audience started to get restive and the folks in back started migrating toward the refreshments. The Happy Hoofer in the green-striped camp chair was pretty burned up. He had been huffing to himself and now he yelled something at the stage, something pretty rough, and he struggled to his feet, cursing. He had been nipping at a beverage of some sort and was glassy-eyed and cotton-mouthed but he managed to tell Jim Dandy to go to hell and the sooner the better. The brother-in-law tried to pull him back down but the Hoofer wasn't having any of it. He told the Doo Dads they were the sorriest piece of business he'd seen in his life and an insult to the town and as for singing, he'd heard drunks in a bar do better than this and how dare they sing the national anthem—he'd never seen any of them around the Legion—no, sir—and had they been to Korea or Okinawa or Guadalcanal or the Philippines? Frankly he doubted it. Buncha draft-dodgers standing up there making fun of this country.

The crowd was awestruck. Simply awestruck. They had never seen anybody do this before, stand up and yell at people at the microphone.

The brother-in-law said to me, "He's gone through a lot lately."

And then the Hoofer bent down and pulled off his shoe and cocked his arm and pegged it straight at Jim Dandy, hard, and it caromed off the mike and konked him hard on the noggin.

"You had no cause to do that," said Jim Dandy. "No cause. We're doing our best up here." He bent and picked up the shoe and flung it high in the air, out into the crowd. "You're drunk and you better sit down before you fall down."

The Hoofer said he'd rather be a little drunk than an idiot by birth like Jim Dandy. He offered to come up on stage and knock his teeth down his throat.

"I think it's time for your friends to calm you down, mister."

But Jim Dandy was looking out in the crowd to where the man's shoe was being passed slowly forward. It was a big brown shoe and people laughed to see it go by. A woman in the front row handed it to the Hoofer, and he wound up again, as if to throw, and Jim Dandy ducked, and the crowd hooted and clapped. Having sat in the hot sun and endured the Doo Dads, now here was some entertainment at last. The Hoofer turned and took a deep bow and there was heavy applause, far beyond what had been heard previously. The Hoofer bowed again, deeply, and whipped the shoe between his legs and hit Jim Dandy just below the belt, and J.D. leaped off the stage onto the man and grabbed him around the neck and they rolled around in the grass for a minute, punching and kneeing each other, until several men stepped in and pulled them apart, and the Hoofer got the last punch and clipped J.D. in the beezer and drew blood. J.D. looked shell-shocked.

"You fight about as well as you sing, ya big nancy," the Hoofer yelled. He was having the time of his life. It was his big day. "No wonder the Army wouldn't draft ya. You're nuthin' but a cake-eater!" And he turned away in sheer triumph and a Legion guy popped up on stage and yelled "How about a big hand for the Doo Dads, ladies and gentlemen!" and there was a very small shriveled shaky hand for the Doo Dads, and then we all turned around and hightailed it out of there, every single one of us.

That afternoon, Ding made a speech in the dugout before the game. He said, "Gentlemen! Listen up. Some of you apparently are hard-of-hearing, so pardon me if I repeat myself. We have certain rules on this team and let me bring these to your attention.

"Number one. There is no gambling by any player on any

game in which he is engaged! This goes for every last one of you. Don't let me hear otherwise or your butt will be out the door faster than you can say Grandma Moses.

"Number two. Drinking in the dugout. Let's keep it down to a minimum. If you can't remember how many strikes are on you, you've had too much. Remember what happened last year. I'm referring to the occasions when someone took a swing and the bat went sailing into deep center field. Let us have an understanding on this matter. A wooden bat in the hands of a drunk is a lethal weapon.

"Spitting. A little *ptui* is fine but I don't want to look up and see you guys standing around with a couple quarts of brown stuff squirting out of you. That stuff kills grass, especially if you've been drinking. Use the coffee can in the dugout. Please. That's what it's there for.

"Profanity. I'm hearing much too much of it on the field. Put a damper on it. This is a family game. Let's not be throwing cuss words and dirty talk around in front of small children. And let's have a little less grabbing your crotch out there. You get set in the batter's box and right away you gotta reach down for the family jewels. Some of you guys reach down there so much, it's surprising you still got two of em left. If there are adjustments to be made in the gonad department, take care of it in the dugout. Let's not look like a bunch of savages and sexual perverts. Okay, let's go play ball."

And they did, and that afternoon, Roger set down the Freeport Flyers 4–1 and looked every bit the up-and-comer and future Yankee, the way he strode on to the field, the sureness of his warm-up pitches, the cocky way with the resin bag, everything bespoke great confidence.

After the game, he climbed up to the press box, his hair soaked, a sweatshirt around his neck, his elbow wrapped in a towel, and Jim Dandy poured him three fingers of whiskey in a Dixie cup.

"There was one of those scouts here today," J.D. said. "Little sawed-off guy, dark glasses, in a nifty blue blazer. Stuck around for three innings. He was taking notes and he was looking at you, buddy."

"My fastball didn't get going until the fourth inning."

"It looked good from up here."

"The change-up was getting them, though."

"And that's your money pitch, the change-up."

"How did your show go today?" said Roger. "I had to miss it."

"It went great. Crowd went nuts. We did five songs and they went nuts for every one." He glanced at me. "That old hometown loyalty. There's nothing like it."

By six that evening, families had staked out the best vantage points on the lakeshore and were deep into the bratwurst and beer, there was smoke and mustard and the sweetness of malt and hops in the air, and a double Ferris wheel turned and a merry-go-round in the middle of Main Street and folks in the buckets of the Tilt-a-Whirl hurtled past the windows of Skoglund's Five & Dime store and the Mercantile. Kids tore up and down the sidewalks, gangs of girls stalked gangs of boys, waving their sparklers. Grandmas and grandpas promenaded on the sidewalks, and little boys darted out of the shadows to throw firecrackers at their feet and see the old folks jump, which some did and others were too deaf to notice. Kids raced up and down the beach, kids splashed in the water. A motorboat skimmed past with a girl in a red two-piece suit on skis. People turned and looked. Nobody from here, that's for sure. David Magendanz, who had just lost the blueberry-pie-eating contest to a fireman from Millet, thirteen pies to eleven, walked slowly by, stunned, red-faced, wondering if he was really going to do what he felt like he was about to do, and if he was, where should he go to do it. There were several exciting dogfights and rumors of a gang from the Cities, youths with shaved heads and teeth filed to sharp points, riding motorcycles, swinging tire chains, but they were nowhere to be seen. At dusk, the fireworks team of the Volunteer Fire Department headed out on the lake in two pontoon boats lashed together, big cartons of bombs and rockets on deck. They anchored in the bay, and dark figures climbed around on deck with flashlights. Roger and Kate and I were parked in the Pontiac behind Ralph's Pretty Good Grocery, facing the lake, me in the back seat, him kissing her.

"I should probably be on my way," I said.

He put his arm around Kate and got her crushed up next to him, his arm tight around her, and he kissed her hard. I said that I'd be running along and hoped they'd have a nice evening. Neither of them tried to persuade me to stay. In fact, I wasn't sure they knew I was there. It didn't seem that they did.

Something was going on lower down, on the trouser level, and Kate whimpered, and he got more excited and shifted himself to the edge of the seat, almost facing her, and put his head down and started kissing the front of her.

It occurred to me that I might wish to stay and observe and take notes.

Her left shoulder was bare now. He had undone the buttons and she was working on his shirt and his hands were busy below and he was saying, *O God my God I love you you are so beautiful,* and his mouth was all over her face and neck and she lifted up a little and I believe he slipped her skirt off her and his hands were working away in that area.

It occurred to me now that if I opened the door I might shock them both and make him mad at me. So I sat tight.

We were parked by Ralph's garbage cans, about a hundred feet from the water, and in front of us a little crowd of families sat on blankets on the dirt under the maple and poplar trees, the kids waving little sparklers. Roger now seemed to have lowered his trousers and she was doing something to him that made him particularly joyful.

I was not certain what I should do. Whether to stay or to leave. I tried easing the door open and the handle made a big clunk. I scrunched down and tried not to look at them. Visions of Uncle Sugar came to mind. My great patron, the giver of gifts, the man who made me a published writer. I knew what he wanted of me— to throw the door open and run and find him and tell him—and I could not do that. Roger's head had now disappeared below the seat back and Kate was helping him unhitch her bra and she tossed it over her shoulder and it landed beside me and now the pace of things started to pick up, the murmuring and the moaning, it sounded like a race to the finish line, and that was when the first rocket went up and then a volley of rockets, shooting straight up into the cosmos, rockets whipping in low trajectories across the water, mighty booms and phosphorus showers of yellow and green and red and lilac, and a bomb went off that lit up the interior of the car, and Kate gasped, and I heard him say, "Let's get out of here and go someplace." And he yanked on his pants, and I eased the door open and dropped out onto the ground and crawled away, and the Pontiac roared, and he threw it into reverse, and backed up, the rear door hanging wide open, and he raced away as the orange Chinese Fountain went up and Eruption of Vesuvius, the Shelling of the Emperor's Palace and Destruction of Peking, and finally the finale, the Cascades of Liberty, spluttered into the lake.

As the crowd turned away, a storm front slipped into town. It got cool fast, and lightning flashed to the west, and then, as the crowds broke and hightailed it home, the rains came down, sheets of rain, and I galloped the last block along Green Street in the rain, and up the sidewalk, the porch lit up, a waterfall from the eaves, a steady thrumming on the roof.

Daddy had come home after the parade, avoiding the Doo Dads debacle, and watched the fireworks from the front steps. He wanted to be where he could see if a stray rocket landed on our roof and get up there with a hose before the whole house was reduced to smoking cinders and his family became a clutch of paupers begging for charity in the streets. The rain took a big load off his mind.

"It was the best fireworks ever," said Mother. She had watched with Flo, sitting on a blanket in the park.

—I saw you with Kate and Roger, she said. What are they up to? You should have invited them over.

—They had other plans.

—Did they go out afterward?

—Yes.

—They say where they were going?

—Not to me they didn't. They were in a hurry.

—Uncle Sugar asked me if you knew and I said I'd ask. Is there something you're not telling?

—About what?

She sighed and went back behind her newspaper. "I meant to tell you," she said. "They arrested Ricky and Dede. At Yellowstone Park."

The young lovers had hitchhiked to Yellowstone and decided to see Old Faithful, and while they sat and waited for the geyser to go up, a woman recognized them, and park rangers arrested them, and they were to be flown back to Minnesota, and Ricky might be charged with kidnapping and auto theft.

"Well, at least they didn't get shot to death," said Mother. "Thank God."

She resumed reading, and a moment later she said, "It's good that they can get away and relax."

"Ricky and Dede?"

"Ike and Mamie."

Ike and Mamie were vacationing in Colorado and Ike went fishing in a creek, old man in rubber waders, up to his waist, casting, a long-billed cap on his old bald head.

Kate and Roger were relaxing somewhere. Lying naked in some secret place along the lake, their great frenzy spent, holding hands, looking up at the sky. I wasn't going to tell anybody, I knew that, even though Grandpa looked down from heaven at the iniquity of the thing and was trying to get my attention and get me to do the right thing, I was not going to do it, and that was that. Rain gurgled in the downspouts and whispered in the grass, a car whished down the wet black street.

22

The Del Ray

The Doo Dads, in their white suits and white bucks and black shirts and white ties, are swaying in unison, doing a finger-poppin version of "My Girl" at the fashionable Del Ray Ballroom ("You're A-OK at the Del Ray"), and Kate and I are dancing, close, her head on my left shoulder, my face in her neck, my nose grazing the short hairs.

> Her skin so soft and fair
> My face buried in her hair
> I don't care if I ever go home
> I could spend the night alone
> With My Girl
>
> All my old friends—out the door
> All the things I did before
> Ever since she took my hand

I've been living in the land
Of My Girl

"Take me out on the veranda," she whispers, and we step outdoors into the glittering summer night, a long trail of light etched from the moon across Lake Elmo to us, and she whispers, "You're driving me mad, the way you put your lips on my neck. Making me think crazy thoughts. There's a whole wild side of me that nobody knows. Except you."

The Doo Dads are singing inside, and we slip behind a potted palm and we kiss, her tongue fluttering in my mouth, and she says, "I want to be yours. Tonight."

"We can't. We're cousins."

"We're not really," she whispers. Our faces an inch apart, our eyes meet unblinking. She says, "I'm adopted. Mother told me. Last week. I was left in a basket on the parsonage steps. My daddy was an Indian and my mama was a minister's daughter. Or so they think."

A few minutes later, we stand in the shadows beside the bathhouse. In the lighted windows of the ballroom, our friends go on dancing.

"Maybe we're too young to be in love," I say. "Maybe we should wait."

And she tugs on her zipper and her dress falls into the sand and she drops her bra and steps out of her panties. "Be naked with me," she says. So I follow suit. She leads me into the warm water and we float together and paddle lazily out to the diving dock and embrace in its shadows, her proud young breasts pressed against me.

"God created our bodies, what is the sin in enjoying them?" she says.

"What if they find out?" I say, my manhood thickening.

She kisses me hard and I grab hold of her firm young buttocks and our bodies meet and then she gasps as we are united and
she moans and thrusts against me, my hardness inside her, and
she thrusts again and again and again and now her fingernails are
deep in my back and her teeth in my lower lip as her body trembles violently and she throws her head back and shrieks—

I could not decide what she should shriek. I left it unfinished.

The big sister came home the day after the Fourth, in a state of anguish. She had gone off to a Bible conference in the Apostle Is-
lands on Lake Superior with Uncle LeRoy and Aunt Lois and, as
Sanctified Brethren liked to do on car trips, Lois and the sister
rolled up Gospel tracts in bright yellow or red or blue cellophane
and tossed them out by rural mailboxes so that when folks came
to get their mail they'd see the shiny thing on the ground, unwrap
it, and read the tract, entitled *Where Will You Spend Eternity?* and
be convicted of their sins and accept the Lord as their personal
Saviour. LeRoy, as the driver, was exempt from this duty. As they
drove along, Lois and the sister tossed out a few hundred tracts,
and then LeRoy started kidding them and referred to it as "gospel
bombing," and made a whistling and exploding sound when Lois
tossed one, and if he saw a farmer up ahead he'd yell, "Git him!
Git that sucker!" and step on the gas, which the sister felt was not
behavior that glorified the Lord, and then, after fifty miles or so, as
tedium set in, Lois gave up tossing tracts and sat in a stupor listening to the radio, a worldly station, not a Christian one, and the

poor sister was left with sole responsibility for the souls of the people of northern Wisconsin. Before, she'd been tossing only to the left side of the car, and now she was responsible for both sides, and LeRoy was driving too fast for accurate tract-tossing, 70 and 75 mph. She planted herself in the middle of the back seat, wrapping the tracts as fast as she could, and threw left and right as they flew past mailboxes; meanwhile, LeRoy and Lois were playing the Alphabet Game and 20 Questions in the front seat as if it were a joyride. The car was hot, the seats sticky, the road a narrow concrete ribbon with asphalt seams that thumped on the tires, and when a semi went by, it almost blew them into the ditch, and somewhere around Hayward, the sister simply felt she couldn't throw one more tract. She begged LeRoy to stop so she could rest and he said, "We'll stop in a little while," and kept right on driving. She was so tired she couldn't make her arm throw and she slumped in the seat, her head resting against the window, and up ahead she saw a man standing at a mailbox looking at mail. She prayed for strength to throw one more tract, and she sat, arms limp at her sides, as he flew past and she caught a glimpse of his face and it was a face full of weariness with sin and hunger for the Gospel. This man in Hayward, Wisconsin, might die and face an eternity in hellfire because she was unable to bestir herself and throw out the lifeline of Good News.

The sister spilled out this whole tearful tale to Mother on the porch. Mother patted her hand and told her not to fret, to pray for the man, that prayer is the real lifeline, but the sister said, no, she felt that this man's soul was on her conscience and that she must—she *must*—go to Hayward and find him. The sister was very dramatic, sniffling and holding her head in her hands and flouncing around and striding across the room and so forth. When

Mother went to get a Bible to read a comforting passage from, I stepped onto the porch. The sister turned a bleary tear-streaked face to me, and I said, "Don't imagine that you're all that important, because you're not, you know."

She tore after me and I dashed across the living room and into the kitchen and out the back door as Mother came trotting down the stairs with the Bible and the sister grabbed the sugar bowl off the table and hurled it at me as I lunged out the back door and she yelled, "God damn you to hell!" and the bowl smashed on the kitchen wall.

I immediately went to work in the garden, laboring quietly over the tomato plants, snitching out the little weeds, and hoeing, and when Mother came out a few minutes later, I was the picture of diligence.

She told me she wished I could be more understanding toward my sister. She couldn't understand why there was so much bad feeling between us. It broke her heart to see family members so angry at each other.

"I'm not angry whatsoever," I said. I smiled at her. "I have no idea why she is. I've stopped trying to figure her out."

Mother sighed. "It's beyond me what to do with you. It's absolutely beyond me."

"Don't worry about it. I'm fine."

It was clear from the sister's syrupy disposition the next evening that she had gone and done an evil deed. Gone was her sour mug and her anguish about the unsaved Hayward man. She was all smiley, as if she'd won first prize in a cuteness contest, and she got lovey-dovey with Daddy after work and poured him iced tea and squeezed the lemon and perched on the arm of his chair beaming at him like a child in a Sunday-school magazine and asking charming questions about banking and what was the best car to buy and why is there a lunar eclipse and got him to tell stories about boyhood on the farm and how hard he worked and how contented he and his brothers and sisters were, playing in the dirt with blocks of wood and stones, wearing hand-me-down clothes, never demanding more. Poor Daddy melted like a pat of butter. At supper he asked if she cared to say table grace. Oh boy, would she! She folded her fat little hands and clamped her beady eyes shut and went to town, thanking God for sending Jesus to die on the cross and also for this macaroni and cheese for the nourishment of our bodies, praying for those who might not have accepted Christ as Personal Saviour, may their hearts be exercised and so forth, and praying for the sick and suffering, and distant loved ones, and classmates, and young people everywhere, the orphans especially, and missionaries in foreign climes, and teachers, and Scout leaders, and also Camp Fire, and then she turned to President Eisenhower and prayed for him, and for those in the Armed Forces, and Those Who Are Lonely and in Distress—it's too bad you can't interrupt someone who's praying and say, "Oh, knock it off, would you?"—and she prayed for farmers, that their labors might be richly blessed, and fishermen, and foresters also, and now she was running out of gas, but she tossed in the Bereft and Bereaved, and the Backsliders, and those on Beds of Pain, and in Prison, and came back to Those Who Had Not Accepted Christ, and finally she said, "We ask it all in Jesus's Precious Name. Amen." And we all took a breath. The macaroni was cold, the cheese congealed.

* * *

And the very next morning Miss Lewis called while I was mowing the grass and asked me to come to her house. I said I was busy and she said it was important and if I couldn't come to her she'd come to me, so I went. She was sitting on her front step, in her slacks and green blouse and sun hat, and she had my story about the Del Ray Ballroom on her lap.

—I hear you have a nice new typewriter, she said. I nodded.

—Is this yours? she said.

I looked at it and saw the part about my manhood being large.

I shook my head.—No, ma'am. I never saw this before in my life.

—It sounds like something you might've written, Gary.

I shook my head. *Not my style at all.*

—Then who do you suppose wrote this?

—I wouldn't have any idea. A lot of people could have. It's really not that good.

—What do you suggest I do with it?

I said she should burn it probably and then be sure to speak to the person who stole it and explain to her the meaning of private property.

I walked home, heart pounding to think of Mother reading about me and my manhood, and the small friendly animals, and in front of the Lutheran church I heard my name called and turned and there was Leonard striding across the church parking lot. He said he wanted his magazine back.

"What magazine?" I said. I wanted him to say *High School Orgies* out loud.

—You know what magazine. The one I gave you a month ago.

—Oh. I forgot all about that.

He said that he didn't like the way I was acting these days, like I thought I was better than anybody else. He didn't think we were friends anymore. He just had that feeling. In fact, he said, I was on his stink list.

—Yeah, well, I've been busy writing for the *Herald Star*. I have a job now. I have no idea where your magazine is. I have better things to do than look at titties.

—Then you better buy me another.

—I wouldn't know where to go to buy garbage like that.

—Then give me the money.

—I'll think about it.

—How much they pay you to write those dumb stories? Fifty cents?

—Fifteen bucks apiece, I said coolly, giving myself a nice raise.

That shut him up for a second. Finally, he said, "I hear Roger Guppy is nailing your cousin." I didn't stop to think, I just grabbed him around his scrawny neck and flailed on him as hard as I could right there in the parking lot of the Lutherans, got him in the gut, in the chops, across the throat, whaled on him with one hand and held on with the other, until he slithered away, and then I cracked him one in the back and let him go. He ran a hundred feet or so across the asphalt and turned and cursed me in a harmless, amateurish way and yelled, "You want to know something? You're nuts. Your whole family is nuts. And you can't write for beans! Anybody could write better than you!" He gave me the finger, waving it high in the air as if that should put the fear of God into me, and turned and slunk toward home. What a pitiful person. To think that I had wasted time on being friends with him. I resolved never to make that sort of mistake in the future.

* * *

I went home and retrieved *High School Orgies* from its hiding place and took it out to the incinerator along with the trash and lit the fire. I had snagged an empty Cloud O'Cheese aerosol can and I tossed it in when the fire was going good, the pages of the magazine curling one by one and blackening in the flames. I saw the librarian go by and the tennis instructor and the English teacher and all their gleaming orbs and lovesticks, and then the Cloud O'Cheese blew up, *whump*, and the orgies were over.

When Aunt Flo came over that afternoon, I was sure Miss Lewis had passed my story on to her. Aunt Flo was no dummy. She could look at that page and see it was Sugar's old typewriter. She sat on the porch with Mother and I said hello and Mother asked me to please leave them alone and I was glad to.

From inside, I heard Flo say, "She is driving them to a nervous breakdown, going around with this Roger. Those two can never be happy together. Sugar and Ruth are sick about it. Ruth said to her, 'I hope you're not doing what I think you're doing.' And Kate went through the roof. She said, 'I love him and there's nothing anybody can do about it.' "

Mother says she thinks Kate is someone who will do the right thing. There is a calmness in Mother's voice that astonishes me.

23

My Girl

The Whippets beat the Melrose Hubs twice the next Sunday *(The Whippet squad crossed bats with the Hubs in a double-decker Sunday last on the home pasture, and after a slugging bee in which backstopper Milkman Boreen cleared the fences twice, notching six RBIs, lifting the locals to a 12–7 triumph, the Dogs swept the nightcapper 4–2 as sternwheeler Roger Guppy bamboozled the Hub sticksmiths with his multifarious pitching)* on a steaming bug-infested night when Roger poured ice water over his head and steam rose from his hair, the Whippets' winning runs coming in the ninth, when Ronnie punched the second pitch into center field and the Hub fielder dove for it and the ball skipped over his glove and rolled merrily to the wall, and by the time the right-fielder dug it out, Ronnie had a double, whereupon the Perfesser sliced one down the right-field line, the Hubs' first-baseman waving a glove at it, and the right-fielder chased it into the corner and snatched at it, threw the ball before he had a grip on it, dropped it, and the Perfesser had himself a double and Ronnie was in like Flynn. Then Milkman banged one straight at the right-fielder, who must've thought the bogeyman was after him, because he stepped back a few paces and let the ball drop, and it bounced over his head, and the Perfesser strolled home with the capper.

Afterward the fans streamed out into the mosquito night, dumbfounded at the turn of the events. Nobody could remember when the boys last swept a twin bill and exerted such dominance. The fans were waiting for Lady Defeat to come and sing her sad song, and instead, there was Mr. Jubilation looking them in the eye. They didn't know what to do.

The ballplayers were in the habit of parking their cars up close to the dugout so as to discourage teenagers from letting air out of the tires or sticking a potato up the tailpipe. Some of the fans gathered there, and when two players finally came out, Milkman Boreen, the black hornrims perched on his big beak, and Ronnie Piggott, jaunty and loose-limbed, there were murmurs of "Good game" and "Way to go," like cricket whispers, and when Roger emerged, the fans could not help themselves, they clapped for him. He tossed his equipment bag into the trunk and turned and nodded to them and said thank you. "You're great, kid," a man said from the dark, and there were murmurs of agreement, and he added, "You're making this town real proud right now. I hope you know how much that means, young fella." It was almost more emotion than you could bear. Roger tipped his cap and got in the Pontiac and drove away. It wasn't until he did that I noticed Kate sitting in the front seat.

* * *

Then they met Albany on a Tuesday night, to make up a rained-out game, and I climbed up to the press box to find Roger conferring with his brother Jim Dandy, who was saying how much money he'd won gambling on that sweep of the Hubs. "Just had an inkling that you guys were going to have you a big night. And, boy, those dairy farmers were glad to take me up on it. O ye of little faith! I was getting five-to-one odds. Raking them in. Lots of sporting money out there."

I stood by the open door and heard everything.

"If you ever have a feeling that it ain't your night and that you might be serving up cheese to the batters, I hope you'll let me know about it," said Jim Dandy.

"I don't know what you're talking about."

"Just give me a sign. Stick your cap in your back pocket or something. Hang your warm-up jacket on the fence."

"I'm not gonna throw a game, if that's what you're talking about."

"Not talking about throwing anything. People suffer mental lapses, that's all I mean, and if you feel it coming on, you could let me know. Happens to the best of them." Then Jim Dandy noticed me at the door.

"Anyway, I've seen those Yankee scouts taking a look at you. Next February you'll be in St. Petersburg, son, impressing the pants off them, and next April, wham, you'll be walking out to the mound in Yankee Stadium, sixty thousand people clapping for you. You'll be scared, sure, but you pitch good scared, you'll win that game, and next morning, you're written up big in all the papers. Just remember, you heard it here first.

"Next year is your year, and meanwhile I got this great song and it's in the can and I need a couple thou to press enough copies

233

to get people's attention. This could be my last ride on the merry-go-round, kid. If it were me, I'd do it for you."

"Where are these major-league scouts?" said Roger. "I haven't seen any."

"They're there. I saw one in Holdingford last week. They come to Avon sometimes. They're there. They're taking notes on you. I seen em."

"Let me think about it," said Roger.

"Don't think too hard, it'll give you a headache."

That was the night I got up the nerve to ask Jim Dandy about writing poetry. It was around the second inning, he was enjoying his fortified tomato juice, and he asked me how everything was going, so I said, "Fine. When you write a poem, do you have the idea in mind first, or do you just start writing and let the idea come to you? I've heard of people doing it both ways."

He said he always had the idea in mind first and usually it was the same idea. "Half of all poetry is about *I love you more than anything* and the rest is about *I love you so much, how come you treat me so bad*. Those are the classics that make good songs that people want to hear."

I asked him what meter he preferred. He said, "This one," And he sang—

> *Love me, baby, love me night and day.*
> *Take me in your arms and never take your love away.*
> *Please, baby,*
> *You know that I love you.*
> *If I ever lost your lovin, I don't know what I'd do.*

"That's your basic verse. You can't go wrong with it."

I asked him what he thought of free verse.

"Free verse," he said, "is what nobody's ever going to pay you to write, so why do it? Get some cash for your trash."

He promised he'd look at my poems if I wanted to bring them around sometime.

That was the night the Perfesser sidled up to Ding before the game and said, "Skipper, I'd like your permission to lead a prayer in the dugout. I think some of the fellows would appreciate it."

Ding rolled his eyes. "Go out and get a hit and you can pray all you want to. Sing hymns too."

That same night, Ding got hit in the head by a foul ball, a screamer, that caromed off the dugout roof and cracked him above the ear as he stood pondering his next move. He fell pole-axed to the ground as the Albany fans jeered and hooted. "Show us your crack again!" they hollered. He struggled to his feet, dazed, and turned to face them and felt the warmth where he had wet his pants. A guy yelled, "Someone spilled warm piss in your lap!"

Roger yelled, "Aw, shut your piehole!" as he helped the crest-fallen manager into the dugout. The fan challenged him to duke it out and Roger ran to the railing and threw a punch and poked him in the snoot before other Whippets reeled him back in. The fan's nose bled all down his shirt and he and his friends were all bent out of shape and hopping around, waving their fists and yelling about how they'd be laying for Roger afterward and punch his lights out.

This was in the sixth inning, the Whippets up by two runs, and after that Roger had no breaking pitch to speak of, nothing but a medium fastball. The Miners feasted on it in the seventh and eighth and jumped ahead. "Get the crank!" yelled the crowd. The Whippets came up in the bottom of the eighth and Roger stroked a lovely triple and stood on third, pleased with himself, and a minute later he trotted toward the dugout, thinking the umpire had called the batter out on strikes for the third out, but in fact there were no outs, Roger had been the lead-off hitter. And it was only the second strike, not the third. The Albany fans sang, "Do it again, do it again, over, over," and one cried out, "Hey, fish head, you been eating Dumb Flakes for breakfast??" All the air went out of the Whippets then, and they collapsed into the arms of defeat. You would not think a player could make such a mistake. "I never saw him lose his concentration like that," said Jim Dandy. Ding sat, nursing a killer headache, moaning. "Guess I was dreaming," Roger said. Dreaming of what? We soon learned what. That was the day he found out Kate was pregnant.

Monday night I called up Jim Dandy and his mother, Mrs. Guppy, answered. "He is over at the Sidetrack Tap most likely," she said. "If you see him, tell him I ain't holding dinner."

"I would also like to express my sympathies to you and the Guppy family and I want you to know your son Ricky is certainly in our prayers," I said.

She sighed. "Well, it's always something, isn't it. A person just never knows. You think you're doing the right thing and then something like that happens. And what can you do? Nothing."

"I'm sure you did all you could for your son and I am confident that someday he will thank you, too."

"We went out of our way for him, that's for sure, gave him

everything and look what he did to us. Oh well, that's the way the cookie crumbles! No sense crying over it."

"Well, we just have to hope for the best, don't we."

"Who did you say this is?" she said. "I don't recognize the voice." I said I was a friend of Ricky's from school. "You're not from the paper, are you?" I said I was not.

Mother and Daddy were heading for Charley's in Freeport, where it was Chicken Pot Pie Night. Two for the price of one. The older sister was at her girlfriend's, holding their pity party. I was shutting off the sprinkler. Suddenly there was shouting indoors: Daddy thrashing around, unable to locate his car keys. Shaking coat pockets, digging in the junk dishes, rummaging on the kitchen counter, tearing into piles of things, like an animal caught on the barbed wire thrashing himself to death, until Mother located the keys in the pocket of a jacket.

When they left, I put on a clean plaid shirt, combed my hair, and headed downtown to the tavern, coming around by the alley and in the back door.

A cloud of smoke and beery air and hamburger grease wafted out like a big belch and I slipped inside and stood by an empty booth in back. The room was dark, except for the yellow and green and orange neon beer signs, and when my eyes adjusted to the dimness, there was the doleful Wally in his white apron behind the bar and Ding, his big gut balanced on a stool next to old Mr. Berge, and Jim Dandy, wearing his best black shirt with pearl buttons, his hair slicked back, looking like he had the world on a string. Next to him was a stack of 45s he was autographing.

He told Wally, "You need to get this one on your jukebox. This is going to be a big one. It's going gangbusters everywhere. Stores are having a hard time keeping it in stock. DJs are going gaga over this. Absolutely bananas. You don't want to be the last one on the bus."

Wally slipped around behind the bar, in constant motion, straightening things, shifting, moving the salt shakers, wiping the counter and the lid of the big jar of boiled eggs, filling the rack of beef jerky, rinsing glasses in the sink below, rearranging the back bar and the cooler.

"People like to hear the newest thing on the jukebox," said Jim Dandy.

"Not everybody. Guys in here go more for the Hank and Lefty stuff. Guys here are still hoping Glenn Miller didn't die in that plane crash."

"Let me play it for you."

"What's it called again?"

" 'My Girl.' "

"Rock and roll?"

"You bet. But it's smooth, it's not a screamer."

He stepped to the jukebox and unlatched the cover and put the 45 on the turntable and pressed a switch. And there were the Doo Dads humming like the Mills Brothers, and the bass going *hmm boom boom ba da da doom doom*, and Earl the Girl cutting loose into his falsetto wail.

> *Saturday I went to town*
> *Met the guys I hang around*
> *Had a smoke and a glass of gin*
> *Waiting until she came in*
> *My Girl*

Is she beautiful? Oh my
I see her and almost die
I would kneel in the street
And place my forehead on her feet
My Girl

Jim Dandy slow-danced to it as if a girl were in his arms and his left hand were stroking her thigh.

"I don't think so," said Wally. "These guys come in here and try to forget women. They already put their forehead on some girl's foot and she gave em a swift kick with it. 'I'm So Lonesome I Could Cry'—that's the song they want. Getting tears in my beer crying over you. They don't want teenager songs. Anyway, we already got two by the Doo Dads."

Jim Dandy smiled. Fine. He didn't care. He was only giving Wally a chance to get in on the ground floor of something that was going to be a major sensation. If Wally wasn't interested, it was no hair off his nose. A guy makes an investment in a tavern like this, you figure he wants to keep up with modern trends and draw the young crowd and make a few shekels for himself. You can't turn a profit on farmers, pal—they will go through the free popcorn like locusts and nurse a 15¢ beer til the paint on the barn dries. Every week or two, they'll splurge on a boiled egg. No, sir, drawing a younger clientele is the formula for success here. Attract young women and young men will spend money hand over fist to make them happy. Throw the bucks in the air! Pound it down rat holes! Appeal to the lass of 18 and you'll be rich in six months! But if Wally's not interested in making a go of it, then that's okay, there are plenty of others who are. Like the HiDeHo. He just figured he was doing Wally a favor trying to clue him in.

Mr. Berge pointed to Wally's belly and said, "No reason for him to worry about business, he looks to be eating regular."

"I am," said Wally, "though for a man with my hemorrhoids, eating regular isn't the fun that it ought to be."

"I know all about that," said Berge. "Had them when I was in the Army. Had a bad habit of reading books in the barracks after lights out. I'd go sit in the can, where the lights are on all night, and I'm on the throne getting engrossed in this book and about six hours later I got hemorrhoids as big as prunes. I could hardly roll out of bed. The docs took one look, said it was the worst case they'd seen, maybe a national record. They took pictures—somebody told me I'm in all the medical textbooks. Sent me to the hospital to get reamed and this lady runs a metal thing up my tailpipe until it about comes out my left ear and after that I never could sing as well as before. Used to have a nice tenor voice and sang at weddings. Now—nothing."

"Get yourself a foam doughnut to sit on," said Ding. "They're a lifesaver. Had a bad case of hemmies myself about three years ago, and some of the boys spooned some Tijuana Cat Whiz into my hot-dog relish. It's made from cactus and it gives you a hard stool. I sat on the crapper, and I cried, it hurt so bad. It was like trying to pass a brick."

Jim Dandy studied Mr. Berge for a moment.

"How much can a good hairpiece cost anyway?" he said. "I would think you could get something for twenty bucks that'd improve on what you got on your head there. That toupee looks like a highway casualty."

"Don't discuss my hair and I won't tell what I saw when I stood next to you at the pisser," said Berge. He signaled for another whiskey.

"You were so drunk you were looking down at your own," said Jim Dandy. "You never saw a well-hung man until you seen a bass singer. That's what gives that deep voice. Extra-large equipment. Ask the ladies. They're the ones who know quality."

Wally pointed a hairy hand in my direction. "Watch your language, there's a youngster here."

The three of them swiveled around and cast their eyes at me lurking beside the booth.

"It's the sportswriter!" said Ding. "Watch what you say."

"How you doing there, Larry?" said Jim Dandy. "You care for a root beer or something?"

I asked if this would be a good time to show him my poems or should I come back later?

He thought about this. "Sure," he said. I handed him a sheaf of poems, four of my best, folded in thirds. He thumbed through them. "This one is about trees, I see. That's nice. I think that I shall never see a poem lovely as a tree. And spring—this is nice."

> O gentle spring, you have banished winter, our angry dad
> Who yelled at us to dress warmly and to do our duty
> And to work hard and save our money as he had
> And now you give us all this vernal beauty
> As a little child is given his mother's breast,
> The precious gift of life without price.
> And now the snowy fields of the Upper Midwest
> Have you turned into a green paradise.

"You got his attention there where you mentioned a breast," said Ding. "Add another one of those and you've got him hooked."

Jim Dandy browsed through the others. "You got any love poems in here?" I shook my head. "Why not?"

Well, the answer stood right there before him. *The World's Strangest Creature, Half Boy, Half Toad. Yes, It Is Alive! It Walks, It Talks, It Crawls on Its Belly like a Reptile!*

Ding took a hard drag on his smoke, pulling the coal almost to his lips.

"If you're looking for help with your writing, kid, you're hollering up the wrong drainpipe. This feller"—he nodded at Jim Dandy—"he's an authority on getting drunk and pissing his pants. He knows as much about writing as I know about the H-bomb."

Jim Dandy sighed and shook his head. "It's the old story! Somebody with talent and ambition comes along in this town and they got to cut him down to their size! That's what small people do. And in ten years this town's going to be even more of a dead end than it is already. 'Cause people like you run out all the talent! Everybody with ideas! You belittle em!"

He turned to me. "This town is one big cemetery, kid. Some folks above ground, some below, but it's about the same one way or the other. The ones above ground can't leave either. They're afraid to. Afraid if they went to California nobody'd know who they are or how smart they are, so they stay home. Plant their feet in the ground and start sinking.

"Well, what the hell," he said. "In six months, when this record hits and I'm in New York on television, it isn't going to bother me worth a rat's ass then, so why should it bother me now? Right?"

"In six months," said Ding, "you're gonna be sitting on the same stool except with more stains on your shirt."

"Small minds! One of these days I'm gonna write a song about it. And dedicate it to you."

24

The English Language

slipped out the back and strolled home, where I soaked a big rect-
angle of lawn so as to soften it and dig out the latest dandelion
assault from the Andersons. When the older sister came out and
ragged on me for my latest story, which referred to Roger as a
horsehide magician and said he *aired the orb for a three-
bagger*, I only smiled and said I was grateful for her interest.

"I don't know what you imagine you'll ever do for a living,"
she said, "but let me tell you: writing isn't it. A word to the wise."

I thanked her for the advice and promised to keep it in mind.

She snorted. She said she didn't see much evidence of my being
aware of anybody except my own stupid self. She said that
Mother and Daddy were worried about how I'd changed and that
it broke their hearts to know the sort of smutty magazines I
brought home and the filthy stories I wrote about myself and my
own *cousin! My cousin! Did I understand what I was talking
about? And did I think they don't know what goes on in their own*

home? Did I take them for utter fools? No, they were well aware of what I was up to and were disgusted by it and ashamed.

I let her blow, and when she was done, I said coolly, "There is no such magazine and no such story." I looked her unblinking straight in the eye and said it without a tremor of a doubt.

"You're not even very good at lying," she said.

"You'll have to be more specific. I'm sorry, I don't follow you at all."

"L-i-e. Know what it means?" She gave me a little shove.

"I have no idea what you're talking about." I smiled sympathetically at her, as if she had gone mad and was drooling.

"The English language! That's what! Listen, jerkhead—I'm on to you. Okay? I read your story, the whole disgusting thing about having sex with your own cousin! My gosh. Does the word *incest* mean anything to you? Do you ever even *glance* at your Bible? Is there no limit to how low your mind goes? Is there?"

"Jerkhead—is that a Biblical term?"

She was poking me in the shoulder, pushing, her voice a little shrieky. "You are about to be exposed for the slimy person you really are," she said, "and all the old ladies who dote on you are going to get a mighty big shock. I hope Grandma and Aunt Eva don't find out. It'd kill the both of them."

I asked her if the story she referred to was the same story Miss Lewis had shown to me last week. The story about swimmers.

That threw her for a moment. She faltered—and I came in with the uppercut. I said, "Miss Lewis asked me if I thought you wrote it."

"You liar."

"I looked at the story and said I was about ninety percent certain you couldn't possibly have written it. I mean there was a lot of stuff about kissing that you wouldn't know the first thing about. And what good would it do you if you did know? Kissing requires two people and there is never going to be anyone who cares to do it with you. You know it and I know it. If you want to know why, ask me sometime and I'll try to explain it to you. It's your personality."

And I turned and walked away. She fumed at me about what a monster I was and how I wouldn't get away with it, and I returned to work on the lawn.

Grandpa looked down, speechless. Jesus had gone back inside to talk to somebody. With the ground wet, those dandelions came up lickety-split, roots and all, and into a bucket, dead soldiers. Mrs. Anderson called out to ask what I was doing. I said I was digging worms. She said, Oh.

25

Poison

I t was the middle of July and Aunt Eva had sent me two plaintive notes on bits of index card:

> *Dearest Gary: I am avidly following your stories in the newspaper thanks to Flo, who is diligent about forwarding copies, and I must say I enjoy them tremendously, and so does Mother. You are making baseball fanatics out of us both. We miss you keenly, Mother & I, & wish you here, tho of course you are all grown up now & busy with your own affairs, but we do wish sincerely that you could spare a day (or two) for yr old relatives. Do let us know when you can visit. All our love, Eva*

> *Dearest Gary, Mother keeps asking when you will honor us with your presence and I tell her that you are occupied with your duties at the paper and all, but do want you to*

know that if you could spare even an hour you would make two old ladies very happy. I am making banana bread and it's not much fun without you here to enjoy a slice of it. Let us have a look at you. Kindly greet your dear family. All our love, Eva

So I hopped on my bicycle and rode out to the farm. Eva was kneeling in the yard, weeding a bed of petunias inside a truck tire, and when she looked up I saw a flash of dread in her face, the old fear of strangers, and then she grinned and jumped up and ran and gave me a hug.

"Let me look at you." She held me at arm's length. "My, you are a feast to the eyes."

She was the only person in the world who'd ever say such a thing to me. Nobody else considered me even a light snack to the eyes. Most people would consider me a light purgative to the eyes.

She led me by the hand and sat me down on the front step and grilled me about the Whippets and whether the Guppy boy was really as good as I said in the paper and could the team win the New Soo crown and go to the State Tourney at Nicollet Field in Minneapolis, and after we exhausted that topic, she asked about the entire family and wanted a day-by-day account of their activities, and then she said, "Come and let's get you a bag of tomatoes to take home. Those town tomatoes taste soapy to me."

We walked down that long dirt road I'd walked with her ever since I learned to walk, and there was the garden, majestic in the sunlight, everything where it should be and always had been since Adam and Eve.

* * *

Grandma was talking about death these days, Eva said, and she was studiously planning her funeral and which hymns should be sung, and who should preach and who should conduct the graveside service and how there absolutely would be no open casket and no flowers—"Give me the flowers while I live," said Grandma, quoting the old song—and which neighbors she wanted to be there and which ones not.

And then Eva said, "I don't think I could survive two weeks around here without Mother," and she sat down in the dirt and got out a hanky and dabbed at her eyes. "I told Mother that if she's intending to go then she can plan mine too. Have a double funeral."

She made me promise not to tell anybody about any of this. I promised.

"A lot of people would clap their hands to see me dead. They could sell off the place and pocket the money and never have to lower themselves to coming out here to visit us poor old hillbillies." I patted her shoulder a little and then she jumped up, mad, and said, "People move to town and suddenly they're too good for the likes of us! Our own flesh and blood. They buy a fancy house and expensive clothes—I'm no dummy, I know how much they pay! All that brand-new furniture. All the luxuries they've got. Think they're better than those of us who have to make do! Oh yes! I know. They see me coming and they get out the Air-Wick and the Lysol! Think they're better than us."

I got the idea she was talking about Mother. I said, "Nobody thinks they're better than you."

"They do so. Some people, you'd never know they were Christians, the way they look down on their poor shirttail relatives. I know what they're thinking. It's a great big chore for them to take

an hour and visit their own family. They come through the door
like they were entering a loony bin and they brush off the chair
before they sit down lest there be spiders. And they'd rather go
home early than have to go out back and use the biffy. Imagine
that. They think they're too *good* to put their little bottoms down
on a wooden seat and do their business in a hole! *Too good for it!*
Too good to eat home-butchering! Have to buy their meat in a
wrapper! My own relatives! I'm just plain ashamed of them. I
wish I'd never lay eyes on them again."

This speech in the tomato patch came out of nowhere. It rocked
me back on my heels. If she was talking about Mother and Daddy,
I didn't care to have to listen to it.

And then she started patting my head and saying how I was her
favorite person in the whole world and always had been like a son
to her, her baby, and the relative who was most *like* her and the
only one she really cared about aside from Grandma and how it
would kill her if I ever turned my back on her as others had done,
and if she thought I would do that, then she'd rather go up to the
house right this minute and drink a glass of poison. "I mean it,"
she said. She kept a big brown bottle of poison in her bedroom in
case of rapists, and if I was intending to high-hat her as others had
done she'd go up there and drink it and ask God to forgive me and
then go be with the Lord in heaven.

"Nothing wrong with wanting to be in heaven," she said. "I
could be there in fifteen minutes. Cast off this old body and get a
new one. What's wrong with that? I'd wait for you there."

This was too much for me. My eyes got red and itchy and I
wanted to run away. She was clutching my arm. She said, "You're
the dearest thing there is, precious. I love you more than I can say,

precious. I want you to promise me you'll always come out and visit, no matter what."

I made a sort of agreeable sound in my throat.

"Promise," she said.

I said that she was wrong about people looking down on her. I said that everybody liked her very much. This was not true, but I said it in a pleasant tone of voice.

"I know all about what people think, they're not so clever they can hide it from me," she said.

She had gotten up from a sitting position and now was kneeling in the dirt, sitting back on her heels, tomatoes in her lap, her old print dress, and her white stockings rolled down to the ankles, her hair wispy under the pins, the blue bandanna scarf, straps of her underthings hanging down and visible in her sleeve, the hair on her arms, her tears, her red nose, the warts on her neck, and suddenly I felt a faint revulsion for her. My crazy aunt. I stood a few feet away, holding my bucket, wanting to go home, wanting not to have heard anything she said, willing it to not exist, crossing it out, hoping she wouldn't touch me again. I had a big urge to set the bucket down and light out through the trees and bike back to town and never return.

"If Mother were to die, you're all I have left in this world. If you turned your back on me, I couldn't bear it. I couldn't."

She sat and sniffled and blew her nose and she clambered to her feet and we walked back to the house and put the pressure cooker on and no more was said for a while. But I was spooked out of my skin. I couldn't put it out of my mind, the thought of her going upstairs and drinking poison from a bottle. Should I sneak up and find the brown bottle and dump it down the biffy? No, I didn't want to be anywhere near there anymore. Even the thought of her death was too much for me. When she went to the cellar to look for Kerr lids, I was halfway out the door to go home, but then Grandma came tiptoeing downstairs from her nap and I had to sit and visit with her, and Eva came back and made tea, and we sat in the front room. Grandma said, "One of these days I'll lay down for a nap and I won't wake up. I look forward to that."

"Now, Mother," said Eva. "Don't talk like that. It scares me silly."

"Someday you'll know what it's like to be old," Grandma said to me. "It's not a whole lot of fun, take my word for it."

I always knew Aunt Eva to be an oddball, what with the backwards psalm, the eighty-seven counties, the hypnotizing of chickens, her fear of strangers, but the talk of poison was in a whole new category of nuttiness. They would be talking about us at the Bon Marché for years to come. The people with the lunatic aunt who drank the rat poison.

I stood at the window waiting for my chance to escape. Grandma heisted herself up and headed for the biffy, and Eva said it again. *If I thought you were going to forget all about me, I'd go upstairs right this minute and take that poison.* She said she'd had a dream that I was grown up, wearing a very expensive suit and tie, walking in a crowd of strangers down a city street where she stood alone on the corner, hungry, lost, scared, and I walked right past her, not recognizing her, my own flesh and blood. She spoke my name and I turned and said, "Who are you?" And she ran away into the woods and the woods stood for her own death. "In the dream I knew I was about to die, and I wasn't afraid," she said. "I was happy to."

And as she said it, I knew that the dream was real. That was exactly what was going to happen someday.

"What kind of poison?" I asked.

"Arsenic."

"Wouldn't that be painful?"

"I don't care. It'd be the last pain I'd ever have to suffer, and it couldn't be anything like the pain of seeing people I love turn away from me."

I got on my bike with a big bag of tomatoes clutched in one arm and I kissed her goodbye and wheeled away and onto the paved road and down the hill and over the crick and I knew that if she took arsenic I didn't want to be around or know anything about it or even attend the funeral. But Grandma looked good, her color was good, her mind was pretty sharp. If she could hold on for another ten years, then I'd be 24 and by that time a person knows what to do about these things. It was a fine day, no time to be thinking about funerals. I rode along no-handed, a talent common among tree toads I'm sure, and as I came to the first mailbox, I took a tomato out and threw it sidearm and missed, but I hit the big yellow sign with the curved arrow and went around the curve fast, still no hands on the handlebars, and hit the curve sign on the other side of the curve. The crowd of strangers in Aunt Eva's dreams was a crowd of friends of mine in some city I hadn't seen yet but would see and would be happy there. *Yes! Happy!* Strangers to her but dear friends to me. People who don't sit around planning their funerals and complaining about the cost of butter nowadays and waiting for the Lord's Return and agonizing over every light left burning in an empty room. My friends will be of another race entirely, a more joyful race, and I intend to be happy right along with them, and if you expect me to sit and weep and mope in the damp and gloom, you've got another think coming, by God—and I hit the stop sign where the township road met the county road, splattered tomato all over, and missed one mailbox and then hit three in a row, for a record of six hits and two misses, and hit the RAIL ROAD CROSSING sign on both sides of the old Great Northern spur, and was coming in sight of town, up to the tree between the road and the swamp where Uncle Al had nailed the FOR ALL HAVE SINNED AND COME SHORT OF THE GLORY OF GOD sign—"Surely," said Grandpa, "surely he has sense enough not to"—and Jesus looked down and said He believed I was going to hit it and of course He, being part of the triune God, was right—the big tomato made a lovely looping arc and splatted right between COME and SHORT and left a bright-red mark like blood, and now I was nine-and-two and the WELCOME TO LAKE WOBEGON was a cinch for No. 10 and the SLOW CHILDREN was No. 11 and just for the principle of the thing, I stopped to throw the last three tomatoes as high in the air as I could, to hear them hit the asphalt. If someone had come by and stopped and asked why I was wasting all those perfectly good tomatoes, I would have said, *Because they're my tomatoes and because it makes me HAPPY!* Let's hear it for Happiness! I'm h-a-p-p-y to throw t-o-m-a-t-o and a *splanch* and a *splinch* and a mighty *spil-woshish*. Grandpa turned away from the window, he couldn't bear to see it. For somebody who was in heaven, he sure worried a lot.

26

Stole Your Undies

The next Sunday, Roger pitched great against Albany and beat the Meinschafters, 7–2, on a grand slam by Ronnie Piggott, who ran the bases backwards, knees pumping high, arms outstretched, waving his cap, whooping like an Indian, and fell on home plate and kissed it and hopped up and did a somersault, he was so pleased with himself. Nobody'd ever seen such showboating by a Whippet before. Jim Dandy sat glumly in the press box and announced the batters and tipped the vodka, and I asked him if he ever heard from his brother Ricky, and he shook his head. "Young Richard is gone. We'll never see him again in this life," he said. I asked how "My Girl" was doing—Big Daddy Fats played it almost nightly on Weegee—and he said that it was going down the toilet, that the distributors and jukebox jobbers and program directors were against them because they were local. "People in Memphis love Elvis, and Fats Domino is a god in New Orleans, but Minnesota? Huh-uh. Don't stand a chance if you're from here. You get no favors. Nix on you. If you were any good, you'd be in New York, not here. That's the psychology." He said that Earl the Girl was talking about joining the Dominos who were on the road with the Crew Cuts and Teresa Brewer. "If he does, we're kaput. *Ausgespielt.* The Doo Dads will be dead." The sound of it made him smile. "Doo Dads dead," he said. "Dead indeed. Doo-dah, doo-dah."

The ump was a squat man solemn as a bishop who called strikes with a motion like someone ripping a cardboard box and yelling "HEE-raw!" and Roger had him ripping boxes all night. Roger was improving every week, you could see it. He had refined his windup so now it looked like a man turning to close a window and then lunging for the door while falling off the stair, and his money pitch was right on the money, curving up and away from a right-handed batter, and the change-up defied the law of gravity, and the fastball blew their hair back, and he tied Albany in knots. One bullet-eyed batter after another stood and waved his little stick and stepped out of the box between pitches and did stuff with dirt and small stones and scratched his heinie and hoisted his testicles and looked down to the third-base coach as if he might have a handle on things, and then stood in to the plate again, and Roger threw another HEE-raw! And another box got ripped. And the batter walked back to the bench and sat down. *Wham bam, thank you, ma'am.*

Kate sat in the front row, her bare arms on the rail, her chin on her arms, not taking her eyes off Roger. I trotted down to visit with her after Ronnie's grand slam and she said she couldn't wait for the summer to end. Why? Too hot. She hated the heat, and hated everyone asking her what she was going to do come fall.

"What are you going to do?"

"Well, see, that's the question I hate. The answer is, I don't know, and I'm looking forward to doing it, whatever it is, that's for sure."

I asked if she still wrote poems. I was only trying to make conversation.

"I'm too busy for that," she said. "I think, before you sit around writing poems about what you feel inside and shit, you ought to go live a little and have some experiences worth writing about someday. So that's what I'm doing. I'm having experiences."

I nodded. I wished she'd say more, but she didn't. What experiences? I wondered, and then I guessed maybe I'd rather not know. So I just said that that all sounded fine to me and that it'd be nice to see her again, but something told me I shouldn't hope for too much. The afternoon we shot pool and kissed in the movie seemed like a thousand years ago. Like something I'd read in a book.

On Tuesday night the team traveled to Bowlus and Roger had the Bull batters corkscrewing themselves into the ground with his fastball and then the change-up winging its way like a silver moth and the batters swinging as if at the moon, saliva churning in their mouths, teeth grinding, their eyeballs ratcheted tight as ball bearings, all of them so PO'ed at the *thought* of losing to the pitiful Whippets, they could hardly see straight. Roger took his sweet time, stopped to carefully tie a shoelace, pat the resin bag and bounce it in his palm, study his outfield, and adjust his pants, then he bent in for the sign, wound up with great gathering force, and threw letter-high, and the batter swung with conviction as the change-up putt-putt-putted across the plate a second or two later. The ump made his strike sign like he was pulling a starter rope on an outboard motor. Different ump. Roger sped up, he slowed down. He worked that Bowlus team like a monkey works a banana.

The sky turned dark in the seventh and black thunderheads floated in from the west like a range of mountains, and when Roger came striding out for the bottom of the ninth, the light was like an old black-and-white movie, as Bowlus's dreaded Hangman's Row of Wagner, Wagner, Schimmer, and Schultz came to bat, the Bulls down by two, the Bull fans standing and pleading, *Doctor, save my baby!* One by one three of the ferocious four came to the plate and stood heavy-browed and fearsome to behold, waving their manly clubs, and the Bowlus fans tightened the imaginary noose and made choking sounds, but it was the hangmen who choked, not Roger. He gave them all his gaudiest stuff and they scowled and swung at the pitch previous and missed the current one and were set down like legless men at a square dance. The last batter, Schimmer, swung hard at two straight ankle-high fastballs, and stepped out of the box and stood, wishing no doubt that he had stayed home with the hogs, and loosened his crotch and stepped back in, and Roger threw him a slow change-up that fluttered homeward and bounced on the plate and skittered off and Schimmer flung himself at it swinging like a ton of bricks and the ump pulled the starter rope and the sky exploded into light, as brilliant jagged bolts of electricity ripped toward the earth, thunder slapping against the grandstand *ker-whammmm*, sheets of rain sweeping across the parking lot, and the Whippets dashed for the bus laughing like children at Christmas, and the Bowlus crowd had to trudge home in the storm, which pitched its tent over the ballpark and dumped the entire contents on their heads. They looked like drowned cats as they straggled past our Whippet bus.

They didn't bother to run, the defeat had taken the will to run right out of them.

It was a festive bunch on the bus. Even Ernie, who had injured his throwing arm in a drinking mishap, was going around back-slapping, and Milkman Boreen and Lyle Dickmeier, the Beer Belly Boys, were passing out boilermakers in paper cups, and Boots Merkel and Rudy and Orv Schoppenhorst and Marv Mueffelman dealt out the cards for a round of Borneo, and Lyle let out a long melodious belch.

Kate was there. She and Roger sat snuggled together in the back. Roger showed her his billfold with her picture tucked in a secret pocket along with a perpetual calendar, a Prayer for Times of Discouragement, and a George (The Ace) Fisher baseball card. The Ace was an Avon boy who pitched three seasons in the New Soo and then went up to the Chicago Cubs for five sterling years in the Windy City. If it could happen for him, it could happen for Roger. The lovebirds whispered and smooched, and Ernie said, in a stage voice, "Ole and Lena, you know—they had twelve kids, be-cause they lived near the train tracks, and when the midnight train came through and woke Ole up, he'd say, 'Well, should we go back to sleep or what?' and Lena'd say, 'What—?' "

"Yeah," said Rudy, "and then he run off with the waitress, but Lena, she had six more kids, because ever so often Ole would come back home to apologize. He never sent her money for the kids, though: he always wrote in the letter, 'P.S. I meant to enclose money but I already sealed the envelope.' "

Ernie told a couple of raw ones about a man and a woman mak-ing out in a car with the gearshift on the floor between them, try-ing to get Roger's goat, but he wouldn't rise to the challenge. I sat next to Ronnie. He said, "I heard Roger got lucky again last night.

Nothing like a piece of fish pie to get a man ready to pitch a ballgame."

The Perfesser chuckled. "I understand that he got her de-pantsed and the stairway to heaven was waiting and he couldn't get his flag unfurled. He reached for the pistol and it was a pistachio."

"Lordy, Lordy."

"Yes, sir." They said this just loud enough for Roger to maybe hear it, but he didn't raise an eyebrow.

The bus chugged through Bowlus, which already seemed chas-tened and diminished by our victory. "Drive around the block again," yelled Ronnie, and Ding's brother Fred at the wheel cranked it and we circled downtown, the windows down, yelling, "Bowlus, Bowlus, you've been beaten! Your pants are gone and your lunch is eaten! We can beat you Sundays and beat you Mon-days! Your ass is bare 'cause we stole your undies! We can beat you Tuesdays and beat you Fridays! We stole your ladies in the little pink nighties! Thanks for the memories, Bowlus!" Round and round the block we went in the rain, past the café full of Bowlusites waiting for the storm to let up and the Big Bowl super-market, where shoppers hustled to their cars with brown bags in both hands, and the taverns with the loungers huddled in the doorway, and we expressed our wholehearted disdain for Bowlus and everything it stood for, even Ding was sort of chanting it. Ronnie yelled, "Let's go get some red paint!" but that was too much, and Fred steered us toward home.

27

The New Day Dawns

The next morning, Uncle Sugar called up and Mother said to Daddy, her hand cupped over the phone, "Sugar's upset. You talk to him." Daddy was reading *Beetle Bailey* in the funny pages and still had *L'il Iodine* and *Peanuts* to go, while finishing his oatmeal and looking forward to his cup of Folger's coffee. He said to tell Sugar to call back later. "Talk to him," said Mother. "He's on the verge of tears." She put the phone up to Daddy's ear and he took it as if it were a live bomb. To have a male relative weep in his ear was nothing Daddy cared to be part of. But he held the phone and heard the whole sad story. Sugar had been in the Chatterbox Café the night before and Mr. Berge walked up to him and said, "What's this I hear about your daughter shacking up with the Guppy boy?" The news was all over town, evidently, if a slow leak like Berge had got wind of it. Daddy tried to pass the phone back to Mother, Sugar's tinny voice sawing away inside, and she shook her head—this was *Daddy's* family, *his* sister's husband,

and he could do some of the listening for a change—and then
Sugar went to pieces and Aunt Ruth came on the phone, all distraught, asking Daddy about mortgaging their house to raise
money to send Kate away to a Home for Wayward Girls in Indiana and Ruth was sobbing and then pausing to mop up the liquid,
and Daddy stiffened as if he were on the electric chair. And then
suddenly I can see why.

It is a dazzling writerly moment for yours truly.

I am—I hesitate to say this, my fellow countrymen, sensing
your views on the matter, but let the truth be judiciously weighed
and a fair verdict rendered—taking notes on paper napkins on my
lap as Daddy listens to Sugar and Ruth. For breakfast, we use
cheap brown napkins, not so soft as the deluxe we bring out for
company, and the cheap ones make excellent notepaper, and I am
jotting down key phrases of conversation with a ballpoint as, with
my left hand, I hold my toast and jelly, and in this state of height-
ened attention, I notice my own father's eyes watering and his
nostrils twitching and a redness spreading on his face, and suddenly it dawns on me: *He dreads tears for fear that he himself
will cry.* And right there Daddy opens to me like a book. All his
grumbling and grouching, his crotchets and glooms and snits and
stews, are mere camouflage for a sensitive heart, and I, a writer,
am afforded this slight insight, and it is my sacred duty to look
upon the heart, as God does, and to reveal it.

I almost burst into tears myself.

The big sister sits crunching her Sugar Pops and reading a *Susan Davis, Student Teacher* novelette and pouting because Sugar's
phone call has taken the focus away from herself and her com-
plaint to Mother about me typing late at night and keeping her
awake. She is oblivious to the deeper things, but I am a writer and

depth is a writer's natural element. We are divers, and divers do not lounge on the beach inviting the admiration of the naïve, we plug our ears and tighten our goggles and go down below.

Mother moves to the sink and washes her cereal bowl and Daddy looks to her for rescue as Ruth's tiny voice gibbers in the receiver, describing the tragedy at their house. Daddy's eyes are red, his lips purse as if he might be losing control, about to blubber at the thought of it—Ruth and Sugar's life plunged into despair by the wild, wild ways of their only daughter—the lost lamb on the rocky steeps and the shepherd parents descending to rescue her—and what if they fail? Their hearts will be broken forever, they will turn to drink, lose their home, wind up at the county poor farm—meanwhile, the big sister is absorbed in the valiant Susan's struggle to persuade the flinty School Board to replace the smoking furnace at Sunnyvale Elementary, and I am writing things on a napkin, and out of the blue Mother says, "I can't get over how beautiful the lawn is."

"Let me have you talk to the boss," says Daddy in a trembly voice and looks to Mother.

She is right, our house is surrounded by the loveliest yard in town and such luxuriant turf, praise be to God.

Why do we keep such a yard? *For the love of our people, that they mayest behold it and feel uplifted by its stately quietness, Selah.*

Why do I take notes on a napkin? *For the love of our people, that our joys and travails may be held up to heaven and to ourselves, that we may see what it means to be human.*

"I don't think it's a good idea to rush into anything," says Daddy, to Ruth, and hands the phone to Mother, who shakes her head and refuses to take it.

May the Lord bless my people at breakfast, their juice, their Post Toasties, their eyes tight and red from unshed tears over the funny pages, the cheap novel open and crumbs of toast falling into the crevice, the low rumble of the man on the radio on the counter giving the weather forecast and a joke or two, the vexations around us, the luxuriant lawn.

And I think a thought to Kate: *Do what you will, park with Roger Guppy on a lonely gravel road and the gearshift between your legs, unbutton your blouse with no bra, your small friendly animals run to greet him, open your mysteries to his throbbing manhood and so forth, come together naked and weeping and greedy in the darkest dark and thrust and pulsate, moan, throb, etc., do what you will and only let me write about it.*

I am the unseen guest, the silent listener. In my house I have many brown napkins. My ballpoint runneth over. Let me watch from the shadows, O daughter of Jerusalem, and hear you sing to your beloved, and I will take you in my own arms, all your words, your lovely visage, your everlasting soul, and bring you to my Underwood.

"What are you staring at, stupid?" says the sister.

Thank you, O Lord, for those who doth persecute and bite and harry, for they only do Thy Will and keep us on our toes.

"Wake up, Shakespeare."

Even the sister is clear to me now—the swift avenging sword of this sanctified sourpuss—she who glories in her skill at hunting the sinner and running him naked up the tree and baying at him there cringing in the upper branches—oh, I do pity her—and may the Lord bestow such blessings and riches on her as to embarrass her poverty and meanness.

"I'm talking to you, Mr. Toad."

"That's no way to speak to your brother," says Mother, ever hopeful that we should be a happy family like those on the radio.

"Mr. Toad is what he calls himself in stories."

"I don't care. It's not nice."

Aunt Ruth's voice is still, finally. She has told Daddy a long story, some true and most of it sheer imagination, about homes for unwed mothers operated by the Salvation Army, and women Ruth once knew who were packed off on the train to spend their confinement in long echoey rooms in musty old mansions behind iron-speared fences and give birth to their babies among rank strangers and sign the babies over to other strangers and return home to friends who now behaved like strangers and how shattering this was and so many of those unfortunate girls never recovered their poise and gumption but accepted any man who showed interest in used merchandise such as they were and thereby they landed in loveless marriages to sour old bachelors—oh, the sorrows that a young woman is susceptible to—and now, finally, Aunt Ruth is finished, and Daddy says, "We'll just have to hope for the best and see what happens." And says goodbye and hangs up the phone.

And brushes the crumbs from the funny pages and starts in on *L'il Iodine*.

And Mother pours him his coffee.

The window is open to the summer breeze redolent of new-mown grass and last night's rain and the Stenstroms' morning glories. The dog sits by the screen door, tail thumping on the stoop. A page turns and Susan Davis, having stoked the furnace and bled the radiators, leads her third-graders through their fractions. A radio quartet sings about a cream that prevents mastitis. Mother runs the hot water and drops a blob of detergent into the stream and our nostrils twitch at the sweet astringent smell. Somewhere my cousin lies in a dim room staring at the ceiling, hearing Sugar and Ruth charging around downstairs like two spooked horses, and the cousin herself a little queasy at the thought of what life might have in store for her. She does bad things. If Grandpa and Jesus are worried about me, they must be really amazed at her. The rock is about to drop. And here, one street over, we wash dishes and attend to *L'il Iodine* and savor the morning coffee.

Whatever happens, I will write it down.

I will write no more poems to please my teachers. I will write no more of boogers and farts to curry favor among the cruel and callow. I will no longer toy with tornadoes and talking dogs and fatal blood diseases as if making a puppet show.

I will sit at the table with my family and write down their sighs, their little pleasures, their kind hearts, their faithfulness. In the face of sin and sorrow and the shadow of death itself, they do not neglect to wash the dishes.

I shove the napkin and pen into my pocket. I take a clean white towel out of the drawer and start drying the plates and cups. "Why, thank you," says Mother. The big sister snorts: "Will wonders never cease!" Daddy turns the page and starts on the crossword. Mother looks out the window over the sink toward her garden of tomatoes, peas, beets, carrots, pole beans, onions, cucumbers, red and green peppers, parsnips, Bibb lettuce, asparagus, Swiss chard, rhubarb, summer squash, resting in the blessing of bright sunshine, awaiting their death and resurrection in salads and soups.

28

The Principle of
Separation

That very night, around 11, Sugar spotted Roger's Pontiac parked up the block, in front of the Fredericksons'. Sugar and Ruth had turned in at ten-fifteen, after the news, but they couldn't sleep, so they listened to the Troubadour, and then a car came slowly up the street, the headlights in their bedroom window making a bright square drifting across the ceiling, then stopped, and the lights went out but the motor was running. Sugar dressed and went downstairs and out to the yard to investigate. He recognized the Pontiac. He approached. The rear window was steamed up. He rapped on the passenger window, and heard rustling and snickering inside, and Roger opened the door and said good evening, and both he and Kate appeared disheveled and Kate's blouse was misbuttoned. Sugar grabbed Kate by the wrist and hauled her out kicking and yelling, and he pointed a big finger at Roger and forbade him ever to see her again. "I will not tolerate you treating my daughter like a common tramp and trollop," he said. He towed her to the house. On the front step she called him a name he hadn't been called since his Army days. He cocked his arm as if he might wallop her and she called him one even worse. He let go. He cried, "Where did you ever learn words like those?"

She said, "I learned them by *living!* That's how. I actually *live* life. Unlike some other people around here who I could name."

"I forbid you to speak profanity in this house. I'm your father. And I forbid you to see that person again."

She said, "Well, Roger's going to be a father too. What about him?"

It was a restless night at their house. Kate threw some clothes in a suitcase and said she was going to run away at the first opportunity and flopped down on the couch to wait, and Ruth and Sugar made a pot of coffee and sat up until 4 A.M., weeping and reading from Scripture and arguing with her about the meaning of obedience, and Sugar even put the Mormon Tabernacle Choir on the hi-fi, as if this might clarify matters. Cranked it up loud and lit several candles, and the room was full of Mormons singing "Lead, Kindly Light" and "How Great Thou Art" while Ruth started making chocolate-chip cookies, and finally, exhausted, talked out, they fell into a fitful sleep until 11 when Sugar brought Kate over to us. Ours was the only house she would consent to stay in.

Sugar brought Kate over and she was put under house arrest in the older brother's bedroom, among his old Science Fair projects including one about the development of the embryo chicken. Mother went upstairs to talk with her. I heard Kate crying. Daddy had stayed home from work. "I laid down the law," Sugar said, "and she defied me and I have to kick her out of the house.

What else can you do?" He looked beat-up, like he'd fallen down the stairs and had a lung removed. "I better go home and shave," he said.

"I thought I'd seen everything," said Daddy, "but this takes the cake."

I asked him, "What's wrong?"

"You know perfectly well."

When Mother came down to the kitchen, she was a little weepy too. She said it was one of the longest days of her life and it wasn't even noon yet. She said, "I don't want you to talk to her. She needs to be alone."

—Is she sick?

—Not exactly.

—Is she in trouble?

—I'll tell you all about it someday.

I was only trying to get Mother or Daddy to say the word *pregnant* out loud.

—What's wrong? I asked.

—Just never you mind.

I asked how long Kate would be staying with us, and she said, "Don't ask so many questions."

Which is par for the course for this family. We believe in secrets. Aunt Eva. A big dark secret. Was she ever normal? Did she have a boyfriend? Did he promise her the Milky Way and lead her down the primrose path and then, once he got what he wanted, fly the coop and leave her to pick up the pieces? And on Mother's side, Aunt Doe, our family martyr. Married to Rex, a florist, and then he delivered a bouquet to a Cuban woman and a week later ran away with her. Drove to Florida, intending to catch a boat to Havana, and they were coming over a hill and the tailgate came loose on a truck ahead and it dumped ten tons of bananas on the road and Rex hit the brakes, the worst thing you can do when driving on fruit, and he skidded into a palm tree and killed himself and Consuela both. Once, at supper, Doe said, "Rex really likes creamed broccoli," as if she were expecting him for supper. It was the first time I ever heard Rex's name mentioned in our house. Everything I knew about him I got from Kate. To Mother and Daddy, he didn't exist anymore. Some things are better left undiscussed and Rex was one of them.

They do not know there is now a writer in the house.

My bedroom was next door to the brother's, and when I put my ear to a certain spot high on my closet wall I could hear Kate's voice. She was saying, "You never loved me. You say you do now but you never said it before, all you did was try to squeeze the life out of me, I don't call that love. You may think it is but it's not. Well, you won't be seeing me again. I'm going away with Roger and have this baby, and if you don't like it, you can stick it where the moon don't shine. I'll show you. I'd be perfectly happy if I never saw you again for the rest of my life."

And then she put her face in her hands and wept long wrenching sobs. It was hard to listen to. Maybe I should've gone and offered her a hug, but it didn't seem my place to do that.

Instead, I sat and wrote a story on my Underwood.

Twilight in August

It was twilight in August and the lady in the white satin dress took off her crown and set it on the bureau. Her hair was a fright, she was bushed, and there was a big grass stain on her dress from when she tripped over the shovel in the cemetery. She had traipsed from one end of town to the other, making appearances at the homes of the sick and the elderly, widows, children, blind people, backsliders, the lame and halt, the faint of heart, and her torch was all used up and so was she. She wanted to go to bed and sleep for a week. She had sung her song for every sad sack in this town and bestowed her light on them and all for what? Did anybody, *anybody*, get any good from it? Usually they just lay and gazed up at her with big watery eyes and winced when she blessed them and on her way out they told her to be sure to shut the door and not let the cat out.

The only food in the house was a can of beans. She had given everything else to the poor. She felt too tired even to light a fire and heat up her humble supper.

She sat on her front steps as the sun descended into the hills and she said, "Lord, I've done Your work and I'm bone-tired. I don't know how long I can keep it up. I'm no spring chicken. Lord, I'm asking You now to give me a nice long rest." She leaned back against the railing and put her hands in her lap and as she did she felt something kick her in the stomach. It was inside her. She held her hands over her belly and she felt the kicks again, hard ones. She asked Him for a nice long rest and He put a bun in her oven.

She wept.

"Thank you, Lord," she whispered. She wondered how she should explain this miraculous event to her neighbors and then she thought, "Oh, what the hell. I'll just go live with the blind for a while."

It was a beans-and-wieners night, and Mother took a plate up to Kate and the rest of us ate in the kitchen. The big sister was secretly gleeful to have a major sinner in the house. I was small fry compared with a Girl in Trouble. A virgin sullied, a soiled dove, a fallen angel. The sister feigned sorrow and concern for Kate and shook her head over the tragedy of it, a young life cast away for a moment of carnal pleasure—but it was all a big play to her. "I don't believe God sends any tribulation except to strengthen us in our faith," she said devoutly, chomping on a wiener.

Mother and Daddy murmured agreement. Miss Priss was in her element. She said, "I really feel that this will draw us all closer to the Lord, especially those who may not have accepted Christ as their Saviour." She herself had felt her own faith strengthened, she said. To see a loved one make a terrible wrong choice should confirm us all who had followed God's Will in these matters. God has made these things clear, and God is not mocked, and those who willfully disobey must be left to God's Mercy and to His chastening rod. It was astonishing to hear a 16-year-old girl talk like a grandpa, but this was Brethren language and we were all steeped in it. You could go around talking normal and suddenly the word *vouchsafe* would come out of your mouth.

She was sailing along full-steam and then Aunt Flo and Uncle Al walked in. Our relatives didn't knock. You heard footsteps on the porch and suddenly there they were, right next to you. Flo and Al sat down, and you could tell it was not a happy social occasion. "You're excused now," Mother said to me in a pointed way. LeRoy and Lois came in. Lois looked weepy, LeRoy was his usual jovial self. "Nice lawn," he said. "How much they pay you? We'll pay more." Sugar and Ruth arrived, their faces pale and drawn, walking on eggshells, whispering as if in a hospital, and Mother brought in folding chairs from the living room. She told me to please go to my room. "We're having a family meeting," she said. The big sister smirked at me with all her might. Evidently she was allowed to stay and perhaps talk about the chastening rod.

I went upstairs and crawled into the upstairs linen closet which was directly over the dining room. An old heating vent brought the voices up from below, like a radio show.

They were still for a while, and then Uncle Al opened the meeting with a prayer for wisdom and the courage to follow God's Will as Thou hast so clearly revealed it to us, which indicated that Al himself was in no doubt about what action to take.

And then Al was talking about the principle of separation. Scripture makes clear we are to separate ourselves from evil and not let it contaminate us. Look at the Lutherans and Methodists: they tolerated false doctrine and loose behavior, like beer-drinking and smoking and card-playing and dancing and movie-going, and now they were no better than the Catholics.

"Most people in the churches don't have enough faith to paint their toenails with," said Uncle Al. "They go to church and sit there in the pews, hoping something will rub off, but they don't have Jesus in their hearts. They don't realize that God would prefer they were out-and-out atheistic communists than be luke-warm Christians like the Laodiceans. God hates a sham. God looks on the heart. God prefers an honest sinner to a make-believe believer. If you attend church just to go through the motions, God'd rather you get you a bottle of bourbon and a whore and go to a hotel and have you a good time." He said that we couldn't overlook Kate's sins or we'd be making a sham of our faith. He read a chapter from Deuteronomy, about how disobedience might cause the Lord to turn His face from you and abandon you to your enemies.

"The Lord will hold Kate to account for her actions, and for bringing disrepute onto those gathered in His Name, but the Lord will especially hold us to account for our exercise of discipline," he said, quietly.

Kate, he said, was 17 and no child and she knew what she was doing when she did it and now she would have to be sent away. There was a home for wayward girls in Indiana. He himself would drive her there if she wouldn't go with Sugar and she would give birth to her baby there and it would be placed for adoption with a Christian family.

Mother said, "Why couldn't we keep her here? We can decide about the baby when the baby comes. And then there's Roger—"

Al didn't like to be questioned once he had explained things and made them clear. He repeated, tersely, what he'd said about separation doctrine, and he added that Kate must show genuine contrition if she didn't wish to be sent away. She must confess how she had rebelled against God's teaching, and she should do it in writing. Immediately. Today.

Mother said, "We're all sinners in God's sight, and there is not so much difference between Kate and any of the rest of us, if you ask me."

I could hear Daddy say, "Excuse me for a minute," and get up from the table and Uncle Al say, "We need you here," and Daddy say he'd be back in a minute and leave the room. Daddy could sense an argument approaching. He couldn't stand to hear high-pitched emotion of any kind, he couldn't bear it.

He shuffled through the kitchen, rattled a pan, opened the back door, and headed for the garage. I guessed he was trying to think of a good reason to be out there. Some urgent necessary thing. Maybe he'd start washing the snow tires or alphabetizing the paint cans by color.

Ruth said she was so upset she couldn't think straight. Roger Guppy was no good and she'd known it since he was a child and threw rocks on the playground and almost put another child's eyes out. She had tried to keep Kate away from worldly influences, a hard thing in this day and age, and the harder she tried, the more Kate resisted. She had searched Kate's room this morning, top to bottom, and found cigarettes, empty wine bottles, books of all sorts—atheist poetry and worldly novels, Hemingway, Cummings, Steinbeck, Kerouac, that whole crowd—and *this*—she was showing them something—and there were low outbursts of disgust and then uncle Al said it out loud. " 'The Flaming Heart'? What sort of thing is that for a Christian to be reading?"

Sugar said, "It's about a tornado or something. The boy is the son of Broadway actors. He's carried away by a high wind and dropped among Brethren. He stays only because the dog tells him to."

"How can a dog tell him to stay?" says Lois, never too swift.

"It's fiction," said Flo.

"Certainly doesn't seem too complimentary to Brethren," noted Al.

"That isn't Kate's," said the big sister. "That's Gary's. He wrote it."

It sounded as if Ruth were paging through it. "It's silly. Get it out of here. Burn it or something."

"It's just been one thing after another," said Uncle Sugar. "I can't tell you what we've been through." His voice shook. He said that Kate had broken his heart in two and that if she couldn't mend her ways it'd be better for everybody if she left and never came back. There was a period of liquid sobbing and shoulder-patting then. And a long honk into a hanky.

Uncle LeRoy spoke up. He said we should be calm and take the long view and not act precipitously in anger, lest we do harm that can never be repaired. People sometimes haul off in a big huff and do more harm than good.

Al said, "I'm not in a huff and it isn't precipitous to insist that Scripture teaching be followed."

LeRoy said, "You are *too* angry, look at you."

Al said sharply that anger was the farthest thing from his mind. "Anger has nothing to do with this."

Al and LeRoy were often edgy around each other. Al was top dog in the Brethren, the leader of Bible reading, the teacher, the explainer, and LeRoy liked to pretend not to notice him.

Flo asked LeRoy what he thought should be done. LeRoy said, "I think the boy ought to marry her." There was silence. Ruth said she could not even imagine such a thing.

I snuck out of the linen closet and knocked on the brother's door and opened it. Kate sat on the bed. I said, "I'm sorry you got caught with my story." She said, "It doesn't matter. That's the least of it."

—They're talking about sending you to Indiana.

—I'd like to see them try.

—They want you to make a statement of contrition. In writing.

—Let em write it themselves.

—If you don't, they'll send you away and you can't come back.

—Who said I wanted to?

I wanted to know how it felt to be pregnant. Could she feel the baby inside? What happened? Where was Roger? Did he know about this? What did he say?

I said, "I could write it for you. I'm a writer." I said, "Just tell me what happened."

She lay back on the bed and pulled the quilt over her. "What do you mean, what happened? I got pregnant, that's what happened."

I said, "But how? When did it happen? Where were you?"

"I was with Roger," she said. "It's nobody's business."

She lay looking into thin air, thinking. Faraway, like ocean surf, the murmur of voices downstairs, our family, trying to piece the world together. She said, "Do you think I'm pretty?" I said yes. She said, "I mean, really pretty?" I said yes. She said, "Do you still like me?"

I took a deep breath. I looked into the air above her head. I told her that I loved her and that I meant it. She put her hand on mine and we sort of hugged sideways, a quick one, a shy hug. I told her that when this all blew over, I'd take her to Joe's Bar and buy her a Martini and we'd dance to the "Hyena Stomp."

* * *

I had her confession sort of worked out in my mind, how she had fallen among evil companions and wasted her inheritance of grace and now was throwing herself on the mercy of those who loved her, though she was not worthy of their love. It was a good confession, contrite but not too abject, leaving certain questions open, and I was all set to type it up, and the next night Roger, who had gone to visit his uncle in Millet and figure things out, called up Kate from a tavern at 10:30 P.M. and asked her to marry him. He said, "I think we should do it. There's no reason why not."

She said, "Have you been drinking?" and he said, "Sure."

She said, "Roger, this is for a lifetime, you know." He said, "Hey. You're telling me." But he told her he loved her and that next spring they'd be in New York City probably and none of this would matter anymore.

29

Sickness and Health

Aunt Ruth hustled around and arranged for the Lutheran church the following Saturday evening, the Lutheran ladies to fix the supper, Pastor Tommerdahl to officiate, bouquets of daisies and lilies from Mrs. Hoglund's garden, Kate's dress to be a refitting of Ruth's old white satin wedding dress, and three bridesmaids including the older sister, and three groomsmen (Ding, Milkman, and Jim Dandy). Mother offered to help and Ruth said she was just fine, thank you. "As long as I've got something to keep me busy, I'm happy," she said. Sugar was having conniptions, she told Mother on Friday, not sure whether he should allow the marriage or not, and he spent Thursday in bed, convinced he was on the verge of a cerebral hemorrhage, and wrote out instructions for the disposal of his goods and chattel, but was feeling a little more chipper today. Ruth, on the other hand, stayed up all night sewing a dress for herself.

"You need your rest," said Mother.

"I can rest when I'm dead," said Ruth.

Kate, she said, now that they were about to lose her, was sweet as pie, helping around the house and being pleasant at the dinner table and behaving as a young lady should behave.

The couple would reside with Roger's parents until they could get a place of their own. The Guppys had a spare room, what with Ricky being in jail.

The wedding day dawned bright and fair. The older brother arrived on the Greyhound from Minneapolis and sat himself down at the kitchen table and ate the eggs and bacon Mother fried for him. He was okay, he said. School was okay. Courses were interesting. Grades were good. Liked his dorm room. It was okay. Roommate was okay. He was never around so that was good. Why was the roommate never around? Had a girlfriend, that's why. The brother smirked. Women. They take up your whole life. The roommate was probably going to flunk out. And for what? Some woman. Hard to believe.

The older brother was not one to regale you with anecdotes about his life and times. He sat, tall, erect, Adam's apple bobbing, chewing unself-consciously, mouth open, cud rolling around, glasses slid half down his nose, and his mind was not on us at all. I doubt he was entirely aware of why he'd come home for the weekend. He was cogitating over some great problem, numbers were jingling in his head, equations circling, theorems pacing back and forth. Mother took his laundry bag down to the basement. He looked up at me as if trying to recall my name.

"Mother has purchased a snub-nosed revolver and she's taken to carrying it in her purse when she goes downtown," I said. "I think we need to keep an eye on her." He grunted and ducked his head and shoveled in a fresh load. "Daddy's hitting the gin something fierce. Drinks it out of a jelly glass like it was lemonade." His eyelids flickered and his eyes seemed to focus for a split-second and then he was gone again, back doing the math. "Sister stays out until three in the morning and comes home with a sack full of money. Ones and fives, mostly. Some tens. I think she's working as a hootchy-koo dancer in Millet and giving hand jobs to the railroad men."

Mother came in and asked the brother if he wanted to take a bath. What she meant by that was that he smelled bad. But he didn't get that either. "Sure," he said, but he didn't budge.

I was chosen to accompany Kate to the Bon Marché Beauty Salon that afternoon to sit with her while she had her hair done, which was a signal honor and I accepted with alacrity, having just learned the word *alacrity*. She asked me to come with because she didn't care to be alone with those old biddies who'd been gossiping about her and Roger for weeks.

Saturday was a big morning at the Bon Marché, what with Saturday canasta and afternoon Mass and all, and Luanne's sister Marilyn was helping out, washing hair at the sink in back. Marilyn did the washing and the bluing and highlighting, and Luanne did the curling and snipping. Mrs. Ingqvist, Mrs. Krebsbach, Mrs. Bunsen, Mrs. Magendanz, sat under beehive dryers along the wall, wrapped in white, reading beauty magazines, their ancient heads getting fluffed under the drying hoods. The whole place had an old-lady aroma, a combination of perfumes and medications and something dry and sour, something left too long on the stove, a cream soup gone bad. Darlene from the Chatterbox was plopped in a styling chair and Luanne was trimming her bangs. Aunt Flo had plenty of stories about Darlene and her string of ne'er-do-well boyfriends and Darlene looked as if each one had taken ten years off her life. She looked 35 going on 72.

Luanne looked up as we two walked in and saw Kate and said, "Well, here comes the bride!" and gave her a big hug.

"You look just like someone ought to look on her wedding day," she said. "Like royalty."

She sat Kate in the second chair while she finished up Darlene's bangs. Luanne said, "I'm so happy for you. Now all we need to do is find a good man for Darlene here." Darlene frowned. She'd been waitressing long enough to know there was no such creature. "You find me a good man, tell him to come fix my roof and put in a new furnace, then we'll talk about it."

Around the room, the ladies chuckled.

"It's supposed to be a hard winter, they say," said Darlene. She was a heavy woman with sore feet who looked like she'd endured a lot of hard winters. About a thousand, maybe.

Around the mirror, taped to the glass, were pictures of Luanne's children and nieces and nephews, her sister who married the dentist and her sister who married Leonard Larsen's uncle and her brother who owns the biggest greenhouse in Oklahoma and the brother who nobody asks about anymore, it would be impolite. He is in Minneapolis, employed at some sort of job. At least you don't read about him in the papers.

—How is your Mother? I imagine she must be rushing around, said Luanne.

—She's fine.

—Lot of work getting married. Where are you kids going on your honeymoon?

—The Black Hills. But after baseball season's over.

—Well, that'll be nice. Not so crowded then. I always wanted to see Mount Rushmore but Bob won't go because it means we'd have to visit his sister in Rapid City. She's the one who can't stop talking. Talks nonstop. Morning, noon, and night. Talk, talk, talk. Bob and I went to Chicago for our honeymoon, he'd always wanted to see a major-league ballgame so guess what we did for three days. Yup. I took along a magazine and read. He said, "The least you could do is make an effort." Our first argument. Stayed in a hotel room that smelled of kerosene. It was on the tenth floor and I couldn't stop thinking, What if the place burned? How would we get out?

She finished up Darlene, curling a row of bangs over her forehead, and fluffed her and sent her away and turned to Kate and studied her and ran her fingers through her hair.

—Is it long enough to have it in a chignon? Kate asked.

—Honey, if you want it in a chignon, that's how we'll do it, and if it isn't long enough, believe me, I have my ways.

She led Kate back to the sink and sat her down and leaned her back and washed her hair. She said, "When I got married, I saw this picture of Grace Kelly on the cover of *Life* and her hair was in a French roll and it was so dainty, I did mine exactly like it, except I used a toilet paper roll for a foundation and I forgot to take all the toilet-paper off. I tripped on the hem of my dress coming up the aisle, and the roll fell out and hung there. I must've looked like Medusa with a headful of snakes. My mother looked up from the pew and saw toilet paper hanging down from my head and she leaped up and pulled out all the pins and my hair hung down like

Spanish moss and that was the final straw, I was all worn out, I'd been up all night finishing my dress, and I stood there and bawled so hard I could hardly get the words out. The minister read as fast as he could go and never looked up. I don't know what Bob thought, he never said. He just took me to that horrible hotel and three days at the ballpark. I haven't been to a game since."

And then Kate started to weep. Softly, but everyone was suddenly quiet. I saw her in the mirror. Her mouth all rubbery and tears shining on her cheeks.

"I'm sorry," she said. "It's nothing. I'm okay." She was reading a story in the *National Enquirer* while Luanne toweled her hair— *Woman Marries Martian, Honeymoons on Jupiter, Gives Birth to 40-Lb. Infant with Glass Head*—she read the headline and started crying. She cried sweetly, like a little girl, very musical. Nobody said a word. It was so quiet you could hear the little alarm clock on Luanne's cabinet next to the comb jar, you could hear footsteps on the sidewalk, music tinkling on a radio upstairs.

A bride crying on her wedding day. It scared me to hear it but the women of the Bon Marché seemed unperplexed.

"I just wish I knew what I was getting myself in for," Kate said and cried a little harder.

"It's okay, sweetie," said Luanne. "Everybody feels that way."

I was getting ready to take Kate away to the hunting cabin up north. To comfort her and protect her from the treachery of the world. To amuse her. To help raise her child. To make everybody happy. To get rich and buy a big house with a swimming pool. A long list of things. If she had said, "Get me out of here, I can't do this," I maybe would've done it, or something like it, but she didn't.

Mrs. Krebsbach said, "Believe me, it's the wedding that's the hard part. You slave away for months to make the damn thing nice and, bang, it's over in thirty minutes and he doesn't notice a thing, all he wants is for you to jump into the sack like Ava Gardner. No, once you're past that, honey, everything that happens afterward is not as bad as you might think."

Kate blew her nose delicately and whispered, "I'll be okay," and Luanne said, "Of course you will," and worked on the chignon, using a wad of cotton for a base. And when it was finished, they all stood round the bride, admiring her hair—all the old sorceresses and priestesses and oracles of our town, stood by her, patting her, murmuring priestessly things, and even knowing what they knew about romance and marriage, nonetheless they wished her the best and hoped she and her husband would be very happy together.

On the way home, I asked Kate if she was okay.

"Are you kidding? Of course not. I'm sick as a dog. If anybody looked at me cross-eyed, I'd toss my cookies."

"What's wrong?"

"I got pregnant, that's what. I've been knocked up!" She shouted it, and it tickled her so much, she yelled again: "I've been knocked up by my boyfriend!" And then she started giggling. "I feel like I could have a diarrhea attack and throw up simultaneously. Empty out from both ends. You ever see a woman in a white dress puke and shoot poop at the same time in a church in front of her entire family?"

Up ahead of us, the Catholic bells were tolling and I said, "Let's go to Mass." I thought it'd take her mind off it.

"Why not?" she said.

"As long as we have to go in the Lutheran church, why not give the Catholics a shot?"

So we went in through the big front door of Our Lady of Perpetual Responsibility, a dramatic moment for Brethren children. The entering of a Roman Catholic church was an act so far beyond the pale, it never had to be mentioned: in that respect, it was like shoving your mother down the stairs or eating ground glass. We swung the door open on its black iron hinges, Catholic hinges, and stood in mute astonishment at the opulence and vastness and sheer color of it, the marble pillars, the gilded folderol in the lofty ceiling, the gold-flecked mosaics in the maroon tile floor. It was a cathedral, with great stone arches and columns and florid scenes in stained-glass windows and statues along the sides, angels and prophets and apostles, faces filled with compassion, extending their hands to bless us. Kate, for all her sophistication, was as stunned as I. We snuck up the side aisle toward the high altar, all pink and blue and pale rose, a flame flickering in a crimson urn. In the pews were scattered fifteen or twenty people, kneeling. I recognized Krebsbachs and Lugers and Magendanzes, people I knew from around town but I had never set foot in their houses. Old Mrs. Luger shot me a suspicious look when we eased into her pew, her at the other end kneeling, us sitting—then Kate knelt, and so did I. (When in Rome.) Up ahead was Father Emil bowing and kissing something on the altar and curtsying and turning, as David Magendanz in a white smock followed him, holding a brass pole with a candle at the end. I had never imagined David in a dress, all those years he was beating up people on the playground.

It was the feast day of St. Joseph the woodcarver, Father Emil announced, a man of great faith who in old age set out to carve his magnum opus, a six-foot oak statue of our Lord kneeling in the Garden of Gethsemane, and he carved it in eight months—and a magnificent work it was—and the next morning he came to his studio to find that the oak had become living wood and sprouted branches and leaves, and his work was deformed. He chopped off the branches and carved a smaller figure, about three feet high, of St. Paul preaching, and it was likewise masterful, but lo, the next morning, the wood had sprouted branches again and the figure was ruined. So he left the branches on it, and carved a miniature figure of himself, the woodcarver, in a tree, like Zaccheus hoping to see the Lord, and this was his great work, and it was only eight inches high. And soon thereafter Joseph took sick and lay on his deathbed in great distress. And his friend Titus the Mocker came unto him and called out, in jest, "St. Joseph!" And the woodcarver whispered, "Not yet." And gave up the ghost.

David Magendanz looked straight at me through Father Emil's peroration on St. Joseph, wondering why I was here, daring me to think bad thoughts about his little gown, and then turned when the priest turned to face the altar, and they both knelt and we read St. Joseph's prayer.

It was not a prayer such as Brethren prayed, asking God for the strength to continue doing the great and good things we are doing now for His sake and to withstand the indifference of the unbelievers around us, no, it was only a prayer for solace and comfort, a prayer for a prayerful heart, and Father Emil read it and didn't try to improve on it with a lot of huffing and woofing.

And then it was time for the bread and wine, and Kate looked at me and we scooted out.

She was married to Roger at 6 P.M. in the Lutheran church, in a white satin dress and a cloud of veil, Roger in a navy-blue suit, his hair cut short, his brother Jim next to him in a white suit. An odd choice, I thought, and then I spotted the other Doo Dads in white suits, sitting in the front row. And next to them, with Mr. and Mrs. Guppy, was Ricky, in handcuffs, and a U.S. marshal next to him. He looked as pale and queasy as in gym class, faced with the rope climb.

I sat between the older sister and Aunt Eva, who didn't let out a peep when she arrived with Grandma, just plopped down next to me and sighed, twice, for the misery of being there and all. The organ played and the minister prayed and a girl sang "Oh Promise Me" and the minister read the parable about the tree bearing fruit and nodded to the Doo Dads, who hopped up and sang:

> If I speak—with the tongues—shang shang shang
> Of men and of angels—oooooooooooooo yes—
> And have not love—love! love!
> I am become as sounding brass
> Or tinkling cymbal.
> Love suffereth long and is kind—so kind!
> Love thinks no evil—no no!
> Love beareth all things—O yeah—
> It believeth all things—
> It hopeth all things—
> It endureth all things.
> And now abideth faith—and hope—and love.
> These three.
> But the greatest of these
> Is love—oooooooooooooooh yeah.

Daddy paid no attention to them, kept his eyes fixed on the floor, and after their quavery last chord, the minister stepped up and asked if there was just cause why these two should not be joined together in holy matrimony. Yes, I thought, there is every reason in the world. But probably they should go ahead and do it since we're all here now.

I could smell Aunt Eva's smell and I was so sorry she was crazy. Maybe that's why she was afraid of strangers, because a stranger could recognize her craziness which we didn't because we were so used to her. I wanted to sit and cry for her. But everything is changed and we can never go back to who we were. The terrible things she dreamed about me turning my back on her are all true. We will never stand in the sunshine again, she and I, and wipe the dirt off a tomato and bite into it and taste the hot juice.

And now I think I am going to cry.

They vowed to love and cherish in sickness and in health and the bride wasn't violently ill and she processed and recessed without sudden unseemly bodily eruptions and Aunt Ruth cried in a stately manner and Sugar blubbered like a baby, and sunbeams streamed in the window and motes of dust danced in them and then a naked girl dove into the water, her beautiful marble buttocks, her breasts like two friendly otters, and took me in her arms. And then the Mendelssohn march thundered from the pipes and I rose and filed out. All of the Brethren looked sheepish to be there in the midst of doctrinal Error, and anxious to leave. To get home and wash their hands and brush Error off their teeth.

Kate stood in the reception line shaking hands, looking unsteady, thin-lipped, Roger looming over her, grinning at his buddies. I hung back, not knowing what to say. The Pontiac had been smeared with ripe cheese, and tin cans and shoes tied to the rear bumper, and she and Roger posed for pictures, her in his arms, and then they headed for the car to get away. "But what about the supper?" cried Aunt Ruth. Kate whispered something in her ear. "Well, that's fine, honey, you go lie down," said Aunt Ruth. "And take some Kaopectate." The couple headed for the door, then LeRoy cried out, "One more picture!" and they stopped and posed, with their aunts and great-aunts and old teachers and the ladies from the Bon Marché. Aunt Eva stood in the back row, her face solemn but trying to smile, everybody trying to be as happy as possible under the circumstances, for Kate's sake.

I followed them out the door and waved as they drove away to live their new life, whatever it should be, and I started walking and wound up at the ballpark, dark, deserted, the streetlight casting a faint glow on the outfield. The long shadow of the grandstand stretched out beyond second base. I walked onto the field. So peaceful. To be alone in the ballpark, the simple grandeur of it, the darkness. The four light standards like rockets against the starry sky, the ghostly white foul lines to the deep corners. I took off my shoes and socks and walked across the infield grass and then stripped off all my clothes and folded them and set them on second base and turned and faced the stands.

A person walks around in a cotton envelope, it's good to open yourself to the fresh air and reveal yourself to the universe. Here I am, all secrets known, all desires revealed, and I am not ashamed. Go ahead and turn on the lights, I refuse to cringe and run away.

I could imagine Ding Schoenecker in the dugout yelling, "Hey! You! Boy! What you think you're doing?" Imagine Miss Lewis pale from shock and requiring smelling salts. Imagine the sister crying out, "See? I told you! Nobody believed me! So look for yourselves!" Imagine a story in the paper, BOY, 14, FOUND NUDE AT BALLPARK, HELD FOR OBSERVATION, PARENTS SAY HE "SEEMED NORMAL." *How could you do it?* they said. *Because it felt good.* And because I am a writer and have to live life.

I jogged out to center field and broke into a run as if chasing a long fly ball and stretched and caught the ball over my shoulder and put on the brakes and pivoted and hurled the gleaming spheroid to second base to catch the winged speedster by inches! I strolled toward home plate, acknowledging the roar of the crowd. The grass was cool and damp. My pecker had jounced around like a jockey in the course of my heroic dash and was now on full alert. I did not bother to cover it. I lay on the grass on my back and it stood like a flagpole in the night and then slowly began to bow to the crowd. I lay looking up at the stars and there were Grandpa and Jesus looking over the parapet of heaven.

"I can't believe him lying there stark naked like that," said Grandpa. "What would people think?" Jesus said that people think all sorts of things. The human mind is like a cloud of gnats. Constant motion. That's why you have to look on the heart. "Oh," said Grandpa. He leaned farther over. The coast was clear. Nobody coming. "Shouldn't we tell him to get up and put on his clothes?" he asked. Jesus said I would put on my clothes in approximately eight and a half minutes. Grandpa said, "I worry about the kid. Lying there with his wiener out. What's going to become of him?" Jesus told him to take it easy and to come away from the window and get back to the singing and hallelujahs and the no-tears policy.